THE GREAT MAN

By AL MORGAN

E. P. DUTTON & CO., INC.
NEW YORK · 1955

FIRST EDITION

Library of Congress Catalog Card Number: 55-5345

AMERICAN BOOK–STRATFORD PRESS, INC., NEW YORK

TO MARTY

CONTENTS

THE GREAT MAN

PROLOGUE

I'M SITTING now in my office on the ninth floor of the Amalgamated Building. It's getting dark. I know if I turn around and look out the window at my back I can see the sun setting behind the RCA Building. I can just barely hear the music blaring out of the loudspeaker in the reception room around the corner of the office. The receptionist always forgets to turn it off when she leaves at six-thirty and it's blaring its jazz to an audience of empty chairs, a bank of closed elevator doors and a photo mural of the New York skyline with the call letters of the station slashed across it in red freehand.

My office looks like hell. It always does at this time of the day. The desk is littered with press agents' releases, clips from the drama section of the newspapers and the first draft of a commercial for the reducing pill that's bought a spot on my show and wants a personal approach in its copy. There's a brand new stain on the rug where I spilled half a container of coffee yesterday morning. A roll of yellow teletype paper that was fresh off the local wire at ten this morning has spilled out of the wastepaper basket. The ash tray with "Stork Club" written across the base is filled with half-smoked cigarettes.

None of this is unusual.

The office looks like this most of the time. Every night at midnight the cleaning women emerge from the subway, attack the chaos and leave it spick and span. Twelve hours later, it's a mess again.

This isn't one of those show-off offices that are kept neat and clean. A lot of work is done here every day. Out of this mess and confusion comes a nightly radio show and when you're always fighting a deadline you don't have time to be a housewife.

I won't be here long. In two hours, I'll pull the string on the light over my head, pick up the script in my top drawer, lock the door carefully and go around the corner to Studio 23. Or maybe I'll just pull the string on the light over my desk, lock the door carefully, throw the key away and catch the first plane headed west.

Maybe.

Then again, maybe not.

That's why I'm sitting here.

I'm trying to figure it out. I'm trying to run up a trial balance, trying to decide what I'm going to do in the next two hours.

This is one of those periods that turn up maybe once or twice in your life, when you sit down, look straight ahead at nothing, turn your back on the sun setting behind the RCA Building and make a decision that can turn your whole future upside down.

Somebody's just turned the speaker in the reception room up full and I can hear Maggie Whiting's recording of "Little Girl Blue."

Count your fingers. Contemplate your navel.

Yeah.

". . . reminder that tonight at 10:00 P.M., the Amalgamated Broadcasting System and its affiliated stations from coast to coast will present a memorial program dedicated to that beloved humorist of the airwaves, the late Herb Fuller. This full-hour tribute to one of the great men of our time will be presided over by your favorite New York reporter, Ed Harris. Remember, that's just two hours from now at 10:00 P.M. This is the Amalgamated Broadcasting System, WBSR, New York."

Like the man said . . . two hours from now.

The Promotion Department knocked itself out. All the station breaks are plugging the show. Marge Kelloway did a wonderful publicity job; she'll have lots of clips for the scrapbook. Like this one from Kilgallen:

"Ed Harris, Amalgamated's Man About New York, will be given the big build-up soon. His appointment as valedictorian on the full-hour Memorial Program for Herb Fuller is the tip-off. The Beloved Humorist, who died early this week, gave Harris his first job in radio and Radio Row is whispering that Harris will fall heir to Fuller's radio and TV shows. It couldn't happen to a nicer guy."

Or this one from Winchell:

"Don't miss the Herb Fuller Memorial on Amalgamated tonight. Ironically enough, the death of his benefactor, Herb Fuller, is almost certain to lift Radio Reporter Ed Harris into the Big Time."

It's hard to believe Fuller died only last Monday, five days ago. And what am I trying to prove, sitting here flipping mental nickels . . . trying to decide what to do. Christ! What's the problem?

All I have to do is pick up that script in the drawer, walk around to Studio 23, spend the hour from ten to eleven reading it into an open mike and then sit back and wait to move up into the upper income brackets.

It's simple.

That's all I have to do.

The only thing that bothers me is . . . can I do it?

MONDAY

It started like any other day.

I had a hangover.

The rain that had started about one in the morning was still coming down. As usual, I couldn't get a cab. You never can when it rains in New York. So I walked, sloshing through the rain in my loafers. One of those goddamned pregnant cross-town buses splashed water all over my pants. I was soaking wet.

My mouth tasted like something they give you to drink when you've got a sore throat. I'd had about four hours' sleep.

All this was normal.

Except the weather.

Some days it didn't rain.

But the hangover was the same. So was the mouth. So was the four hours' sleep.

It was an occupational disease. Some people in radio get ulcers.

I just suffer from a bad case of Chronic Hangover.

Peter, the Amalgamated doorman, was all decked out in his rain outfit: hip boots, raincap, coat and striped umbrella.

I nodded to him.

"The Book of the Month to you," he said.

That was the same too. He always said it.

Most of the time you laughed.

It was a ritual, if you worked at Amalgamated. Along with

your group insurance policy, you inherited Peter. Not Pete. Never Pete. Always Peter. He was funny. He was a character. You always laughed at him.

NBC has its chimes.

CBS has Godfrey.

Amalgamated has Peter, the court jester of the network.

"Come on, peasant," he said. "You're late punching your time clock."

Yeah!

Sometimes you do that to Peter. You make believe he isn't funny. You make believe you're not charmed by him. You make believe he isn't a character and part of the ritual. But he knows you're kidding. That's part of the game.

This morning he knew I wasn't kidding.

I walked across the lobby telling myself that it was a childish thing to do. After all, the guy makes forty-five, fifty bucks a week; if he wants to think he's funny, if he wants to be a character, don't be a bastard about it . . . give him his kicks. You can't get many on fifty bucks a week these days.

"Well, you silly bastard," I said to myself, a bad habit that goes only with the worst hangovers, "Now you'll have to slip him a quarter the next time he gets you a cab. And for Christ's sake laugh when he tells the driver, '79 Wistful Vista, peasant.' "

The lobby was crowded. So was the local elevator. I crowded my way in and waited. Nothing happened.

Artie, the starter, was giving me the business.

I'd turned him down the day before. I'd gotten a little sick of his putting the arm on me for a buck or two every other day, gotten a little sick of his always having his hand out, palm up, always needing another couple of bucks until tomorrow and always forgetting to pay it back. I'd gotten a little sick of accepting it as semilegitimate graft.

"Hey Artie. How about it? Let's go."

He turned his back on me.

The elevator smelled wet.

John, the elevator operator, was auditioning, facing front, singing. He always sang. Badly.

I reached into my wallet and pulled out a dollar bill.

I rolled it up into a ball and threw it in the general direction of Artie.

"O.K.? Can we go now?" I asked. "If you need any more just let me know."

Nobody said a word.

The buzzer clicked and John closed the door and we started up.

I got off at nine.

The receptionist smiled at me.

She was new. I smiled back.

"Can I do anything for you, sir?"

Couldn't she just!

"It's all right, honey, I work here. I'm Ed Harris."

"Oh, Mr. Harris," she said, "I'm sorry. I just started work here this morning. Excuse me, please."

"Sure, just remember my face next time."

She smiled again and I walked past her.

She was right smack in the mold. A typical WBSR receptionist, as distinctive as a Ford hubcap. They all look like they're just fresh out of Sarah Lawrence. They all have blond hair and cute fannys. They all smile. They all last about two weeks.

On the way into my office I passed Lillian's desk. That was another ritual. Lillian's a buck-toothed girl from Mount Vernon who works for Don Carter, the sales manager.

"Hello, dahling," she said, the way she'd been saying it to me every morning for the past four years.

I figured, what the hell, I'd already committed sacrilege

with Peter and Artie, I could stop and play the game for a couple of minutes.

"Hello, Sexy," I said. May God forgive me. "Hello, Sexy." Lower this time. More intimate.

I looked at my watch.

"I have fifteen minutes free around one-thirty. Think you can make it?"

She leered.

All twenty-five teeth of her.

"The question is, dahling," she said, "can you make it?"

I leered back at her and got as far as the door to my office.

"One-thirty," I said. "You bring the blanket."

Ginny, my secretary, was opening the mail at my desk. She didn't look up when I came in. She has a morning disposition that's almost as foul as mine. I hung my coat up on the rack and stretched out on the couch.

"Mr. Moore's been on the phone all morning. He's sore about your play review last night."

"Isn't that too bad?"

"He said he saw the play last night too and thinks you were unnecessarily rough on it."

"Isn't that too bad?"

"You're real clever this morning."

Ginny got up and went out to her desk in the outer office. I went over to my desk, sat down and looked over the mail. I don't know why. I wasn't expecting a check, the only reason I can think of off-hand to get off a couch to look through a pile of mail on a desk halfway across the room.

Just as I figured, it was the same crap. The same avalanche from the press agents. The same crap. One pink-enveloped job was set aside. Ginny had written across the front, "For Your Memory Book." I opened it.

"Dear Mr. Harris," it said, "I listen to your broadcast every night. What an exciting life you must lead! All the first nights! All the parties! One minute sitting at the ringside for a championship fight, the next racing across town to cover a fire or a murder. I don't usually write fan letters but I just had to let you know how much I enjoy listening to you, just had to let you know that you bring joy and excitement into the life of one of your faithful listeners. God bless you."

I buzzed for Ginny.

"Ginny, you'd better order me some breakfast."

"I already did. Bromo, tomato juice and black coffee. Right?"

"Right."

"It's on its way."

"Thanks, honey. This time, I'll bring the blanket."

"Save it for Lillian. She has no basis for comparison."

"O.K. You'd better get Moore on the phone. We might just as well start the day off."

Sid Moore is the manager of the station. His success has gone to his midsection. Back in the days when I knew him first, he was a salesman running his tail off at the agencies along Madison trying to peddle spots on our wake-up show. He was lean and hungry. They made him head of local research and he immediately put on fifteen pounds. He added fifteen pounds with each promotion. Now that he's on his way to becoming a V.P. of the network, he's beginning to look the way Johnny Weismuller did when they made him give up playing Tarzan.

Sid's a bastard.

A real hustler but a bastard.

Most of the time, we're polite to each other, but we're not fooling anybody. He'd like nothing better than to throw me out on my can, but as long as the Pulse and the Neilsen stays up around 3.4 and the show is sold out there isn't much he can do about it. He's a bastard but a self-centered one, out to make a rep for himself around the network and as long as the Ed Harris "Metropolitan Memo" can help him, it doesn't really matter to either of us how we feel about each other's guts.

I knew as soon as I picked up the phone that he was in one of his needling moods.

"Ed, boy, how are you?" he asked.

"Fine, Sid. A little tired. I had to make the rounds of the clubs after the opening last night. Didn't get much sleep."

"You still knocking off that French broad that Warner's is promoting?"

I let that one go by.

"I wouldn't mind some of that myself."

"Have you looked at yourself in the mirror lately, Sid?"

"Seriously, Ed . . ."

"Who isn't serious?"

"I wanted to talk to you first of all about a change of time. Nothing definite, just wanted to kick it around a little, try it on for size. Now, I'm just talking off the top of my head, but it seemed to me that we're missing a bet by having you on at eleven-forty-five. Doesn't give you a chance to really do much work on your play reviews. After all, you don't get out of the theater before eleven-fifteen. That hardly gives you much of a chance to really get some sort of perspective on the show you've just seen."

"That's what is known as first impression, Sid, a fresh immediate reaction."

"Yeah, I see what you mean, Ed, but I was thinking about a change. I figured we're missing a big chunk of audience by not putting you on later. Most of the theater crowd hasn't gotten home by eleven-forty-five. It's just an idea. Nothing definite. I just thought I'd touch base with you on it."

Christ! Six miles from the Polo Grounds and we're touching base. How goddamned cozy.

"Look, Sid," I said. "Let's talk about it later. Maybe over lunch."

The kid came in with my breakfast and I paid him.

"Fine, Ed. That's not really why I called you. About that play last night . . ."

"I understand you were there. You should have looked me up. You could have had a drink with Frenchie at intermission and forgotten to come back."

"Now, Ed . . . it wasn't that bad."

"The hell it wasn't."

"I wanted to talk to you about your review because . . ."

"All right, talk."

"Not on the phone. Why don't we have lunch together and talk it over quietly?"

"Go ahead, Sid. What I want is that first impression, that fresh, immediate reaction."

"There's no reason to get nasty, Ed."

"Who's getting nasty? What's on your mind? Go ahead, kick it around . . . try it on for size. You might even try touching base with me on it."

"Relax, Ed. Why don't you order yourself a nice big breakfast?"

"I'm eating it now."

"I didn't say I didn't like your review. I just said I thought you were being unnecessarily harsh."

"Which theater were you in last night? Look, Sid, a girl meets a boy. They fall in love. He goes away. She discovers she's pregnant. She can't find him. She has the baby out of town and pretends it's an adopted child. Shall I go on?"

"I know, but I still think you were unnecessarily harsh. As a matter of fact, I thought one of the girls in the cast was quite good."

"Really?"

"Yes. The kid sister. Harriet Conway, I think her name was."

"Harriet Conway you know damned well her name was."

"All right, Ed, let's stop talking around it. You know goddamned well she's the niece of Chuck Conway of Flexiwoven. You know goddamned well Don's been having a rough time holding onto the Flexiwoven account for the Phillips show. How do you think he's going to feel about the station after you go out of your way to pan hell out of his favorite niece in her Broadway debut?"

"I didn't go out of my way. I said she was lousy. And she was."

"And how many times have I told you that I don't like words like lousy used on our air?"

"You ought to be glad I changed it. Originally I planned to call her performance——"

"Aren't you getting a little too smart for your own good?"

"Sid, I'm having some people drop into Schrafft's window at one-thirty. Do you think you could possibly make it?"

He hung up.

What a goddamned fool I was.

Rating or no rating, some day I was going to push that fat slob too far. Maybe this was the time.

I had no illusions about myself. I knew any guy who spoke the English language and had nothing against going to all the openings, knocking around the nightclubs and putting spots on his liver could step into my spot. I was just another fair-to-middling-sized wheel in local radio. No Fuller, Godfrey or Berle. Just another guy making a buck doing something that fifteen hundred other guys on Manhattan Island could have done just as well, given the chance. And someday Sid was going to give one of them the chance.

The interoffice phone buzzed.

"Mr. Moore's secretary called. Mr. Moore wants you to meet him at the Pig Pen at one for lunch."

"Roger."

"No, Sid."

"Very funny."

Well, I'm off the hook. We'll have a couple of drinks, eat lunch, bat it around, try it on for size, turn a few wheels, and I'll wind up with the Conway dame on my show tonight as my special guest. We'll turn that mountain into a molehill before we get around to coffee.

I finished my breakfast, went through the rest of the mail, talked to a few press agents on the phone and at twelve-thirty called Nicole Duval at her hotel. I find it hard to get worked up over French starlets at twelve-thirty, but dated her up for after the broadcast anyway. By midnight, I knew, I'd be feeling differently about the whole thing.

The Pig Pen is a restaurant in the basement of a brownstone on Sixty-First Street. Its name is Marcel's but nobody around WBSR ever called it that. I guess Gordon Austin, the assistant to the general manager, gave it that name. Gordon is a kind of apprentice Sid Moore. He comes in a different container . . . five foot four and very thin . . . but the contents are exactly the same. Same clichés, same hustling. Same bastard. Like John, the elevator operator, Gordon's always auditioning. But he's auditioning for an audience of one. He trots out all the new dirty jokes, pat phrases and ideas and all he wants in return for his research and energy is a pat on the head or a smile from Sid. A couple of years ago, when the Madison Avenue crowd was discovering hand-painted ties, Gordon spent a week end designing a special one. It had a microphone rampant on a field of corn. He had Countess Mara run up six of them for him and handed them out as Christmas presents. It was a big success. I still have mine home in my top bureau drawer.

The crowd at the station always ate in the same restaurant. For a while it was Feller's. They all had their own individual reasons.

"No matter what else you say about Feller's, they make the best soup in New York."

"If you're like me, you're very particular about the way your martini is made. Joe, behind the bar, does something really special with the rind of a lemon. That's the only reason I go there."

Most of all, they liked it, I guess, because it was like a gathering of the clan. The same reason the sports writers go to Leone's or Toots Shor's. The same reason the theater crowd goes to Sardi's or the circus people go to the Belvedere Bar. Everybody spoke the same language. If you used phrases like "across the board," "conflict" or "live piping to CRI," people knew what you meant. The booths were comfortable if you wanted to sit around after lunch playing Gin for a couple of hours after you'd polished off five or six of those special martinis that Joe, behind the bar, fixed up with that special knack he had with a rind of lemon. But after a while, with nobody saying a word, giving a signal or sending a memo to anybody else, they shifted to the Wagon Lit, a restaurant just down the street from Feller's. It had a buffet lunch, booths and its bartender, Jerry, also had a special way with a lemon rind in a martini.

Sid was the discoverer of Marcel's. He had a date one afternoon with a V.P. and didn't want to run into the rest of the mob, so he headed east across Park and discovered Marcel's. He kept going there and one by one the rest of the crowd followed him. Marcel's became the logical successor to the Wagon Lit. At first they said, "Meet you at Marcel's." Then they said, "Meet you at the joint." Gordon came up with the final refinement: "Meet you at the Pig Pen."

The Pig Pen, like its predecessors, was more than just a place to eat. It was a special little microcosm all by itself. You did business over lunch. The salesmen sold spots to account executives and time buyers from B.B.D.&O. and Esty. You played the match game. You had a phone brought to your table and called your bookmaker in Jersey. You shoved the needle into anybody that was taking pot shots at your job and, fortunately for Marcel, an Italian who spoke with a carefully acquired French accent, Lew, the bartender, had a special knack with a sidecar. He put just a dash of vodka in the mixer. It made all the difference in the world.

That Monday, the Pig Pen was jammed.

Marcel greeted me at the door, guided me past the suburbanites standing four deep waiting for tables and led me to Sid, who was in his usual place, just next to the bar. He was studying the hors d'oeuvres tables.

"Feeling better?" he asked.

"Much."

"Good."

"Where's Gordon? Don't tell me he's learned to eat by himself."

"He's bird-dogging the Tommy Carter Show. It took a nose dive in the rating last month. Gordon's giving it the ear for a week or two."

"We'll miss him."

Marcel handed both of us the menu, hand-printed and about the size of the Herald Tribune.

"Gentlemans, the turkey ees veree good today. Mostly light and dark meat."

Sid ordered onion soup and the filet mignon Wellington. So did I. Plus a couple of Lew's special sidecars.

I waited for Sid to bring up the Conway dame. I was going to be a little tough about it, not give in until dessert. He surprised me.

"Getting a little sick of the show, Ed?" he asked.

I didn't want him to continue on that track.

"Look, Sid, about the Conway dame—I'm sorry the whole thing came up. . . ."

"Who's talking about that. You're absolutely right, Ed. She was lousy. I blew my top on the phone this morning because Don was pressuring me. I guess Chuck Conway was pressuring him. To change the subject, I've been talking about you to the boys upstairs."

"Yeah?"

"I think you have a chance of making it, Ed. Twelve years ago Herb Fuller was just where you are now . . . a medium big shot on local radio. Nobody ever heard his name west of Madison, New Jersey. But he had something. He was ripe for the network build-up. I think maybe you are too."

Maybe he meant it. If he was just getting the Conway dame on the show the hard way, he was certainly giving it the full treatment. I didn't say anything. I dipped into my sidecar.

"You know, Ed," said Sid, "it's a long shot. The boys upstairs figure the first thing to do is work out some sort of a gimmick format. Maybe a kind of fake show business clinic. Maybe a giveaway show. Maybe almost anything. But a gimmick. Something that isn't too new or too unusual. The Yuks will eat up the same old bait and maybe they'll swallow you along with it."

"You make me sound like a real hotshot . . . sort of a cross between a worm and an old piece of squid."

"That's just about what you are now."

"Thanks. Did you happen to look at this month's ratings?"

"Ratings! What do they prove? One or two phone calls can mean the difference between 3.5 and 2.7."

"I wish you'd remember that the next time the rating drops."

"Look, Ed. Twelve years ago Herb Fuller was exactly where you are now. I spoke to the boys upstairs about him and they said, sure, find a gimmick show. I found one. It caught on and so did Herb."

"America's beloved humorist."

"Sure. He can't sing very well. He isn't very funny. But right now he's the hottest performer in the country. You know how much he grossed last year, before taxes?"

"Two hundred thousand?"

"He makes two hundred grand on his records alone."

"That should make me a cinch, Sid. I can't sing at all and I'm not the least bit funny."

"I'm not kidding, Ed. Fuller's secret is very simple. He's a Yuk. He's king of the lodge. He's the Grand Imperial Yuk. He's so corny he's clever. With you I think we need a different approach."

"Like what?"

"You know what you've got?"

"Four hundred and fifty-seven bucks in the bank."

"You're a snotty bastard. You're bright, you're mildly clever, you have a good voice and you know how to put words together. But above and beyond all that, you're a snotty bastard. And maybe the swing is about due. Maybe, for a while, the snotty bastards are going to inherit the top ratings and the big billings. Maybe that's the kind of a format we need. Maybe the Yuks are getting a little fed up with the sweetness and light and the homey touch. Maybe they'll buy a little snottiness."

"Why bother with me? Why don't you cash in on the trend?"

"See what I mean? A snotty bastard. Another guy on the verge of a break, playing footsie with a big build-up, would rupture himself being nice to the guy that can do those things for him. Not you. Not lovable old Ed Harris."

"Seriously, Sid."

"Who isn't being serious?"

"I've heard this build-up talk before. Like nine years ago when I came out of the navy."

"A pink-faced lieutenant-commander with a letter of introduction. I'll do anything, you said—anything. So they sent you down to me. After all, they said, Sid Moore's an old friend of yours. You used to know him before the war when he was a salesman and you were the fastest mailboy Amalgamated ever had. Go down and see Sid, they said, he'll do something for you. And I did, didn't I?"

"Sure."

"You're damned right I did. I didn't stick you in any mailroom either. I stuck you in front of a microphone. You weren't such a snotty bastard then, were you?"

"Do you really like these sidecars with vodka in them, Sid?"

"Sure. Lew has a knack with them. They're great."

By this time we'd finished our soup and Marcel brought the filet mignon Wellington. He always served us personally. WBSR was responsible for half his business day in and day out and he fawned on Sid and Gordon. When I was with Sid, I got the benefit of the reflected glory.

We ate in silence for awhile.

"Ed, I'm very serious about the things I said earlier. I have spoken to them upstairs about you. What I'd like you to do is kick around a couple of ideas for a format, then come in and bounce them off me. Meanwhile, how about switching your show to twelve-fifteen? I really think we'll pick up a chunk of audience."

"It's all right with me, and if you're serious about the format deal I'll see what I can come up with."

"Don't wait too long. Now, will you do me a favor?"

"Have her in the studio at eleven-thirty."

"Like I said, Ed . . . a sweet reasonable guy. That's your great charm."

Marcel came over to our table carrying the phone like it contained the head of John the Baptist. He plugged it into the wall next to the table and handed the receiver to Sid.

Sid didn't say much into the phone. Just "Hello" and then he listened. The blood drained out of his face and he lit a cigarette, took two puffs and then crushed it out in the ash tray.

"What time?" asked Sid and listened some more.

"Get two reservations on the first plane going up there. Cancel the Harris show tonight and have the music library set up a fifteen minute disk show in place of it. And listen, Gordon, don't say a goddamned thing to any reporters until I get back!"

He hung up and lit another cigarette.

"What happened?" I asked.

"I told that dumb son of a bitch. I told him. No, he had to make like Barney Oldfield."

"Fuller?"

"He crashed just outside Hartford, Connecticut."

"Dead?"

"Not yet. They took him to the hospital. In bad shape. Listen, I canceled your show for tonight."

"So I heard."

"You and I are going up to Hartford on the first available plane. Gordon's working on the reservations now. We'll go back to the office and pick up a minitape. When Fuller regains consciousness I want you at the bedside with a recorder. We'll have to do some sort of a memorial show, if he dies, and this could be what we've been looking for."

"What are you talking about?"

"The gimmick . . . the format . . . the big splash . . . what we were talking about for the last hour and a half."

"I hate to bring this up, but suppose he doesn't die?"

"He'll die. But he'd better not die before we get there. He'd better not."

We got out of the Pig Pen fast. Back at the office I picked up the minitape, a battery-operated, portable recording machine, about the size of a large shoe box. I used it a lot covering fires and plane crashes. This was the first time I was taking it to a death bed. Gordon had our reservations and we had forty minutes to catch our plane.

By the time we got to the airport, the afternoon papers had the story. Most of them just had the headline, "Herb Fuller Crashes! In Critical Condition." The *Journal-American* ran a picture of Herb in his Cadillac convertible and had evidently replated the front page fast with a hashed up rewrite of what must have been the standard obit. There weren't many details. Sid had been on the phone talking to the hospital in Hartford and all he knew was that the car had suddenly swerved, hit the side of a railroad embankment and turned over. Fuller had evidently been plastered all over the landscape and, while Sid was talking to them, they were preparing to amputate the right leg just above the knee.

On the plane, on the way up to Hartford, Sid was full of plans.

"They'll have to let me into the act this time," he said.

"Who will?"

"The Network."

When he used the word you could almost hear the capital letter.

"That's been bothering me, Sid. What do you have to do with Fuller anymore? He's network property. You have no claim on him at all."

"No?"

"Do you?"

"Listen, Ed, I found him. He was a broken-down lush, working on a 200-watt station outside Boston. I brought him down to New York and shoved him down their throats. I was a salesman then, I had no business poking my nose into the program end, but I convinced them that Fuller had something, so they put him on as our morning man. Brother, was he lousy!"

"Like the Conway dame?"

"Not that bad, but lousy. I wet-nursed him, bottle-fed him, got him off the booze and worked my tail off peddling spots on his show. First thing you know, he had all the other local morning shows backed right against the wall. He had them where the hair is short. I started branching out with him. I hired two guys to write gags and feed him jokes. I created him out of a booze bottle in Worcester, Mass., and I only made one mistake."

"What was that?"

"I never figured him for anything but a local phenom. I figured after he hit locally and got me two promotions, I'd gotten everything out of him there was to get. How wrong can you get?"

"Who could guess? Right now, if you'd never heard of him, would you pick him out of a general audition?"

"No, I guess not. Every once in a while a pebble on the infield bounces one over your head. That was a million-dollar boot. I got caught looking at the third strike that time."

"Completely?"

"Well . . . no . . . not completely. I didn't take my bat off my shoulder, but I had another lick coming. I raised hell when the network wanted to take him over. I told them it wouldn't go. He's strictly a local wheel, I told them . . . but they said they wanted to carry the ball for a while, so I went out and dug him up a format and for that they gave me a piece of him. Not a chunk. Just a piece. But it's enough of a wedge to get into the act now. Maybe, now, finally, I'm going to make something out of Fuller. They're throwing side-arm but I've got my switch hitter up."

"Now you're going to make something out of Fuller?"

"With you. Look, Ed, don't get any illusions about yourself. You just happen to be handy. But before I move a muscle, before I call a signal or open up a hole for you to go through, we sit down, the two of us, and sign a contract. And this time, I want a chunk."

"What would a chunk of four hundred and fifty-seven bucks come to?"

"Right now Fuller's got a potful of radio and TV shows, right?"

"Right."

"And they're up for grabs. Somebody has to do them. Maybe you. Why do you think I had you bring the cheese-box along?"

"To record the sound of the splash as you siphon out the last drop of the Great Man's blood."

That stopped Sid for a minute.

"Listen, wise guy," he said, and he was mad, "stop being a snotty bastard for a minute and listen to your old coach, Sid. From now on, you're the official chief mourner, intimate grief-stricken friend and maybe even pallbearer, if I can work it. When he dies you stick the best piece of black silk you can find around the sleeve of your coat and go into mourning for your good, true and intimate friend, Herb Fuller."

"You know how intimate Herb Fuller and I are? I used to deliver his mail. He once gave me a bottle of scotch for Christmas, me and the rest of the mailboys."

"From now on, Herb Fuller is the best friend you had in the world. He gave you your first job in radio and you're not ashamed to wear that black silk band around your sleeve in his memory."

The hostess came down the aisle and leaned down.

"Will you fasten your safety belts please," she said. "We'll be landing in ten minutes and it may get a little bumpy over Hartford."

We fastened our safety belts, put out our cigarettes and leaned back. I suddenly remembered something.

"Remind me to make a phone call when we get to Hartford, will you, Sid?"

"Sure. Who to?"

"Nicole. I'm supposed to pick her up at midnight. I don't suppose we'll be back by then."

"You and I are mapping out a campaign that will make Grant, Lee and Napoleon look like a trio of Fort Benning ninety-day wonders and all you can think about is a broad."

"A French broad. There's a difference."

"You're going to have to lay off that for a while. Until Fuller's good and dead and good and buried, you're going to lead the life of a Trappist monk."

"Aren't you carrying this period of mourning a little too far, Sid? What the hell does Nicole have to do with my good, dear intimate friend, Herb Fuller?"

"You think this is all a gag. You think it's just batting practice. Old Sid's just hitting fungoes. I'm damned serious."

"So is Nicole."

"She'll keep."

"Sid, you don't put something like that in an icebox for a while and find it there when you go back for it."

"I'll tell you what I'll do, Ed. I'll take her off your hands for a while. That'll keep the rest of the wolves away. Then when it's safe for you to do a little coo-shaying again, I'll deliver her back to you in good condition."

"I think you're serious."

I knew damned well he was serious.

"Why not?" he asked. He was smiling sort of tentatively. That gave him a chance to retreat if I really got tough about it.

"I thought you said you wanted a chunk instead of a piece, Sid."

"It was just an idea."

"Sure. Touch base with somebody else on it."

"Take it easy, Skipper. I was kidding."

"You're a very funny man. A little disgusting but very funny."

"She must really be something to get you so hot under the collar."

"Let's get that straight. She is something, something that, at the moment, is mine. I like it that way. We like each other fine and as long as we're going to work together, let's straighten something out right now. You haven't anything I want, I haven't anything you can have. We're not playing Switch."

"O.K., take it easy, Ed, boy. You scored. You don't have to kick the extra point. Take it easy."

The plane started heading down. No matter how many times you fly, this is still a tough couple of minutes. You grit your teeth, press your feet against the ledge under the seat in front of you, swallow air and sweat it out. Not Sid. He just kept talking.

"There may be some reporters at the airport. I had Gordon phone ahead and set it up. Keep your mouth shut and put a solemn look on your kisser. And curb your natural instinct to smile into their lenses."

"We come to bury Caesar, not to laugh at him."

"There'll be more reporters at the hospital."

"Keep my mouth shut and put a solemn look on my kisser."

"Right."

"Suppose they won't buy me upstairs on the network?"

"They'll buy you. Maybe not right away, but they'll buy. There are plans underway already to do a big memorial show for Fuller when he dies."

"If he dies."

"He'll die. You don't plow into a railroad embankment at eighty-five miles an hour and come out of it alive. I'm running the memorial show and you'll be on it. If I can swing it, you'll be the only one on it . . . maybe a couple of recordings of Fuller's top shows . . . but nobody else. I'm just thinking out loud, ad libbing right now, but whatever we do or however we do it, I promise you this will be the big splash, the gimmick, the beginning."

We were only a couple of hundred feet off the ground now and I thought, "Christ, if we crash that'll be the last thing I'll ever hear—a Moore cliché."

We didn't crash. We bounced twice when we hit the runway but we didn't crash. When we taxied up to the terminal there were three lone photographers waiting for us. I looked solemn and kept my mouth shut while they shot us getting out of the plane.

Gordon had screwed up the arrangements. He was supposed to have a car meet us at the airport and drive us to the hospital. It wasn't there. We grabbed a private cab and right away the driver wanted to talk.

"You wanna ride past the place where Fuller's car hit?" he asked.

"No thanks," said Sid. "Just get us to the hospital."

"You from New York? Friends of his?"

"Close, personal, you might say intimate, friends."

"Gee, that's tough. I hear he was loaded."

Sid leaned forward.

"Listen, goddamn it, you drive and keep your big mouth shut. Who cares what you hear?"

"O.K. I was just talking."

"One of the sweetest guys that ever lived, am I right, Ed?"

"The sweetest," I said.

"The sweetest guy ever lived and before he's even cold in his grave, you buzzards are spreading lies about him. Don't you know that Herb Fuller never took a drink in his life?"

"Is that right?" said the driver. "I don't know how people can go around spreading stories like that. I told the guy at the lunch counter he was fulla crap."

I thought Sid was pouring it on a little. We didn't say anything to each other on the way in. I looked solemn and tried to figure out how much of what he'd said coming down on the plane was the old high-pressure malarky. Sid lives in a world where you're never caught without a plan or an angle and this build-up routine might have been just so much reflex action. But why bring me along and why the minitape? And they would have to do some kind of a memorial program to Fuller if he died. It didn't figure all the way. But one thing I was sure of. Sid wasn't kidding about Nicole. I made a mental note to call her the minute we got to the hospital. Well, maybe not the minute we got there. It wouldn't look right to fly up from New York and rush to a phone to call a dame in New York. I'd have to wait awhile and maybe slip into a pay phone later. I had until midnight. It was just a little after six now.

I was surprised to find there were no reporters in the lobby of the hospital. It seemed to me that even in Hartford, Connecticut, they'd put a death watch on a guy like Herb Fuller. The reception room was empty too. Sid went over to the desk and identified himself and asked if he could see Mr. Fuller.

The girl behind the switchboard asked him to wait a minute. A couple of minutes later a doctor wearing an operating-room gown came over to us.

"I'm Doctor Connors," he said. "Are you Mr. Moore?"

"That's right."

"New York called and said you were coming. Would you come into my office for a minute? There are a few routine questions I'd like to ask you."

"This is Ed Harris."

We shook hands and followed him down the corridor to his office.

"Mr. Moore, you were a close personal friend of Mr. Fuller's as well as a business associate?"

"Yes."

"Would you care to contact his wife or would you want us to do it?"

"He's dead?"

"Oh, I'm sorry. I thought you knew. He died a little less than an hour ago."

Sid blew his nose. I watched him carefully. I figured, if he cries, I cry. He didn't.

"Frankly, Mr. Moore," said the doctor, "he didn't have a chance. It's a miracle that he was still alive when they got him here. I don't think there was a bone in his body that wasn't broken. His right leg was almost severed and he'd lost a great deal of blood. We did an amputation immediately and started a transfusion, but he died before it did any good."

Sid blew his nose again.

"Did he regain consciousness at all, Doctor?"

"Well, I suppose you could say so. He wasn't lucid, if that's what you mean. But, in the strict sense of the word, he was conscious."

"I hope you won't misunderstand what I'm about to say, Doctor. But Herb was more than just a business associate of mine. I discovered him seventeen years ago. We were very close. Ed here got his start in radio through Herb. They were inseparable. Both of us feel a keen sense of personal loss, but I think everybody in America that ever laughed at him, chuckled with him or was moved by his simple humanity lost a friend tonight."

"I suppose you might say that, Mr. Moore. Mrs. Connors and I enjoyed his programs very much."

Sid was moving into high gear now. You could almost hear the harp glissando in the background and violins picking up the main theme.

"He was more than just a performer. He was a real integral part of American life. Dr. Connors, the Amalgamated Broadcasting System will want to do a memorial program for Herb. Coast to coast. A tribute to a great American. Mr. Harris here, who knew Herb better than most of us were privileged to, will narrate it. What I wanted to ask you was this, Doctor. You were fortunate enough to spend his last minutes with him. Could you tell us if there were any final words? Did he say anything—just before he died?"

I unpacked the minitape, plugged in the mike and handed it to the doctor.

"I'll want that as part of the memorial program, Doctor," I said. "I wonder if you'd mind repeating his last words for us."

The doctor started to say something and then stopped.

"It's all right, Doctor," Sid said. "Don't let the mike frighten you. If you don't get it right the first time we can always do it over again. It's a tape recording. We can wipe it clean."

"It isn't that, Mr. Moore. It's just that I don't think you'd really be interested in what he had to say."

"Look, Doctor, suppose you let us decide that."

The doctor shrugged his shoulders.

"All right. It was just before we gave him the transfusion. He was mumbling. Aside from the injuries he was in a considerable state of shock. He kept trying to say something, so I leaned over and then—just before he died he said one word."

"What was it?"

"He said—he said—'Sh . . . '"

Before he even finished the word I was afraid for a minute I was going to laugh. I didn't. We thanked the doctor, told him we'd contact him from New York about the body and went back to the airport.

We got back to New York around ten that night. I left Sid at the Airline Terminal on First Avenue and I agreed to be in his office at ten the next morning.

I caught a cab and went up to Nicole's hotel.

I was two hours early but she was expecting me. At least, I guess she was. She was in bed.

I didn't feel a bit like a Trappist monk.

TUESDAY

READING the papers Tuesday morning, as I did over the eighty-five-cent breakfast in the Lexington Avenue Childs, you'd have thought nothing else had happened in the world. The *Times* gave it the two right-hand columns on page one. Their headline was explicit: HERB FULLER, RADIO AND TV PERFORMER, KILLED IN AUTO CRASH

It wouldn't have occurred to anybody but the *Times* to put the parenthetical description in. It was a little like saying "Douglas MacArthur, army general" or "Pius, well-known church figure."

The *Herald Tribune* put it in a three-column spread at the bottom of page one.

The *Daily News* had a black headline and two pictures: one of Fuller in front of a mike, the other a shot of the wreck . . . an A P wirephoto. The *Mirror* had the same two pictures and on page four they had the first of an eight-part bio of Fuller by Bob Considine. It was juicy.

Nick Kenny had a poem about how Heaven was a happier place now that Fuller was there.

Winchell did a piece headed: "Herb Fuller—American."

The *News* had gone to the most trouble. They'd lifted out their centerfold and had a black-bordered page of Fuller pictures. They also had one of their special "Subway English" editorials.

HE'S DEAD!

People stopped total strangers on the street yesterday afternoon and said, "He's dead. Herb's dead." And you shook your head a little and walked on, feeling like you'd lost a close friend or a member of the family.

Sure, he was just a clown.

A comic.

His jokes were stale and his face wouldn't win any beauty contests.

But Herb Fuller was a great American. We like stale jokes and we don't have any silver loving cups on our mantel either.

We understand Abe Lincoln used to sit around the parlor of the White House and spin some mighty corny yarns. And you know what he looked like.

Like an American.

And like Abe Lincoln, Herb Fuller was as easy and as comfortable as an old shoe . . . as familiar as your old pair of suspenders. The sophisticates, the city slickers, the wise guys laughed at his corny philosophy but he didn't let that stop him. He believed in his country and loved it and wasn't ashamed to say so . . . to an audience of thirty million of his fellow cornballers.

In a way, Herb Fuller was a sort of composite American . . . he was all the corny Americans from coast to coast who think going to church on Sunday is important . . . who think raising a family is important . . . who think saying that this is a great country and a great flag is important.

We'll all miss him.

An important piece of America was destroyed on that lonely railroad embankment in Hartford, Connecticut.

We'll miss him but we won't soon forget the things he believed in, talked about and loved.

May his soul rest in peace.

Amen.

Amen, indeed.

I slid my check and a dollar bill across the cashier's desk.

"He's dead," I said. "Herb's dead."

The girl looked at me.

"Who?" she asked.

"Herb," I said.

"Oh," she said, handing me my fifteen cents change. "You mean that radio comic. I heard it on the air last night."

"He was a great American," I said. "Like Abraham Lincoln. Ugly but great."

"He wasn't so ugly. I see fifty people a day come in and out of this place are uglier than he was."

"Listen, sister," I said. "He didn't have any silver loving cups on his mantle."

"I guess not," she said, giving me a queer look. I had the feeling she was trying to decide whether or not to call the manager. I smiled and walked out onto Lexington Avenue. It was a beautiful day. I felt fine. No hangover. And I'd gotten to bed early the night before. Of course I had to get up at two-thirty and go home, but I'd sure gotten to bed early.

On the way over to Amalgamated, I decided to try making up for yesterday by being nice to Peter and Artie. I didn't have to try at all. Funny what a couple of lines in a couple of columns can do for you. I noticed the difference immediately when I walked into the Amalgamated Building. Peter held the door open for me.

"You'd better move your tail, peasant," he said. "You can be replaced, you know."

It was a subtle difference. Yesterday morning I was just another guy to be greeted with "The Book of the Month to You." This morning I'd moved up a couple of thousand dollars a year. I was now a "You can be replaced" man.

It was a subtle difference but anyone of the agency, radio, TV crowd would have noticed it and been impressed by it. They used to say in Marcel's that you could tell from Peter's greeting how much an Amalgamated employee made a year.

The huge grinning picture of Fuller in the chrome frame that's been hanging in the Amalgamated lobby for as long as I can remember was draped in black. When I walked into the elevator Artie gave me the big smile and sent the car right up even though there were only two other passengers, both over-age delivery boys. It was five to ten by the reception room clock on the ninth floor, so I decided to stop off in my office first. On the way I got the big smile from the new receptionist and a broad wink from Lillian who was busy on the phone. The March of Events, however, did nothing to soften Ginny's regular morning disposition. She nodded at me and went right back to her container of coffee.

I looked through the mail on my desk, hurriedly. Nothing there of any importance, except a bill from Goldfarb for the twelve corsages I'd sent Nicole in the last month. Meat prices certainly were going up. Ginny came in with my usual breakfast. I downed it out of habit.

"You'd better get a move on," she said.

"I know. I can be replaced."

"You're due in Mr. Moore's office five minutes ago."

"I know."

"The big brass from the Network have been floating in since nine-thirty. Are you the heir apparent, like the papers say?"

"Ask me that same question in two hours. I'm going to give it the old college try this morning."

"Big deal. How was Hartford, Connecticut?"

"Lovely place."

"That's the trouble with you. No small talk."

"Look, Ginny, let's call a truce this morning. I'm nervous. I'm not up to ad libbing on this level."

"The brass got you worried?"

"To be perfectly honest with you for the first time in our

long relationship, I'm scared silly. To use a Sid Mooreism, I'm gonna boot this grounder sure as you're a foot high."

"That's two Sid Mooreisms."

"Do I look all right?"

"You look lovely. Did you see Fuller last night?"

"He was dead when we got there. Did you ever meet him—Fuller?"

"Once. Before I worked for you I was in the typist pool. One day I got sent up to work for the Great Man for a couple of days."

"And?"

"He made a pass at me almost immediately. He was a real bastard."

"Did you happen to notice how much he looked like Abe Lincoln?"

"It's funny you should mention that. I always thought he looked more like George Washington, with just a touch of Huck Finn thrown in."

"As easy and comfortable as an old shoe or your favorite zipper."

"A real bastard."

"Well, I might as well get into the meeting. Don't commit yourself until I get out. Who knows I may want to make a pass at you."

"I'll enroll at Berlitz while I'm waiting. They have a very good French course."

"Very funny."

Ginny took the mail off my desk and left the office to sort it at her desk, just outside the door. I sat down for a couple of minutes. The truth was that I was frightened, bad. I had a cramp in the pit of my stomach. This was the time I had to play it right. This was the time I couldn't afford to screw it up. I finally got up, straightened my tie in the mirror over the coat rack, pulled up the corners of the show-off handkerchief in my breast pocket and walked down the hall to Sid's office.

Sid gave me the cue as soon as I walked in the door.

I took a quick look around. I recognized two V.P.'s, the Chairman of the Board, the President of the network, the network program director, the guy from William Morris who handled Fuller, the head of the Press Info Department and Nick Cellantano, Fuller's personal press agent. Big brass. Very big brass.

Sid came from behind his desk and took my arm, like I was his pregnant aunt from Peoria trying to cross Fifth Avenue at five o'clock.

"Glad you could make it, Ed," he said. "You feeling better?"

"Yes, Sid, thanks," I said, playing it by ear. "I feel fine now."

"I had a mighty sick boy on my hands last night," Sid said to the rest of the room. "I think, in a purely personal way, Ed feels this more than any of the rest of us."

I kind of half smiled. I figured I underplayed that bit fine. A regular Spencer Tracy.

"I don't know whether you know everybody here or not," Sid said, leading me to a chair between the two V.P.'s. The only one I knew to speak to was Nick, but we all nodded as we were introduced as if it was an unnecessary formality.

Sid sat behind his desk again.

"I hope the rest of you will bear with me while I bring Ed up to date," he said. "Ed, here's the way it stands. Fuller's body is over at Campbell's now. They've put one of their best men on it. Fortunately, the face wasn't bruised. We decided on a half-open coffin . . . something simple but expensive . . . red maple, wasn't it, Harry? I guess it's as obvious to you as it was to us that we couldn't just bury Herb, like that. The people wouldn't want it that way. First off, we thought of St.

Patrick's. It seemed to some of us that it was an ideal place . . . large, centrally located and you know—it has a certain dignity. We thought we'd have him lie in state for a couple of days in the center aisle and let the public file past. Like they do in Westminster Abbey. They wouldn't buy it. They were nice about it, but they wouldn't buy. I think they were afraid of the crowds, but the clincher for them was that Herb wasn't a Catholic. Harry, did you ever find out what he was?"

Harry Connors, the head of Press Info, consulted a piece of paper he had in his hand.

"I don't think you could honestly say he was anything."

"Anyway," continued Sid, "when they vetoed the Cathedral, we had a couple of other ideas. Yankee Stadium—the Polo Grounds was out because the Giants are in town this week—anyway, we agreed that maybe the Stadium wasn't quite dignified enough. We discarded Madison Square Garden for the same reason. Finally, Harry, here, came up with the best idea of the lot. We had the carpenters working all last night on Studio 41. They turned it into a chapel, stained glass windows and all. Did a hell of a job. We'll cancel all broadcast tickets for the next week and move the ushering staff over to 41 to handle the crowds. We'll move the coffin in there this afternoon and open it up to the public daily from nine to five. We've arranged for a change of flowers every four hours, the Religious Department has set up a rotating schedule of choirs—all denominations—so that there'll be some singing group working all the time. The mikes will be hidden in the flower beds. TV is clearing fifteen minutes a night from now on, until the funeral Saturday morning, and we'll have a different preacher in every night delivering a eulogy. How many stations have we cleared for it?"

Harry Connors looked at the paper in his hand again.

"Fifty-four at the moment," he said. "The rest will come

into line. I think it's safe to say, Sid, that we'll have the basic TV network riding with us on this."

"Good," said Sid. And I sat there admiring the way he seemed to have taken over.

Charley Carouthers, the network's program director, cleared his throat.

"Our feeling is," he said, "that this whole thing must have a great deal of dignity to it. If we use showmanship, nobody but us should be aware of the sweat that goes into it. We can't make a circus out of Fuller's death. On the other hand, we have a certain responsibility to Fuller's memory and, to be mercenary for a moment, the amount of billing he's represented to this network. As far as all the other shows on radio are concerned, network and local, the policy is hands off—strictly. No mention of Fuller's death, no tributes, no cheap maudlin sentimentality. We'll pick up that nightly sermon from Studio 41 for radio, full net. As far as Fuller's shows are concerned, the thinking seems to be to go along for the rest of the week, with old transcriptions. We've been listening to tapes of old Fuller shows all night and we've come up with a dozen of his best with Herb right at the top of his form. We've edited out any topical references and we'll put them on the air starting today. It seems to me that this is the best memorial to Herb Fuller, the way he'd have wanted it."

Charley stopped and blew his nose. Well, I figured, that takes care of me.

"Now, Ed," said Charley, stowing his handkerchief away in the inside pocket of his jacket, "let's get around to you."

About time.

"Sid," he nodded to Sid, "Sid, as you probably know, has no right being in this picture at all. He's local. This is strictly, it would seem on the surface, a network operation. However, the thinking seems to be that since Sid found Fuller in the first place and since he has a certain claim that I won't go into here, we'd bring him into the picture."

"And he brought you into the picture."

It was like the voice of God.

If you worked at Amalgamated, that's exactly what it was. It was the first time I'd ever heard Philip Carleton, president of Amalgamated, speak. Charley shut up. I figured the star halfback was about to run with the ball.

"Sid was all for moving you right into Fuller's shows," he said. "Immediately. I'm against that. Ed, I'm going to be very blunt with you, maybe brutally frank. Do you mind?"

"Do I dare?"

This merry sally was greeted by quiet laughter.

"Let me tell you why, Ed. Sid's a good boy. I like Sid, but I'm still running this network."

Sid jumped into the breach.

"I didn't mean anything by it, Phil. It was just a suggestion."

"That's all right, Sid. I'm not chastising you. I'm just being blunt and frank. I like running this network and I intend to continue doing it. My way. And my way is keeping Ed under wraps temporarily. As of right now, Ed, you don't have the stature to step into Fuller's shoes . . . or his shows. It would do all of us a lot of harm if we overlooked that fact."

Sid jumped in again. It seemed to me he was taking a lot of chances. God has a big right hand just made for slapping people like Sid Moore down.

"Let me tell you something about this boy Ed Harris, Phil. Nine years ago he was just another guy in a sailor suit with a ruptured duck and a set of discharge papers in his pocket. In those nine years he's built himself up into the best cleanup hitter our team has ever had. You have to admit one thing, Phil. Remember, I picked Fuller. Remember, I had to stuff him down your throats, starting at the local level right on up to your office. Remember, Fuller's billings have kept this network in the black for the past ten years. I think Ed Harris here can do the same thing."

"I'd be the last one in the world to belittle Ed's potential, Sid," said Philip Carleton. "I think he's doing a tremendous job locally. We've had our eye on him for a long time."

A hell of a long time.

"Just remember something else, Phil," said Sid. "This time I have a contract. This time I'm part of the package. This time I go with the crackerjack box. I'm the prize you get."

Carleton ignored that.

"It would be a great mistake to move him into Fuller's spot immediately. Face it, Sid, we're salesmen. We have to create a market for our product before we start selling it. I think people might resent Harris if he stepped into Fuller's spot immediately. He's big in New York but do I have to remind you that New York isn't America? I think we have to prepare them for Harris. We have to give him a foot up the ladder. That brings us around to the memorial show."

Now we were getting somewhere.

"Charley, do you want to carry the ball on this?"

Charley blew his nose again, replaced his handkerchief and carried the ball.

"All right, Harris, this is the way it goes. We've cleared the full network for a special memorial show on Friday at ten. Radio only. Our original idea was to put on an all-star show . . . like those Heart and Cancer benefits . . . every big name in show business . . . some government names . . . good ones. Sid, here, sold you instead. Maybe he's right, maybe he isn't. It depends on what you can come up with."

Sid jumped in again.

"Ed and I had a long talk on the plane ride back from Hartford. We were both pretty broken up after we left that hospital and we talked a lot. Charley, this time I think you're playing the brass when you should be orchestrated for strings. I think you're overselling what you've got. What you've got is Fuller. Or at least, the Fuller that the public knew. He had heart and humor and the common touch. Did you see that editorial in the *News* this morning? You have Abe Lincoln and you're trying to sell him like Martin and Lewis. He'd be the first one to give the loud Bronx cheer to a big, splashy, Ziegfeldy production and the Great American Public knows it."

Sid had their attention now.

"Ed, tell them what you told me on the way back from Hartford last night."

Like I said, Sid's a real bastard. And can he throw you a curve when you're all set for a fast ball!

From here on in, I had to really play it by ear.

"I want to do something simple," I said. "Because that's the kind of a guy Herb Fuller was. Simple. Maybe I'm wrong, but I think his basic appeal was that everybody listening to him felt this guy wasn't much different from himself or her husband, or her brother who tells off-color stories and puts a lampshade on his head when he gets loaded at a party."

I was making it up good.

"That was his real claim to greatness. He was the common man with his voice amplified. If you're a skinny little runt you can't fool yourself that you look like Robert Taylor. You know that Ava Gardner wouldn't give you a second glance. But with Fuller it was different. He was just like you and you were able to identify yourself with him. You could believe that the things that happened to him could somehow happen to you."

I had them with me. I didn't know where we were going but they were along for the ride.

"I knew Herb about as well as any of you in this room, maybe better. He was the best friend I ever had."

This was the payoff. This was where my bluff could be called. I looked them over carefully. Nobody said a word. Nobody jumped up and said, "You're a goddamned liar."

"That's the kind of memorial program I'd like to do. I'd like to get out my tape recorder. I'd like to cover the Fuller story like a blanket between now and Friday. Talk to everybody that knew him . . . knew him when he was a dirty-faced kid selling newspapers, talk to his teachers, talk to his family, to Fran and the kids, to the guys in the orchestra, the vocalist from California he turned into a star, to the people everywhere who were a big part of Fuller's life and who knew him as only a very few of us were privileged to. I think that would truly be a memorial to him . . . to give that side of a great man to the American public."

I stopped. I decided to shoot the entire wad.

"I think," I said, "I think Herb would have liked that kind of a memorial."

There was silence for a full minute. Nobody said a word. I was watching only one man, Philip Carleton. The rest didn't matter. He did. I knew this was, to use a cliché much older than any of Sid's, It.

"I'll buy it."

Three words.

"I'll buy it."

Worth on the hoof about five hundred grand a word.

"O.K., Harris. It's your baby. You're on your own. Nick will turn over all the bio material on Fuller. Call on anybody at Amalgamated for anything you need. Good luck."

The tension in the room disappeared completely. Nervous smiles broke out on faces. The decision had been made. Carleton had made it. Nobody else was going to have to hold the bag if I turned out to be a bust. I was God's responsibility. They could all afford to be generous and mildly pleased. The thing that still bothered me was trying to figure out how Sid rated this much attention. He'd literally stuffed me down all their throats. The brass had come to *him*. The meeting was in *his* office. He was either the power behind the throne or knew where some body was buried. He'd sure impressed hell out of me in the past hour.

Sid looked as if he was about ready to hand out cigars. He was flushed and happy.

"You and Nick might as well run along now, Ed," he said. "You might as well get started right now. We'll cancel your show for the rest of the week. Nick can fill you in on the biographical material, maybe give you some leads. If you want to take an Ampex machine instead of the cheese box, Gordon can set up an engineer to go with you on your tape jobs."

"No thanks, Sid," I said. "I think I'd rather use the minitape. People have a habit of freezing up when you have a formal setup with an engineer. I would like someone to set me up some time in a tape room so I can listen to some of Fuller's old shows."

"Just lay off the stuff that's going on the air in his regular spot this week."

"I will."

"Fine. Good luck."

I shook hands all around. Philip Carleton patted me on the shoulder. I'm ashamed to say I liked it. Nick and I headed for the door.

"Oh, Ed," said Sid, "stop off at Eleanor's desk on your way out. She has some papers I want you to sign."

"Sure. And—thanks for everything—all of you. I'll do my best."

They smiled at me again and Nick and I went out the door. I stopped at Eleanor's desk. The papers were just what I thought they'd be . . . contracts. Personal management contracts that tied Sid and me together for the rest of our natural lives. He wasn't letting this one get away. The way the contracts were worded, he got a chunk of me from now on. Everything I did—if I won a two dollar bet on a horse—he got a chunk of. What the hell, without him there wouldn't be many chunks. I signed them. Nick smiled at me.

"Taking the oath of office?"

"My marriage license."

We took an elevator down to his office on the fourth floor. It looked more like a large closet than an office. There were no windows, no ventilation and his desk was set down in the middle of large file cabinets and iron tiers that stretched to the ceiling and contained back numbers of newspapers.

"Where do you want to start?" he asked.

"At the beginning. Give me everything you have on Fuller."

Nick pointed to the twelve file cabinets.

"You couldn't read it all between now and Friday night."

"Then just give me the meaty ones."

"They're all meaty. Suppose we start with the official Amalgamated bio."

He handed me a mimeographed sheet.

"This was the first piece I ever filed on Fuller. This is the Gospel according to St. Nicholas. Look it over, just don't try to verify any of it."

I looked it over.

It was headed: Herbert Fuller.

"Herbert?" I asked.

"There was a big discussion when he moved up to the network. They thought they might call him Herbert. Give him more dignity. When they decided to stick with Herb, nobody ever got around to running off a new bio. There isn't much in it anyway."

I glanced through it.

Herbert Fuller

Born: January 2, 1908, Cedar Rapids, Iowa.

Father: James Fuller, carpenter.

Mother: Mary Fuller, housewife and Sunday School teacher.

Education: Public School, Cedar Rapids High School. Radio School, Great Lakes Naval Training station.

Military Service: Enlisted in United States Navy September 1, 1926. Discharged September 1, 1933.

Marital status: Wife, Frances Fuller (nee Wiley), two children, Herbert, Junior (Born September 29, 1938), Harold (Born July 2, 1941)

Residence: New York City.

Program: "Herbert Fuller's World" Friday Evening 9:00–9:30 P.M. EST, Amalgamated Broadcasting System.

Photographs supplied upon request.

Nick was right. There wasn't much in it.

"Suppose I dig out all the important magazine breaks first? There are seven *Life* pieces . . . a couple of *Look* articles and a long piece on his World War II stuff in the *Times* magazine section. Will that be enough for a starter?"

"Fine."

Nick started pulling folders out of the file. I picked up one at random. It contained a piece *Life* did just after he'd started his network show. It was about Herb and Rickie Tyler and it was headed, "Her Boss Keeps Her in Stitches."

"Whatever happened to Rickie?" I asked.

Nick stopped pulling folders out of the file and sat back in his chair.

"Look, Ed. Let me give you some taboos before you get going. Lay off Rickie. As far as Amalgamated is concerned, she's dead."

"O.K."

"And lay off Fuller's old lady. Do a nice little story on Fran and the kids, talk to Steve and the boys in the band,

Carol, maybe Sherm Billingsley at the Stork and that cowboy actor he used to run around with—what was his name?"

"Ted Stoughton."

"Yeah. Ted Stoughton. Talk to people, but don't dig too deep. It'll just confuse you. You're doing a puff piece. Remember that. It'll save you a lot of trouble in the long run. You're doing a puff piece, like I've been doing for the last fifteen years."

"How did you get mixed up with Fuller in the first place?"

"Supply and demand. I needed a job, he needed a press agent."

"Did you like him?"

"He was the Great Man, wasn't he?"

"Did you like him?"

"That wasn't what I was hired for. There were a hundred and fifty million people that liked him. One word from him and they'd switch their toothpaste brand, their cheese, their shirts, maybe even their politics. I worked for him. I drafted some of those hundred and fifty million into his army for him."

"What *did* happen to Rickie?"

Nick lit a cigarette. Not the kind Fuller sold on TV. He noticed me looking at the pack.

"Man has to retain a little of his integrity somewhere along the line," he said, passing one to me.

"What happened to Rickie?" I repeated.

"I get a letter from her once in a while. She's living down in some southern town. She did all right for herself on the deal and not all of it will show up on her income tax form."

"When did they bust up?"

"Officially?"

"Or otherwise."

"Officially they parted amicably last September. Let that be an object lesson to you, your potential highness. Maybe in a couple of months they'll be measuring your can for a throne. Don't get your meat where you get your bread and butter. I've seen that secretary of yours. Don't get screwed up the way Fuller did. And Ginny's too nice a kid to go through what Rickie went through before she got her pile and got out."

"What'd she go through?"

"Look, all this has nothing to do with a puff piece. Sometime you and me will sit down and really talk about the Great Man. Right now, let's get to work on his monument."

Nick went back to the files.

Twenty minutes later the end of his desk was piled high with folders. This was only the cream of the file cabinets.

"That'll start you off," said Nick.

It was twelve-thirty. Nick suggested lunch.

We went to O'Leario's. That dated Nick. Nobody's gone to O'Leario's in the past five years. Nothing is as dead as last year's fad joint. Five years ago, if you rated at all in the New York smart set, you had to have lunch at O'Leario's at least once a week. Not any more. O'Leario's didn't exist any more. Suddenly it went out of style and it was like reading last year's best seller. It just wasn't something you did. Nick was a little apologetic when he suggested it.

"I like the place," he said. "Especially now that the fairies and the boys in the pin stripe suits have stopped going there."

We had beer with our lunch. That had gone out of style too. Now that it was no longer stylish and glamorous, O'Leario's looked like just what it had been all the time, a dingy Third Avenue bar.

Nick was talkative. He filled me in on the people on Fuller's show and gave me names and addresses.

We finished up our lunch and had some Irish coffee. I don't know what's so special about Irish coffee, except that they put a big slug of John Jamesson in it. I wondered what it would taste like with a big slug of vodka in it. This might be just the thing to introduce at the Pig Pen next time I had lunch there.

Nick was in no hurry to leave and we just sat smoking our cigarettes and sipping our coffee. Finally he looked at his watch.

"I'm wasting your time, telling you stories about Fuller you can't use. That's what always happens when somebody gets me started on the Great Man. I got a cockeyed theory that if we'd started ass backwards at the beginning and built him up as the bum he was, told the truth, he might have been an even bigger sensation. Reverse English is sometimes very effective."

"Nick, what do you think I should do first? How do you think I should start on this?"

"You really want my opinion?"

"I really want your opinion."

"O.K.," he said. "I think you're crazy if you don't just sit down and bat out the whole thing from the clips and the official bio material. The trouble with Fuller is you're gonna sit down with the people that knew him, they're gonna start talking, you'll be fascinated but you won't hear a goddamned thing you can use on the air. And all of a sudden you'll wake up and find out it's Friday night and you won't have any show. Save yourself a lot of headaches. Don't expose yourself to Herb Fuller, the bastard. Stick to Herb Fuller, the legend. It's cleaner."

"I have to get some tape. I thought I'd fly to Connecticut and get Fran and the kids . . . maybe get Eddie and the band and Carol."

"Fran and the kids, O.K. But you'd better be ready to tell them what you want them to say. Eddie and the band will be fine. Eddie's one of the few people in this world that really liked Fuller. Except of course the hundred and fifty million members of the Great Unwashed who adored him. Lay off Carol. She's hitting the bottle again and she's still peed off at Herb over their last set-to."

"What happened?"

"See, you're getting interested. Believe me, you couldn't use it on the air. You couldn't even use it on the telephone. Don't get yourself confused about Herb Fuller. At least not until after the memorial show. And since when were you and the Great Man so chummy?"

"Since Sid Moore said we were on the plane going up to Hartford."

"That's what I figured. What's Sid's angle in this?"

"Me. A big chunk of me."

"I don't mean that. Where does he rate getting in the middle of the whole thing?"

"I don't know."

"For a long time, he and Fuller weren't even speaking to each other, if they could avoid it. I don't get it."

"Neither do I."

"Fuller's big business. Without him, Amalgamated is a fifth-rate network. How does a big slob like Moore call the plays on something like this? You know, the last time Sid and Herb were still working together was during the war. Remember? They ran that Blood Bank gimmick and they paid it off with Fuller taking a pint of blood donated by a listener over to Europe to be given to a wounded G.I. Remember that stunt?"

"Vaguely."

"Sid went along with Fuller on it. But after that they busted up. Sid became a big wheel in local radio and Fuller went it alone. It doesn't figure."

"Well . . ." I looked at my watch. It was ten after three. I had to get going. We argued over the check. I finally paid it.

In the cab, on the way over to the Amalgamated Building, Nick tried to convince me again that there was an easy way to do the memorial show.

"Christ," he said, "you've got no problem. There's enough crap in those files to fill the Sunday *Tribune* from the front page right through the Real Estate Section. Just remember you're doing an obit and nobody ever says anything bad about anybody in an obit. If you can manage it, just go on thinking, between now and Friday night at ten, that Herb Fuller was America's beloved humorist. A great human being."

"I'll try."

"That's all we can really ask, isn't it?"

I paid for the cab. There wasn't even an argument this time. Nick got off the elevator on the fourth floor and I went up to the ninth to my office. I had to get myself organized, get the show in some kind of tangible form before I started running around with the minitape. I spent an hour going through Nick's clippings and then I ran up a tentative dummy of the show.

HERB FULLER MEMORIAL SHOW

OPENING: OPEN COLD WITH THIRTY SECOND TAPE EXCERPT FROM FULLER SHOW. (To be selected—have Ginny set up tape session)

HARRIS: (March of Time kind of . . . "This week, as it must to all men, Death came to Herb Fuller" intro. Keep it simple and sharp.)

BIZ: (SEGUE INTO SOUND FROM OPENING)

SOUND: BARK OF DOG. (Audition dog bark in sound effects library)

HARRIS: That's a boxer named Donnie. He can't read the papers. He doesn't have a radio in his kennel. He doesn't know that a world-famous, internationally beloved humorist named Herb Fuller is dead. Even if he did, it wouldn't have meant anything to him. He doesn't know any Herb Fuller. Any world famous, internationally beloved humorist. He does know that something is missing. Nobody's patted his head. A part of his world has disappeared and he doesn't understand.

There are others who feel that a part of their world has disappeared too. Others to whom the world is suddenly become a sadder place because the friendly, warm, funny, human guy they called Herb Fuller is dead. Tonight, I'd like you to meet some of them. And maybe in the process, you'll see a different side of a man somebody once called "one of the great human beings of our time . . ."

(MORE ALONG THESE LINES . . . CAREFUL ABOUT SPREADING IT ON TOO THICK. HAVE GINNY CHECK REFERENCE ON THE NAME OF THAT BOXER. DONNIE OR DANNY?)

MUSIC: FULL ORCHESTRA UP FULL WITH FULLER THEME.

HARRIS: Your ear is tuned to sixteen bars of music. An ordinary banal piece of music. Written in 1942 by Steve Parsons, the drummer in Eddie Brown's band . . . Title: Blue Dance. An ordinary sixteen bars of pop music, but to a hundred and fifty million Americans it was as familiar and as readily identifiable as a signature. It was Herb's theme music . . . that opened and closed his radio and TV shows every week. To his hundred and fifty million listeners and viewers, Herb Fuller was a friend . . . a friend they'd never met . . . but no less a friend for that. To Eddie Brown and his orchestra . . . to Bob Prince, Bill Farrell, Carol Carson and the rest of the people they called the "Fuller Family" he was bossman, father-confessor and friend. Sure. They all made a good living, being part of the "Fuller Family." Sure. Their pictures were in the papers and the magazines. Sure. The autograph hounds followed them after a broadcast.

But they had fun.

Doing their job.

That was the key to their relationship with the feller they called . . . only half jokingly . . . the "Great Man."

They had fun.

They're not having much fun this week.

They wear a kind of stunned look.

They don't quite realize what has happened.

They have to keep reminding themselves that a big part of their lives crashed into a railroad embankment in a Connecticut town called Hartford.

They're remembering things this week . . . each of them . . . each member of the "Fuller Family." Remembering their own personal . . . things . . .

TAPE: FULLER AND CAROL CARSON DUETING ON "HOW COME I LOVE YOU?" . . . HOLD UP FULL . . . FIFTEEN SECONDS

IN THE CLEAR THEN DOWN TO B.G. BEHIND AND OUT ON CUE.

HARRIS: Ten years ago, a teen-age kid named Carol Carson was working after school as a carhop in a Pasadena drive-in. If you asked her what she wanted to do with her life when she got out of school, she'd have looked up at you with those big brown eyes and said she didn't know.
But she did.
Inside herself, she knew.
She wanted to sing.
She knew she could but it wasn't something you talked about.
Then one night she was at a party. You know what high-school parties are and somebody dragged out a home recording machine and asked her to sing into it. She didn't want to.
She was shy.
She was afraid.
But you know how kids are. They talked her into it and once she opened her mouth, she forgot about being shy and she sang her heart out.
She sang good.
Real good.
The next day, as a joke, a friend of hers took the record and mailed it to Herb Fuller.
Herb listened to it.

TAPE: CAROL SINGING BY HERSELF WITH PIANO B.G. CHECK THROUGH EARLY FULLER BROADCASTS FOR THIS. IF NECESSARY, HAVE CAROL COME IN AND DO IT FOR THIS SPOT.

HARRIS: He liked it. He sent her a train ticket to New York. A round-trip ticket. She only used it one way. Two months and four auditions later she was a member of the "Fuller Family" . . . with a full network tuned in . . . listening to that voice she knew was good when she was balancing trays as a Pasadena carhop. To Carol Carson, Herb Fuller was more than just a celebrity . . . more than just the guy who gave her the big break. He was the father she lost at the age of seven.

(HOLD . . . PLAY PAUSE)

This week, for the second time in her life, Carol Carson lost a father.

How does she feel about it?

In her own words . . . about like this:

TAPE: CARSON TAPE . . . KEEP TO FIFTY SECONDS AT OUTSIDE.

I ran out of gas about here, but it was a start. That's the way I work on a script. Once you get it started . . . it doesn't matter whether it's exactly right or not, you're on your way. I knew a lot of it needed pruning, but the shape was there . . . the format. I had the attack set. From Carol, I'd go on through Eddie and the orchestra . . . run in Fran and the kids . . . use old Fuller tapes . . . then go back to pick up the bio . . . the kid days . . . the start in radio . . . the navy . . . the war, and finally the pay-off with a montage at the end of all the voices . . . coming in . . . going out . . . cross-fading like hell. One thing I did need was a terrific pay-off tape. Something Fuller himself had said on the air. I'd have to sweat through lots of transcriptions of his shows to find it . . . but it had to be something with an impact and a sock. A pay-off.

By now, it was after seven and I went down to the Rose Room, the restaurant in the basement of the building, and had a quick dinner. I finished about eight and went back to the office and picked up the minitape. I checked the batteries, put a clean reel of tape on and stuffed the pockets of the carrying case with five blank reels. Then I picked up the phone and dialed "Operator."

"Honey, this is Ed Harris. Do you have Carol Carson's home phone number?"

"Just a minute, Mr. Harris."

I lit a cigarette and waited.

The operator came back and gave me the number. I dialed it. The phone rang six times before it was picked up.

"Hello."

Her voice sounded sleepy.

"Is this Carol Carson?"

"Yes. Who's this?"

"This is Ed Harris at Amalgamated. I don't know whether or not you remember me, but we met a couple of times in the Rose Room."

"Sure. I remember you. So?"

"I'm doing a show Friday night on Amalgamated. A sort of memorial to Herb. I want to get some tape with the Family and I wondered if you minded my barging in on you tonight?"

"Come on over."

"Over where?"

She gave me the address and I wrote it down on the inside cover of a match box. It was in the forties . . . way over east.

I thanked her.

"It's very nice of you to let me move in on you this way," I said.

"What's nice? Hey, maybe you can tell me something."

"Maybe."

"You know they canceled the show all week. Do you know whether we'll get paid or not? I called AFRA this afternoon but they didn't know. Do you know?"

"I'm sorry. I don't know."

"Just thought I'd ask. Another thing. You're coming over, you can do me a favor."

"Sure. Be delighted."

"Stop at a delicatessen and pick up a couple of bottles of soda . . . large size . . . also some ice. My refrigerator's on the blink. And you might pick up a bottle of Scotch while you're at it."

"Right," I said and hung up.

I suddenly remembered something. Maybe it was the low tones in Carol's voice. It reminded me.

Nicole.

I called her and told her I didn't know when I'd get up to see her but to sit tight and I'd call her later.

I picked up the Scotch, the ice cubes and the soda, grabbed a cab and went over to Carol's.

It was a reconditioned brownstone.

She had the second story.

She was wearing a green sweater and a pair of slacks. Tight slacks. On her it looked fine.

The place was a mess. The ash trays were overflowing with butts and there was a big puddle of liquor on one of the end tables. I could see into the bedroom and the bed wasn't made. It smelled like the place had been shut up for a month.

Carol was a little loaded.

Not much.

Not falling down drunk.

Not even sloppy tight.

A little loaded.

Like maybe she'd slept off the original load and was starting on her second go-round.

I gave her the packages, the three bottles of club soda, the bottle of Scotch, and the large container of ice cubes. She opened what looked like a closet door in the living room and it turned out to be one of those five-by-five kitchenettes. There was only room for one so I stood at the door while she mixed two drinks.

"I hope you like Scotch," she said.

"Sure. I drink anything."

"That's where you make a big mistake. Stick to Scotch."

"Why?"

"Did you ever hear of an alcoholic that drank Scotch and soda? It's a civilized drink. You see somebody guzzling straight rye or bourbon on the rocks, right away you figure he's bucking for A.A. But it doesn't matter how much Scotch and soda you drink. Nobody ever thinks you're an alcoholic. They figure if you are you'll be drinking rye or bourbon."

"That doesn't sound very convincing to me."

"So? You want a big one or a small one?"

"Medium."

She mixed the drinks. One was medium. Mine. The other was practically all Scotch. Hers. She carried the drinks over to a table next to a large gray sectional couch. We sat down.

"So?" she asked. "So?"

"You want to know why I'm here?"

"I know why you're here. You're doing the Fuller memorial show Friday night."

"Right."

"And you brought along your little tape recorder. You want me to say something appropriate about how lost I am without the Great Man. Right?"

"Right."

She took a big slug of her Scotch.

"You know what he used to call this couch?"

"What?"

"My sexual couch."

"Oh."

"It's a joke. It's a sectional couch. He used to call it my sexual couch. He was a very funny guy, the dirty bastard."

At this point we were sitting at separate ends of the couch. She put her feet up and stretched out at her end. Her feet were in my lap.

"Do you mind?" she asked.

I didn't mind a bit. I said so.

"Is it true," she asked, "that you're going to inherit his shows?"

"It's a possibility. Maybe it depends on how the memorial show goes. Maybe it depends on a lot of things that are going on behind the scenes that I don't know anything about."

"Are they going to keep the Family together? Me and Eddie and Bob?"

"I don't know. Probably."

"Sounds like a good deal for you," she said. "How does it feel to fall into a million dollars? Are you sure you didn't jimmy the differential or screw up the carburetor or whatever the hell you do to make a car go into the side of a railroad bank?"

She finished her drink at one gulp. She got up and went into the kitchenette.

"Are you ready for a refill?" she yelled.

"No, I'm fine."

While she was mixing her drink I put the minitape under the couch, turned it on, plugged in the mike, a small black lapel mike about the size of a half dollar . . . and put it casually on the couch where it would pick up both our voices. I don't know why I did it this time. I'd done it in the past when I was dealing with somebody that had mike fright. Just turned it on without their knowing it and picked up a lot of usable stuff. From the way things had gone up to this point, it didn't look like I was going to get any usable stuff out of her, but I figured, what the hell . . . turn it on and see what happens.

Here's the Ediphone transcript of what did happen:

GIRL: You sure you don't want your drink freshened up?
MAN: No, thanks.
GIRL: (FIRST SENTENCE INAUDIBLE) You sure you don't mind my feet in your lap?
MAN: Not a bit.
GIRL: So you're taking over! Does that mean you're taking over everything that used to belong to Fuller?
MAN: Maybe not quite everything.
GIRL: I used to belong to Fuller. Once in a while, I used to, that is. When it was raining and he happened to be in the neighborhood. You never knew when he was going to show up. One night he came in here at five-thirty in the morning, crocked to the ears. You know what he said?
MAN: No.
GIRL: He said, "I was in a cab and I suddenly got the yen for it. I made the driver pull over to the curb and I looked at the lamppost. It was Fifty-fourth Street and Second Avenue. You were the closest, so here I am." He was full of compliments like that. You ready to step into his shoes in the bed department too? You know, you look something like him. You're not as flabby as he was. You're maybe ten years younger. There's a strong resemblance.
MAN: Thanks.
GIRL: I understand you got a French girl you're shacking up with. (THREE WORDS INAUDIBLE) . . . French girls. He's been on the French kick for years.

I think it started when he made that trip to Europe during the war. The show was crawling with French broads. I think the French counsel put it in the passport regulations. If you were a French broad coming to the States, you headed right for Fuller after you cleared customs. We had more French girls than a USO piano player. Herb even went to Berlitz for four months and got private lessons in French. Then he hired himself a tutor to teach him the words they don't teach at Berlitz. You want to do me a big favor?

MAN: Sure.

GIRL: Get the Scotch and the ice in the kitchenette.

MAN: Sure.

(TEN SECONDS DEAD TAPE)

MAN: You want the soda?

GIRL: Not unless you do. I've reached that familiar point where I don't bother with the refinements. To hell with the soda. I hate it anyway. I only drink it for appearances. The Scotch is the important thing. Come on, sit over here.

MAN: Right.

GIRL: Right. Right. Everything's right with you.

MAN: Sure.

GIRL: Me too?

MAN: You wouldn't be making a pass at me, would you?

GIRL: Right. Mr. Harris, you hit that one right on the head. Right. Right. I'm making a pass at you. Shall we be logical about the whole thing. Right? Logical. You heard me sing?

MAN: Sure. I've heard you sing.

GIRL: I sing like ten thousand other girls knocking themselves out at one-nighters and smokers. I sing good. But not great. Good but not great. My last pay check was eleven hundred bucks. I don't sing that good. Eleven hundred bucks a week is a lot of singing. And you heard those impersonations I do. Or maybe I get eleven hundred bucks a week because I play the concertina. You got me it's like you got Phil Spitalny's all-girl band. He heard me doing those impersonations one night, the next thing I know, he got me doing them on the show. One night he came in here and threw a concertina in my lap. "Learn to play it," he said. Eight lessons later I'm playing it on the show. It got so I was afraid to break wind around him . . . afraid he'd have me doing it on the air. Eleven hundred bucks a week . . . Because I'm Lily Pons? Because I'm Peggy Lee? Because I'm Evelyn and her magic violin? No, because Herb Fuller likes to sleep with me. Sometimes. When he's in the neighborhood. Or because the Queen Mary is late. I'm a convenience. And I sing good. Eleven hundred bucks a week.

MAN: Is that the way you look at it?

GIRL: That's the way I look at it. It's a good thing I can sing. Otherwise I'm just a whore. This way I'm a whore-singer. That hyphen makes a big difference. Pour me another drink. No ice. Just Scotch.

MAN: Don't you think you're getting a little drunk?

GIRL: I like it that way. Don't worry about my passing out on you. I don't do that. I don't get sick either. Or loud. It doesn't affect my abilities as a bed companion either. People that used to know me say I'm shy, quiet and reserved when I'm sober. Or don't you like sober, quiet, reserved girls, Mr. Harris?

MAN: You like to think of yourself as a pretty tough little broad, don't you?

GIRL: I am a pretty tough little broad. You can kiss me now if you want to.

MAN: Thanks.

GIRL: O.K.?

MAN: O.K.

GIRL: So?

MAN: So?

GIRL: Just window shopping?

MAN: Just window shopping.

GIRL: You got a better deal than I did. I earned my eleven hundred bucks a week. Brother, how I earned it! All you have to do is get on the air for an hour, tell the world what a great guy Herb Fuller was and you're in the chips.

MAN: Pretty soft, huh?

GIRL: Pretty soft. Give me your glass.

MAN: A light one.

GIRL: Right. You got me doing it. Right. Maybe you ought to hold onto that on the air. Right. Right. Right. A catch phrase. I can hear the kids of America picking it up. Right. Right. Right. You may be the Joe Penner of your time.

MAN: Not the Herb Fuller?

GIRL: I hope not. You didn't really know him, did you?

MAN: No. I didn't really know him. I'm beginning to now.

GIRL: How are you at tightrope walking?

MAN: Never tried it.

GIRL: You better learn. You're gonna have to walk the biggest tightrope in the history of the world. You're going to try to be what Herb Fuller was without being what Herb Fuller was, if you know what I mean.

MAN: No, I don't know what you mean.

GIRL: I don't know either. Maybe you have to be a good

unadulterated bastard like he was to be as big, as famous and as successful as he was. Which came first, the celebrity or the bastard? Was he always a bastard or did he become one after he hit the jackpot? Can you hit the jackpot and not be like him? I don't know. Maybe you'll find out. I don't think you're a bastard yet. Give me another drink. And for Christ's sake have one yourself. I'm not going to take advantage of you if you get loaded.

MAN: Why did you sleep with him?

GIRL: You mean at first or later?

MAN: Both.

GIRL: The first time, there was nothing I could do about it. After that it was a kind of job insurance. Like social security. It wasn't so bad. Except when he was really drunk. I got used to it. What you don't know, Ed, is what it was like to be a member of the "Fuller Family." You did what he wanted you to do. You sang for any outfit he wanted you to sing for . . . for free. If he wanted you to sleep with him, you slept with him. Sure, you were a celebrity . . . you made a lot of dough, but he never let you forget that everything flowed from him and he could cut it off and throw you back where he found you any time he wanted to. It'll be the same way with you, if you take over for him. We'll do the same for you, if you want us to. We may even like it a little more. You're an improvement. We might even like it a lot. Take a good look at me.

MAN: I am.

GIRL: Inventory. Sure, I'm a little drunk. Not too much. Not enough to make me unattractive. Nice hair, regular features, good teeth. Good body. Nice build. He used to call them my Lucky Strikes . . . round, firm and fully packed. Right now, you wouldn't find it exactly a chore to make love to me, would you?

MAN: No. I wouldn't find it a chore at all.

GIRL: I wouldn't find it any chore at all right now to let you. To help you do it. I think we'd both enjoy it. But we're not going to, unless you insist. You know why?

MAN: You tell me.

GIRL: Because I'd never know whether I was doing it because I wanted to or because I wanted to pay a premium on my job insurance. And neither would you. I don't know why he wanted me in the last couple of years. He said once he liked two kinds of women, he couldn't keep his hands off them. He liked them young and unspoiled. He liked to break them in. He couldn't keep his hands off the young kids. Once out in Detroit he got clipped by a high-school kid who came around to his hotel for an autograph. He gave her an autograph all right. It turned out she was fifteen. He gave her an autograph right smack on the bottom of a big fat check. The other kind he couldn't stay away from was the French women. He said you never knew what they were going to do or how they were going to do it. Me, I didn't qualify on either count. I wasn't fresh or unspoiled any more . . . or French. But I was convenient. I was an old established firm and I guess I gave good value.

MAN: How about the first time?

GIRL: You oughta get this down on your tape recorder. When it happened to me I thought it was unique. I found out different. Fast. I saw it happen to other kids after that. I was eighteen when I sent Fuller that recording of my voice.

MAN: You sent him the recording?

GIRL: Sure. I'd just gotten out of high school. My mother was nagging at me to get a job. There was no money to send me to college. I took typing and shorthand in High School so my mother kept after me to get a job as a secretary or a typist.

MAN: What about your father?

GIRL: He died when I was seven. He was killed in a saloon brawl. Somebody poked an icepick in his guts. I don't remember much about him, except that he used to shout. He and my mother used to fight all the time. I guess he was a lush. Anyway, I made this record in one of those penny arcade places. I sang "Tea for Two" and I sent it off to Fuller. I wrote a letter saying I was deaf and blind and I sent the record and the picture. I figured they'd find out right away that I was a phony but maybe I could get to New York before they did. I had to get away from Pasadena.

MAN: Did you have a boy friend?

GIRL: I know what you're driving at. Sure, I had a boy friend. A couple. Sure, we used to neck and pet and play around. I was eighteen and I'd had my share of guzzling in the back seat of a car. Anyway, they fell for the letter and I got a train ticket to New York. Round trip. Of course they found out I was a phony at the first audition, but Fuller was there and he followed me out to the elevator when I left. He dated me up for dinner. I had sixty bucks I'd talked my mother out of. Anyway, Fuller took me out to dinner. At the Stork. He introduced me to Sherman Billingsley, Eddie Rickenbacker and a couple of other people. I was really living. It was a long way from the drive-in at Pasadena. Anyway . . . fix me another drink, will you?

MAN: Sure.

GIRL: Anyway, after dinner we went up to his place. He still had that apartment on Riverside Drive, right across from the Palisades Amusement Park. I knew what was on his mind, but I figured I could handle it all right. I was a veteran of the football team at Pasadena High. I figured if I had been able to handle them, I could handle him.

MAN: You're sure you want this drink?

GIRL: I'm sure. I couldn't handle him worth a good goddamn. I won't say he raped me. Not quite. He would have, but I finally just gave up and figured what the hell, sixty bucks doesn't stretch very far in New York. After that first time, it was easy.

MAN: You mean you were a virgin?

GIRL: I was a virgin. And for a couple of weeks he was crazy about me. He moved me into the apartment. He used to come over between rehearsals. He did everything but give me chalk talks about sex. He learned me good. Then he got me a singing spot on a local station . . . one of those independent 200-watt jobs that nobody listens to. I didn't get paid for it, but he said the experience would do me good. I didn't need money, anyway. He was handing it out and living at his place I didn't have any expenses. Then he moved me in here. He bought me some clothes and gave me a regular weekly allowance. It came in the mail every Friday. Cash. He sent me to Bobby Watkins to take voice lessons. Then he put me on his show. We went along like that for a couple of years. My singing got better and I became part of the "Fuller Family." He knew my singing wasn't going to set the town on fire so he kept figuring out new things for me to do. He dressed me up in funny costumes and had me doing commercials. I did those lousy impersonations. I played that lousy concertina and then when we switched over to TV, I took dancing lessons and he even had that fairy dance director work out routines for me to do on the show once a week. I was so goddamned versatile it'd scare you. I was getting pretty versatile in bed too. Maybe too versatile. Maybe there wasn't anything else he could teach me. Believe me, there wasn't anything I could teach him. After a while he stopped coming to the apartment regularly. He didn't stop altogether but he sort of slacked off. First it was once a week . . . usually when he'd fly down from Connecticut the night before the nighttime radio show. Then he'd miss a couple of weeks. Then finally there was no pattern to it. The only thing was, I'd damned well better be there when he arrived. Once I went to the Music Hall for the nine o'clock show and when I got back to the apartment around midnight he was sitting there, sore as a boil. He told me what the score was. "Don't forget," he said, "You belong to me any time I want you and when I want you, I want you here waiting for me. You just be here." He made it plain. Very plain. As a matter of fact he socked me, split my lip. There wasn't any way to get away from him. He'd fixed that. I couldn't get a job singing with a band or on another show. The word had gone out. The only way I could get away from him was to go back to Pasadena. I didn't want to do that. Of course all this time he was knocking around with five, ten, fifteen, Christ knows how many other girls. But he wanted me available, warming up in the bull pen . . . any time he was in the neighborhood and felt like tearing off a quick piece.

MAN: How did you feel about him?

GIRL: When? Then? Or at first?

MAN: At first.

GIRL: At first I was flattered. You know, at first he took me around and showed me off. He was interested in what is laughingly referred to as my career. He gave me the big rush. I wasn't in love with him, if that's what you mean. Never. It took me a year to really learn to hate him. Christ, he was repulsive.

MAN: But you let him go on making love to you?

GIRL: Sure. By then I'd come to terms with myself. Like I said . . . it was job insurance. Lots of people do lots worse things than that to hold onto their jobs. He had a couple of others, but he started coming around again every week or so. What he didn't know was, I was starting to branch out on my own. To understand that, you have to believe that I hated Fuller. You have to believe that there wasn't even any physical pleasure in sleeping with him. So I started sleeping around. Oh, I was careful about it. I made sure Fuller was out of town first. I started drinking pretty heavy too. I'd come a long way from Pasadena.

MAN: Yes, you had.

GIRL: Does this disgust you?

MAN: No, not particularly.

GIRL: It disgusts me sometimes. When I'm relatively sober. That's why I'm not sober much.

MAN: Doesn't the drinking interfere with your singing?

GIRL: I'm careful about that. I never drink too much except over week ends. Did you ever hear of joy poppers?

MAN: No.

GIRL: Those are people who take drugs for kicks. They're not addicts because they don't have to take a shot of heroin every four hours, or every afternoon at five . . . or even every two days. Maybe they'll do it just on week ends, for kicks. In other words, they can lay off the stuff if they want to. I'm that way about drinking. I drink just enough to keep me happy. I don't really tie one on except over week ends or like now when I don't have a show to do for a week or so.

MAN: Did Fuller ever find out you were playing around?

GIRL: Sure. Fuller was the Great Man. He found out everything. At first I was careful. Sometimes it would be a guy that picked me up in a bar. Sometimes it would be one of the guys in the orchestra. They were safer. They were as dependent on Fuller as I was. They were a lot safer. But then I outsmarted myself. You now Harry Townes?

MAN: The announcer? Yeah, I know him.

GIRL: You know, the one thing I couldn't figure out about Fuller was this. He liked them young and fresh and unspoiled. And then he made them different. He didn't like them anymore. He had to go out and find some new fresh ones. But he wouldn't let the old ones go completely. This city is probably full of girls just like me who used to sit around at night wondering if he was coming to see them . . . wondering if he might just happen to be in the neighborhood. Maybe we ought to form a club.

MAN: What about Harry Townes?

GIRL: Yeah. Harry Townes. Fill my glass. How drunk am I?

MAN: Fair to middling drunk.

GIRL: You find me attractive?

MAN: I find you very attractive.

GIRL: But you don't want to sleep with me?

MAN: Not unless I'm pushed to it. Not tonight if I can help it.

GIRL: Not even if I tell you this one is absolutely free. No strings. No job insurance. Just because we both want to.

MAN: Neither of us would be sure it was absolutely free.

GIRL: No. You wouldn't make me sit around waiting for you whether you showed up or not, would you?

MAN: No.

GIRL: You wouldn't poke me in the snout because I went to the Radio City Music Hall, would you?

MAN: No.

GIRL: This French girl . . .

MAN: What about her?

GIRL: You like her because you like her . . . or you like her because she's French?

MAN: I like her.

GIRL: You treat her good?

MAN: Sometimes. I try to.

GIRL: Listen, I haven't got a bad voice. People know me. I get lots of fan mail. Given half a chance I could straighten up and fly right.

MAN: I'm sure you could.

GIRL: He didn't care what they looked like, as long as they were French. You know something? I think somebody fixed the car up so it would crash. If I knew how, I'd have done it. I used to sit here sometimes thinking of how I could kill the dirty bastard and get away with it. I never figured it out.

MAN: What about Harry Townes?

GIRL: You've got a one-track mind, lover. Straighten up and fly right. Straighten up and fly right. You want to see me do a strip tease? It's more difficult when you're wearing slacks. I could . . .

(INDISTINCT MUMBLING . . . CRASH OF FURNITURE)

MAN: Are you all right?

GIRL: Sure. Help me up. What'd you put in that Scotch?

MAN: Scotch.

GIRL: That'll do it every time. Harry Townes. Harry Townes. Do you mind if I put my head in your lap?

MAN: What about Harry Townes?

GIRL: Harry Townes was a nice guy. A sweet guy. Except for Fuller, he was the only permanent man I ever had. We loved each other for a while. We said the hell with it. To hell with everything. Fuller included. I had five thousand dollars in the bank. Harry was free-lancing, averaging three-fifty a week. To hell with Herb Fuller. So he moved in here. We mighta even got married.

MAN: What happened?

GIRL: The Great Man happened.

MAN: What could he do?

GIRL: You have a very soft lap. Pardon me, I don't mean to be rude, but you have a very soft lap.

MAN: What did Fuller do?

GIRL: Little Old One Track, aren't you?

MAN: Carol . . .

GIRL: You don't want to sleep with me?

MAN: No. Not tonight.

GIRL: I never knew the joke that went with that. All my life I've heard people say, Not tonight, Josephine, and break everybody up. It must be a very funny joke. I've always wondered. Do you know what's so funny about it?

MAN: No.

GIRL: How can you find out a thing like that? You can't call the Public Library and ask them to please tell you the dirty joke whose punch line is, Not tonight, Josephine. You can't write to the Answer Man. How do you find out a thing like that?

MAN: You ask Herb Fuller.

GIRL: Sure. Right. Why didn't I think of that? If there's a dirty joke he didn't know, it wasn't dirty. I missed my chance. Now the bastard's dead. I'll never know the joke. You're sure you don't know it?

MAN: I don't know it.

GIRL: Would you ask around? And if you ever found out you'd tell me, wouldn't you?

MAN: Yes, I'll ask around and if I find out, I'll tell you. I promise.

GIRL: Good old Ed. Sweet darling Ed. Do you know something?

MAN: What?

GIRL: You're a very exciting guy.

MAN: Now wait a minute. Let's get . . . (INDISTINCT . . . TWENTY SECONDS OF DEAD TAPE)

GIRL: You're still going to play hard to get after that?

MAN: Carol, listen to me. What about Harry Townes?

GIRL: A sweet wonderful guy, Harry Townes. I think we were in love with each other. Honest, I do. I think we were in love with each other. We mighta got married. But Fuller found out. You know what happened?

MAN: What?

GIRL: All of a sudden Harry lost his commercial shows . . . one by one. They dropped him. They said they were changing the format . . . or they wanted a lighter voice . . . or he was too well known . . . or he was identified with a competitive product. You know the routine. He tried to get back on staff at Amalgamated. That paid a hundred and a quarter a week. They wanted no part of him. Funny coincidence, wasn't it?

MAN: Yeah. Funny.

GIRL: Funny ha-ha. Then the money stopped coming in the mail every Friday. The landlord came around to collect the rent. The department stores started sending bills. Then I got dropped three days a week from the Fuller show. They said it was for balance. Remember? We had a French torch singer on then. They said it was for balance. Then I got dropped from that. Temporarily they said. All this time, Fuller didn't say a word. My five thousand lasted about four months. Harry took the hint right away. He went to Philly. Got a job with NBC there. I finally went back to Herb. Christ, I did everything but get down on my knees to him.

MAN: And?

GIRL: He took me back. Nothing ever gets away from him. He didn't want me. He just couldn't let anything that used to belong to him get away. That's when I started thinking up ways to kill him. The dirty bastard. The dirty, no good, effin bastard.

MAN: I'm sorry, Carol. I'm very sorry.

GIRL: You're a sweet wonderful guy, Ed Harris. You wouldn't go to Philly, would you? You wouldn't run away from me like that, would you?

MAN: No, I wouldn't go to Philly.
GIRL: Kiss me. Please. Kiss me. Hard.
(TWENTY-THREE SECONDS DEAD TAPE)
GIRL: You know something?
MAN: What?
GIRL: I'm gonna rape you.
MAN: What makes you think you'll have to?
(FORTY-SEVEN SECONDS OF DEAD TAPE)
GIRL: Carry me in the bedroom, darling.
MAN: Put your arms around my neck.
GIRL: I could very easily (REST OF SENTENCE INDISTINCT) (REST OF TAPE ROLL BLANK. END OF TRANSCRIPT)

WEDNESDAY

I GOT into the office early Wednesday morning. I still had a lot of the clips Nick had dug up for me to plough through. It must have been a little after six when I walked into the lobby of the Amalgamated Building. The sky was just beginning to get light.

I felt awful.

I also felt a little panic-stricken about the way the week was getting away from me. Here it was Wednesday, just barely, but Wednesday, and I was only fifty-odd hours away from the memorial show. I was sure wasting one hell of a lot of time gathering a lot of material that I couldn't possibly put on anybody's airwaves.

In all the time I'd been at the station, I'd never been in this early before. It was a strange new world. I saw people I'd never realized existed. Joe Talley, our early morning man, our wake-up disk jockey, was sitting in his office, laboriously writing down his ad libs, gulping black coffee and getting himself into shape to sound like he'd been up for hours and was proud of it. There are two distinct ways to do an early morning disk jockey show. You either have to be full of pep and vitality, radiate good cheer, charm and fellowship or try the other end of the stick . . . bitch like hell about what a terrible way this is to earn five hundred bucks a week. Talley did it the hard way. He was the goddamnedest cheerful bastard in the history of the world. I waved to him as I passed his office.

"Hi!" I said.

"Balls," he said.

I saw porters who filled the water jugs, the early morning mailboy crew and the Air Conditioning Man who checked each office with a thermometer in his hand to make certain that the temperature was at a certain level. What the level was or what he did if the temperature was above or below it, I haven't the faintest idea, but he poked his head in my room and consulted his thermometer four times. He pursed his lips, puckered his brow and walked out shaking his head. I wasn't surprised.

By nine-thirty, when Ginny showed up, I'd been through just about everything Nick had pulled out of the files for me. The morning mail had two items of interest. One was a press release from Nick Cellantano. Clipped to it was a note from him saying, "It's a living!" This is what it looked like:

FROM: Amalgamated Broadcasting System
Radio Press Information Section
Nick Cellantano

For Immediate Release

"Great Man Hunt"

Ed Harris, conductor of "Metropolitan Memo," one of New York's most talked about radio shows, is currently engaged in a Great Man Hunt. This Friday at 10 P.M. (CNYT) Harris will be in charge of the "Herb Fuller Memorial Program" to be carried by the full Amalgamated Broadcasting System's radio network. Since the death of America's beloved humorist earlier this week, Harris has literally spent every waking minute exploring the life of Herb Fuller. He has gone back to visit and talk with people Herb knew personally, armed with his minitape recorder. He's spent hours with close personal friends, Mrs. Fuller and their children, and, of course, the entertainers who made up the world-famous "Fuller Family." It's been a labor of love and dedication to Ed, who got his first big break in radio through the late, beloved humorist they called the "Great Man."

"There's something about this assignment," said Ed, "that makes me feel very humble. I've always known that Herb Fuller was one of the great performers of our time but the closer I get to the real Herb Fuller, the human being, the more I realize that here was one of those rare people who come along maybe once or twice in a generation."

Asked about rumors that he may be groomed as Fuller's successor on radio and TV, Harris says, characteristically, "That's like asking a rookie just up from the Pony League if he's stepping into Babe Ruth's shoes. I have a lot to learn and if I can be half the performer and a third the human being Herb Fuller was, I'll be more than satisfied."

–30–

I chucked that one in the wastepaper basket.

Right underneath it, in the pile of mail on my desk was a plain envelope with no return address on the outside addressed to me and marked personal.

I opened it.

"Dear Ed," it said.

"We've never met, but I think we should. I've been reading in the papers that you're doing the Fuller memorial show this Friday and are being groomed to step into his shoes. I might be of some help to you on both projects. You can reach me at the Astor any time up to Friday morning."

It was signed, "Rickie Tyler."

Ginny brought in my usual breakfast.

I had my usual hangover.

My mouth tasted like the inside of a dirty canary cage.

I had Ginny call Goldfarb's and send two sets of a dozen roses. One set to Nicole because I hadn't seen her the night before. One set to Carol because I had.

At a little after ten, Ginny buzzed the interoffice buzzer.

Before she could tell me why she'd buzzed, I told her to jot down on her calendar a note reminding me to call Rickie Tyler at the Astor.

"Eddie Brown is here and would like to see you for a couple of minutes. Shall I send him in?"

"Sure. Send him in."

Ten seconds later, the door exploded inward. I'd seen Eddie Brown around the building, but this was the closest I'd ever been to him. He was rather awe-inspiring. Remember the costumes the old burlesque comedians Rags Ragland, Peanuts Bohn or Bert Lahr used to wear? Dressed for the street, Eddie Brown could have walked onstage in any house on the Columbia Burlesque Wheel and been in costume. He had a checked suit on, with green as the dominant color, bright tan shoes, multicolored socks, a bright pink hand-painted tie with his name spelled backwards, a pale green shirt with pointed collar tips and a bright Kelly green pork-pie hat perched on the back of his head. He was really something to see.

He walked on his toes, in a funny, feminine, mincing way.

"Hi, kid," he said. "I hear you're doing the show on the Great Man. I figured you'd want to see me. You got your tape recorder handy? I have an hour and a half before my recording date. What do you want from me? I can tell you anything you wanna know about the Great Man. I knew him better than most of the slobs around town that stuck the black ribbon on the sleeves. Me and him been buddies for a long time. You're looking pale, kid. You taking care of yourself? Well—let's go. Get your tape out. I'm set. I'm fast with the ad lib. Variety said me and Phil Harris were the two fastest talking orchestra leaders in America. Did you see that piece? It was in the last Anniversary Issue. Anything you want, just tell me how long and I'll hit it within two seconds. Herb used to say I was like a walking stop watch. Great time sense, I got. I guess it's got something to do with rhythm. Well? What's the bit?"

He paused for breath.

I jumped in before he could start all over.

"Eddie, I've been meaning to look you up this morning."

"Well, here I am, kid. Anything you want, don't be afraid to ask it."

He took a pack of cigarettes out of his pocket, selected one, wet it carefully on one end, put it in his mouth and lit it. It was the brand Fuller plugged on his TV show. He extended the pack toward me.

"Be my guest," he said.

I took a cigarette and lit it.

"How long did you know Herb?" I asked him.

"A long time. I knew him when he was working on that two-bit station up in Massachusetts. I was playing trumpet with a pickup band used to hit the roadhouses up in that neck of the woods. Me and him used to go drinking together once in a while. Then I came down to New York. After Herb showed up, him and me started knocking around together again. When he got that network show of his, he asked me how I'd like fronting the band. I liked it fine and we been together ever since."

"Did you like him?"

"Did I like him? You outta your mind? I adored him. Lemme set you straight on one thing right from the beginning. Herb Fuller was the sweetest, straightest, greatest guy ever lived. Not just for what he did for me. You shoulda been around him like I was. You shoulda seen all the things he did for people. Did you ever drop around the studio after one of our morning shows?"

"No."

"They used to be lined up, maybe fifty or sixty guys, all of them with their hands out. Sure, Fuller made a pile, but I know something about what he did with it. Every morning, Rickie, when she was still around, used to cash a check for two hundred bucks, in small bills, fives and tens. She'd put the tens in one of his pockets, the fives in the other, and after the show Herb would come out and go down this line. He'd listen to all of them—listen to their T.S. stories and according to how tough it was he'd reach into one pocket or the other and hand out a five or a ten. You never heard about that, did you? You're damned right you didn't. Once some smart-alecky guy from *Time* was doing a story on Herb and wrote it up. Herb hit the ceiling. Said it would make the guys feel self-conscious. Said it was nobody's business but his. He raised enough hell that they killed the story. You never heard about that, did you?"

"No, I didn't."

"Lotsa things about Herb you never heard. A guy gets as big as he is, it gets smart to put the knock on him. I can tell you, Herb Fuller was the sweetest, straightest, greatest guy ever lived."

Neither of us said anything for a minute. Eddie walked over to the window and flipped his cigarette out and watched it fall to the street.

"It's none of my business," he said, "but just what are you figuring on for this memorial show you're doing?"

"I'm not quite sure myself," I said. "I've been talking to people that knew him . . . I've been getting tapes with them . . . somehow it'll all go together and turn into a show."

"You've been digging around in Fuller's life?"

"A little."

"And?"

"And what?"

"And what've you been finding out?"

"A lot of things."

"Yeah?"

"Yeah."

"Like what?"

"Like a lot of things."

"You never knew Herb, did you?"

I hesitated for a minute.

"No," I said, after a pause. "I never knew him at all."

"And you're trying to find out what kind of a man he was in five days. You're trying to add him up and come up with a final judgment all in five days. Suppose somebody didn't know you was trying to find out what kind of a guy you were. How would you feel if he devoted just five days to it? How could he find out much about you that way?"

"That's the way it has to be, Eddie. Look, I didn't ask for this job. I didn't ask to do this memorial show. They told me I was doing it. So I started doing it the only way I knew how. I started reading the press notices."

"Great! That'll tell you a lot. God forbid anybody should judge me by what's been written about me."

"I talked to people that knew him. Tried to get their slant on him."

"That's fine, but it depends who you talk to. Who did you talk to?"

"Sid Moore, for one."

"Great. A sharp little operator who's sore because he let a couple of million dollars get away from him. As a matter of fact, they haven't even talked to each other for the past couple of years. Getting a line on Fuller by talking to him is like doing a piece on the Constitution from the files of the *Daily Worker.*"

"I talked to Nick Cellantano."

"Another smart move. I suppose you didn't know that Fuller's been keeping Nick on the payroll for the last year and a half even though everybody's been screaming for Nick's scalp. Nick's been goofing off ever since I can remember. A real no talent guy. Everybody's been telling Herb to get rid of him. Herb used to say, Hell, I don't need a press agent. I'm one of those guys that just get publicity without trying to, but Nick has to eat. Leave him alone. I'll bet Nick didn't tell you that Fuller's been paying his salary personally for the past two years. Not Fuller Enterprises—or Amalgamated —or anybody else—just Herb Fuller—out of his own pocket. You know how much publicity Nick Cellantano's gotten Fuller. *Niente*. Nothin'. But Fuller wouldn't fire him."

"In that case I'd assume that Nick would be very grateful."

"Sure. Grateful. Come off it, Harris. The guy you do the biggest favor for is the guy that's sharpening the biggest knife for your back. I'll bet Nick's been nice to you, hasn't he? Helpful as hell. I'll bet he showed you a whole pile of clippings and told you how he was responsible for them, didn't he? I'll bet he just happened to suggest that he could do the same for you when you step into Fuller's shoes. I'll bet he gave you an earful about what a bastard Herb was."

"I gathered he didn't like him much."

"You gathered right."

"Neither did Carol."

"Oh, sure, you talked to Carol. Kid, I don't blame you. In your place, me, I'da talked to Carol too. I'll bet she gave you an earful."

"She gave me an earful."

"God forbid you was God. God forbid you'd judge me by what you hear from a tramp bottle baby. I suppose she told you how Herb ruined her when she was just a sweet young kid from Pasadena, didn't know what it was for and this monster he ruins her. I suppose she told you that?"

"She told me that."

"Lissen. I was around when this kid turned up. She hung around the studio all the time, throwing it up in everybody's face. Finally one night Herb decided what the hell—it was there, he might just as well try a little of it. She was an innocent kid! Oh sure. Did she happen to tell you why she left Pasadena? I'll bet she did. The cops picked her up shacked up with some married guy in an auto court. The guy paid off plenty to hush it up and gave her railroad fare out of town. So she wound up here. Sure, Fuller was knocking it off now and then. Sure he put her on the show. My own personal opinion is that in addition to knocking it off whenever he wanted to, he liked the kid, felt sorry for her. He even let her do those lousy imitations. Figured it might catch on. He had her doing the commercials and tap dancing. She even played the goddamned concertina on the show. The way she played it you'da swore she got it too close and it was squeezing her boobies. He was strictly good to her but she didn't see it that way. She pranced around the studio like she was Queen of the May. Then she started sleeping around. I don't think there's anybody in the band that hasn't had some of it."

"You included, Eddie?"

"Sure. Me included. Free lunch is free lunch. Then she started drinking. She'd show up with half a bag on. Herb took a lot from that broad. Why he didn't haul off and paste her one, now and then, I couldn't figure. Finally it got to be too much even for Herb. He dropped her from the show—first just a couple of times a week, then finally he dropped her off completely. But she came around and begged him to take her back. And he did. For a while she even laid off the sauce. For a while."

"You think that's why Carol hated him, because she's just a tramp? A bottle baby?"

"Hated him? She was crazy about him. Where would she have been without him? He made a star out of her. I don't know what she told you, but just remember something, Harris. Fuller's dead. While Fuller's around, the kid is a celebrity. The kid has a job. The kid isn't just a tramp on the booze, running away from a morals rap in California. But Fuller's not around any more. Then out of the blue, you pop in. You're gonna be around. Get the idea?"

"She's just a tramp, is that it? She's not a tramp because Fuller made her one? She's just a bottle baby? She's not an alcoholic because Fuller made her one?"

"Come off it. She's been on more beds than a traveling salesman's suitcase. Didn't you knock her off?"

He had me.

"Didn't you? You're goddamned right you did. The first five minutes you spend with Carol, you know it's there if you want it. By ten minutes you want it. By twenty minutes you have your hat on and you're in a cab headed home."

"Let me ask you something, Eddie?"

"Sure. Anything."

"How much do you make a week?"

"Now?"

"Yeah. Now."

"Sixteen hundred. Sixteen fifty. Maybe more if I've got a hot record going for me in the juke boxes."

"You're doing pretty well?"

"Sure. I'm doing fine. Why? What's the bit?"

"How much were you making when you were just playing trumpet in the house band at Amalgamated?"

"A hundred and a quarter. Oh, I get it. You figure I'm not so different from Carol. You figure I think Fuller's a great guy because he added fifteen hundred bucks a week to my salary check. Is that it?"

"Maybe. It's a possibility."

"Look, kid. What are you trying to do, write an exposé? I had the funny idea you were doing something called the Herb Fuller Memorial Show. I had the idea you were going to do the pulpit bit. What are you trying to prove?"

"I'm not trying to prove anything. I'm just trying to find out what kind of a guy Herb Fuller was. I'm just trying to do a job that was dumped in my lap."

"If you don't mind my saying so, kid, you're goin' about it in a cockeyed way. You're not gonna find out much about Fuller by talking to Sid Moore, Nick Cellantano or Carol Carson."

"Maybe not. And yet I learned a lot talking to you."

"Lissen, Ed. Lissen to me for a minute. You take anybody. Me, you, Christ himself. You sit down with five people and talk about him. When you finish, you gonna know what the guy was like? Hell, no. You're gonna know what five people thought he was like. And their opinion of him is gonna be influenced by something good he done for them, or something lousy he done to them. You happen to pick five people who liked him, you come away feeling he's ready for a plaster Paris base in St. Patty's. You talk to five other people hated him, you come away figuring he's Adolf Hitler. Who can tell you the whole truth—the final truth—the real truth about anybody? Who can, kid? Can you tell the real truth even about yourself? Nobody can. Maybe God. But nobody else. So, you got a simple problem. Herb Fuller is dead. Friday night at ten o'clock you gotta do a radio broadcast about him. Do you do it the easy way? The right way? No, right away you gotta louse yourself up. Right away you begin to thirst after the truth. Who are you, the Supreme Court? The Draft Board? Just tell the people what they want to hear about him. That he was a great guy, the sweetest, straightest, greatest guy that ever lived. Why do you think anybody's gonna be listening to that memorial show Friday? To hear exactly that. And it also happens to be the truth. My truth. Maybe not Nick's or Carol's or Rickie's, but mine. And it better be yours, too."

"You mentioned Rickie. What was her truth?"

"Look, kid, don't make things complicated for yourself. You're a nice-looking guy. They tell me you got some talent. You've been given a gold lifetime pass on the gravy train. Stop playing Mr. District Attorney. Besides," he added looking at his watch, "I got an orchestra waiting for me in a recording studio in a couple of minutes. You wanna do a tape with me, let's get to it."

"O.K., Eddie. You're probably right. Let's get to it. But—sometime, when this is all over, will you sit down with me and really talk about Herb Fuller?"

"Sure, kid. Ain't I been doing it? I couldn't tell you any more about him than I have. He was the sweetest——"

I finished it for him.

". . . straightest, greatest guy that ever lived."

"Right," he said.

I got the minitape out and plugged in the mike.

"Now, what exactly do you want?" he asked.

"I want about a minute. Just a kind of impression of Herb . . . working with him."

"Minute? You want some schmaltz? Something simple? What?"

"Anything you want to do."

I checked the tape reel. It was full.

Eddie Brown took another cigarette out of his pack, went through that same strange motion of saturating the end with spit before putting it in his mouth and lit it. He let the smoke curl slowly out of his nose.

"I'm set," he said. "Roll it anytime you're ready."

I turned the machine on and threw him a cue.

"What was Herb Fuller like?" he said into the microphone. "That's a hard question to answer—or maybe—it's the simplest question in the world. You ask fifteen people, you get fifteen different answers. All I can give you is my own answer. And my answer is kinda special. You see, I never had a father. My father died when I was a kid. In a way, Herb was kinda like that father I never had. He was big and warm and you felt kinda reassured just because he was there. You knew you could go to him with anything that was on your mind . . . anything that was worrying you . . . and you knew no matter what it was, he wouldn't get mad . . . he wouldn't be shocked . . . he'd just look at you, with that look he had, and then do something about fixing everything up. He was also like the brother I never had. He cared about you . . . as a person. He cared what happened to you. It's a good feeling to know that there's someone like that around. Like everybody else that knew him, I'm gonna miss him."

I looked at the stop watch in my hand.

He had a time sense all right.

I'd asked for a minute. He'd hit it right on the nose. I turned the machine off.

"O.K?" he asked.

"Fine," I said.

"Anything else, don't hesitate," he said and held out his hand. I shook it.

"I hope we're gonna work together," he said. "I think we'll get along."

"Thanks, Eddie," I said.

"Nothing," he said. "Nothing."

He waved his hands, turned around and walked out of the office. From the rear he was every bit as awe-inspiring as he was from the front. His buttocks jiggled from side to side like a fat dame wearing a pair of tight slacks.

I sat for awhile after he left, looking out of the window. I was thinking about Nick and Carol and Eddie, trying to fit what they'd said into some sort of a pattern. Ginny interrupted me by buzzing the interoffice squawk box. I picked up the receiver.

"Sid Moore called. I told him you were busy recording and he said to call him back when you finished."

"Right. Get him for me, will you?"

"Rickie Tyler called too."

"Did she say what she wanted?"

"No. She just said that she wrote you a letter and just to tell you she called and that you can still reach her at the Astor."

"Get Sid for me first, will you?"

"Sure."

While I was waiting, I turned on the portable in the office. It was a quarter to eleven. I'd forgotten about the special Fuller tapes we were carrying all week in his regular spot and it was something of a shock to suddenly have him come booming out of the speaker on my desk. He was singing the song that sold a million and a half records for him.

Ginny buzzed me again.

"Yes?"

"Sid Moore."

"Thanks."

I pressed the button on the base of the phone.

"Hello, Sid," I said heartily.

I was getting hearty as hell. Next thing you know, I'd start shaking hands with the salesmen.

"How's it going, Coach?"

Well, Sid hadn't changed. Not a bit.

"Fine," I said.

"I'm not trying to pressure you, Ed, but it is Wednesday. Have you got anything I can look at yet? Got any tapes I can hear?"

"I have a rough, first draft of the show," I lied in my teeth. "I have a lot of wonderful tapes."

That was certainly true. Like the one with Carol, for instance.

"Wonderful," said Sid. "Wonderful. When can I see the rough and hear the tapes?"

"I'd rather you waited until it was in a little better shape."

"Like when?"

"Like pretty soon."

"Look, Ed. This is Wednesday. Tomorrow's Thursday. The day after that's Friday."

"And then comes Saturday, Sunday and Monday, which is usually followed by Tuesday and right after that damned if another old Wednesday doesn't crop up again. Isn't it fascinating?"

"I'm not trying to push you, Ed, but we're in the seventh inning, kid, and the light's going."

"Where is it going?"

"You really got a first draft written?"

"That's what I said."

"I know that's what you said. I'm asking if you really have one or if you've been goofing off with that French broad of yours."

"Sid, I've been a Trappist monk."

"Don told me a good one this morning. Did you hear the average man's definition of the perfect wife?"

"No," I said. "What is the average man's definition of the perfect wife?"

"A nymphomaniac who owns a liquor store."

Sid laughed. Juicy. Then he got down to business.

"Look. I'll tell you what. Come on up to the apartment tonight. Any time. I'll be there and we can go over the rough together. Just give me a ring a half hour or so before you figure on coming up."

"Doing a little homework, Sid?"

"I think I'm gonna be scoring tonight. I've been dancing off third for a long time. I think I'm finally going to make it across the plate."

"Don't be too sure," I said. "You know, the best planned lays of mice and men gang aft agley."

Sid erupted again. Juicier.

"That's great. I gotta tell that one to Don. The best planned lays. That's goddamned clever."

"Yeah."

"You want me to fix something up for you? Maybe that's what you need, a little relaxation. Might do you a lot of good."

"I thought you said I had to be a Trappist monk."

"I got the strangest little device up at my apartment. I think they call it . . . a window shade."

"I don't know whether I'll have anything to show you tonight, Sid."

"Don't give me that, Skipper. You goddamn well better have something to show me tonight. Look, Ed." He lowered his voice. He was being solicitous.

"Look, Ed," he said. "You need any help? We got a couple of guys warming up in the bull pen we can throw in for you. You want a couple of researchers to dig around for you? Maybe you want me to call the newsroom and have them turn a couple of guys loose with a tape recorder to do some of the tapes for you?"

"No thanks, Sid. It's all under control. Besides, this is the kind of stuff I have to do myself."

"What time do you think you'll be around the apartment tonight?"

"Oh, maybe around ten-thirty, eleven. I have a tape-editing session after dinner. Depends on when I finish that. I'll call you."

"Be sure and give me that half hour stand-by. You been up to Studio 41 yet?"

"No, I haven't had the chance. I've been up to my ears."

"I think you oughta go up there, Ed. Take your minitape along. Do some interviews with the slobs standing on line. I understand there's been a block-long line all day long—like it was the Music Hall on Easter Week—with God on the stage and Greer Garson on the screen."

"I don't know if I can spare the time."

"Are you out of your mind? Spare the time? What the hell kind of a memorial show are you going to do without some tapes with the slobs? Besides, where the hell is your sense of public relations? You gotta show up there. You make the time. Get up there today and don't go wearing any bright seven-dollar neckties either."

"Sure, Sid," I said.

That frightened me a little. It was the first time I'd given in like that without an argument. It was a good idea, going up to 41 to pick up some tapes. God knows I needed some good fat slob voices for the show, but a week ago I'd have said no on general principles the first time Sid got that command tone in his voice. The Fuller bug was getting me quick. The road map to Easy Street maketh the snotty meek, turneth away wrath and maketh me goddamned humble.

"Sure, Sid. I'll get up there this morning."

"I'll have Hymie send a photographer up to get some shots of you interviewing the Grand Unwashed Public. How are you going to handle your tapes on the show Friday night?"

"I figure I'll edit them down first. I have about two and a half hours of tape already. I'll probably wind up with about seven hours' worth and I'll cut them down to about eighteen minutes. I'll make up a show reel and then pipe them over, cut by cut, to Zeke Frank at Carnegie and get them on a sixteen-inch platter. We can handle that better in the control room."

"You don't want to play them right off the tape? You won't lose as much quality that way."

"No. I think I'd better dub them onto wax. It makes it easier for the engineer handling the air show."

"Whatever you think best. Oh, I forgot to tell you. I spoke to Fran on the phone. I figured with the time limit what it is there wouldn't be time for you to go see her. She isn't coming down to New York."

"She isn't what?"

"She isn't coming down to New York."

"That's just dandy. How the hell am I going to do a memorial show without the bereaved window sobbing her way through a music cue? And won't it look a little funny her not being here for the funeral?"

"Let me worry about that, kid. You worry about the show. I'll handle the rest of the bit."

"Since when have I become the junior partner?"

"That's exactly what you are, baby. Or didn't you read that nice, fat, fine-printed contract you signed? From now on there are some major changes that you might just as well get used to. Number one, I don't want any more snotty talk from you. Not to me, I don't. Number two, start thinking of yourself as a sort of Howdy Doody . . . right out there in the public eye getting all the applause, but just remember who's pulling the strings. Number three, I can pull the rug out from under your well-shod little feet any goddamned time I feel like it."

"Leaving you with a handful of limp strings and a big, fat, fine-printed useless contract which I'm sure you'll figure out a use for."

"I've had my share of big-headed, ungrateful bastards."

"Who's big-headed?"

"Don't get the idea you can push me around, Ed. Don't get that idea for a minute."

"Look, Sid. Let's call a truce until after Friday night. After Friday we can go back to hating each other's guts. We just don't have the time for it now."

Look at me. A regular Ralph A. Bunche.

"O.K.," said Sid. "O.K."

"Now, is there anything else you forgot to mention to me?"

There was a moment's pause. Sid was letting his blood pressure go down, draining the anger out of himself.

"About Fran," he said. "I sent a crew up there this morning with an Ampex machine. Fran and the kids did their tapes already. We're going to have them piped in over the closed circuit early this afternoon. You'll have an Ediphone transcript on your desk by three o'clock. O.K.?"

"Sure. O.K. But how do we know she'll do anything we can use? That's why I have to do these tapes personally, Sid. I have a concept of the show in my head and I'm able to guide them into the right channels in front of the mike."

"You've never met Fran, have you?"

"That's a line I'm getting a little sick of. Every time I talk to somebody about Fuller, sooner or later they say, You never met so and so, did you? No, Daddy, I never met Fran."

"You can relax about her, Coach. Fran knows exactly what we want. You probably won't have to edit a word of it except for timing purpose. This is a bright little dame who knows exactly what she's doing every minute. What time shall I have the photographer pick you up at 41?"

"In about an hour. I have a few things to clean up here and then I'll go to 41."

"Right. See you tonight, *chez moi.*"

I hung up.

I turned the volume on the radio up good and loud. Another Fuller tape was coming out of the radio speaker. The voice was getting on my nerves.

I turned off the radio.

Ginny came in and stretched herself out on the couch. She kicked her shoes off and pushed the door to the office closed with her stockinged foot.

"Katzenjammer?" I asked.

"The Katzen-goddamned-jammer I ever had."

"It's getting to be a national craze."

"You don't mind if I conk off for a half hour, do you? Actually, you can figure it's my lunch hour if you want to be lousy about it."

The phone rang.

Ginny turned her head and brushed the hair out of her eyes. She didn't move from her prone position on the couch.

"If that's for me," she said, "just tell them I passed out. Tell them we're having a double funeral for me and Fuller."

I picked up the receiver.

"Hello," I said.

"Mr. Harris, please," said a very precise voice on the other end of the phone.

"Speaking."

"This is Paul Beaseley."

"Yes, Mr. Beaseley?"

"You know who I am?"

"No, I'm sorry, I don't."

"Paul Beaseley of Worcester."

"Worcester, Massachusetts?"

"That's right. Now do you know who I am?"

"No, I'm afraid I don't."

"It doesn't really matter, Mr. Harris. I'm in the building, up here on the tenth floor visiting Mr. Cutler. You know who Mr. Cutler is, don't you?"

"No, I don't."

"Mr. Cutler is Amalgamated's regional representative for the New England area."

"Oh, is he?"

"Yes."

"That's fine, Mr. Beaseley. Just fine."

"I can be down in your office in a couple of minutes."

"That's fine, Mr. Beaseley, but just why should you want to come down to my office in a couple of minutes?"

"This is Ed Harris, isn't it?"

"Yes. And this is Paul Beaseley, isn't it?"

"That's correct."

"Of Worcester, Massachusetts?"

"Correct."

"Just a minute, Mr. Beaseley."

I put my hand over the mouthpiece.

"Ginny, who the hell is Paul Beaseley?"

"Search me."

"We haven't time. Do I know any Paul Beaseley? Of Worcester, Massachusetts?"

"No."

"You're sure?"

"I'm sure."

I took my hand from over the mouthpiece of the phone.

"Mr. Beaseley," I said, "I wonder if you could tell me what it was you wanted to talk over with me?"

"You really don't know who I am, do you?"

"You've forced it out of me. I really don't know who you are."

"I own WGHP in Worcester."

"That's a radio station, is that right?"

"Of course it's a radio station. It's an Amalgamated affiliate. I've owned it, outright, with no mortgages, for the past eighteen years."

"I don't mean to sound rude, but exactly what has that to do with me?"

"You are Ed Harris, aren't you?"

"Just a minute, Mr. Beaseley."

I put the phone down.

"Ginny," I said, "come over here and tell this man that I'm Ed Harris, will you?"

Ginny got up, walked over to the phone, picked it up, said, "He is Ed Harris," put the receiver down again and went back to the couch. She didn't open her eyes at all in the process.

I picked up the receiver.

"Convinced, Mr. Beaseley?"

"Completely," he said. "I didn't doubt you seriously."

"Now," I said, "would you please have somebody at your end vouch for the fact that you're Paul Beaseley?"

Ginny laughed. With her eyes closed.

"That's perfectly ridiculous," said Mr. Beaseley, "I'll be down in a few minutes."

And he hung up.

"That was Paul Beaseley," I said.

"Of Worcester? Ed, when you take over the Fuller Empire, do I get a raise?"

"Sure, I guess so."

"Don't you know?"

"I'll find out. Remind me of it next week after all this is over. How much does Amalgamated pay you now?"

"Fifty-eight bucks a week."

"How much do you want?"

"How much can I get? Seventy-five? Eighty?"

"That's the proper attitude all right, all right."

"Eighty I think would be a nice amount. Do you think I could get eighty?"

"How do I know?"

"Fuller used to pay his girls himself. He took them off the Amalgamated payroll and paid them himself, out of his own pocket."

"He expected certain extra services out of them, I'm told."

"I could learn dictation."

"Look, don't bother me now. I'll see what I can do about getting you more money."

There was a knock on the door. I got up and opened it, after waiting out Ginny, who rolled back toward the wall and closed her eyes again.

A little man in a shiny dark blue suit, with a high celluloid collar and a string tie, was standing on the threshold. He was holding a green-looking derby under his right arm and wearing a kind of tentative smile.

I put my arm around his shoulder and gave him the big smile.

"Paul," I said. "Paul Beaseley! I can hardly believe it. After all these years! I'd have known you anywhere."

His smile got a little more tentative.

"I'm afraid you're making some sort of a mistake," he said in the same precise voice he'd used on the phone. He enunciated. "I'm afraid you're making some sort of a mistake," he repeated.

"You mean you're not Paul Beaseley? You mean I've mistaken you for my good friend, Paul Beaseley? Impossible. No two people could look so much alike. You're not Paul Beaseley?"

"Oh, yes," he said hurriedly, "I am Paul Beaseley."

"That's what I said. Paul Beaseley of Worcester, Massachusetts."

"We never met, you know, Mr. Harris. You are Mr. Harris, aren't you?"

"Ginny?"

Ginny didn't even turn around or open her eyes.

"He is Ed Harris," she said.

Mr. Beaseley noticed her for the first time. The tentative smile disappeared. Ginny's dress had slipped up a good eight inches and there were two fingers of white skin visible on her thigh above the top of her stocking.

"My secretary," I said. "Very capable girl. I'm thinking of giving her a raise. She performs a great many extra little services for me."

"Oh," said Mr. Beaseley. Then he remembered his manners. He shifted the derby under his left arm, walked over to the couch and extended his right hand.

"How do you do?" he said.

Ginny got up.

"Excuse me," she said.

She left the room. Hurriedly.

"Very reliable girl," I said.

Mr. Beaseley smiled. It was the kind of a smile he could have taken back any time the occasion demanded it.

He sat down on the edge of the couch.

"Well, Mr. Harris," he said.

"Well, Mr. Beaseley?"

"You're probably wondering what I'm doing here?"

I leaned over, looked over my shoulder and then lowered my voice to a whisper.

"As a matter of fact, Paul, why are you here? Didn't you get the last ten thousand I left in the hollow tree trunk?"

"You're joking, Mr. Harris," he said.

"I'm joking."

"I thought so."

"You were right. Now what can I do for you? What are you doing here?"

"It is true that you are doing the Herb Fuller Memorial Show on Friday night?"

"It is true."

"Excellent. That's excellent, Mr. Harris."

"I'm glad you're pleased. Now what exactly can I do for you?"

"Don't the call letters WGH–P mean anything to you?"

"I'm afraid they don't, Mr. Beaseley."

"I gave Herbert his first job in radio. I thought I might be of some little assistance to you in your task."

"You might indeed," I said.

I was getting interested.

"Excuse me for just a minute, will you, Mr. Beaseley?"

I buzzed for Ginny.

"Yeah," she said. "What can I do for you now that I'm practically an eighty-dollar-a-week executive-type secretary?"

"Set up the minitape. Put a new reel of tape on it and then bring it in."

"Right."

I turned back to Mr. Beaseley. Mr. Paul Beaseley of Worcester, Massachusetts.

"Mr. Beaseley, I've been talking to a great many people who knew Herb Fuller very well. I think perhaps you can fill in some of the gaps for me."

"Herbert and I were very close. Of course, that was a good many years ago."

"I wonder if you'd mind just sitting back and telling me some of the things you remember about him."

"Not so fast, Mr. Harris. I'm a businessman. I have something you want. I don't expect to make you a present of it."

"You want some dough? Is that right, Mr. Beaseley? You'd like a little dough?"

"Oh no. Of course I don't want any money. I'm afraid you misunderstand me."

"I'm trying not to. You don't want any dough. What do you want?"

"Well . . . I want you to be sure, somewhere in your broadcast, to work in the call letters of my station."

"I don't understand."

"We take our call letters rather seriously up in Worcester, Mr. Harris. You see, most stations just pick their call letters out of mid-air. Out of the blue, you might say. Oh, sometimes they take the first three letters of their city and put a W or a K in front of it. Or they get cute and spell out four-letter words."

"Four-letter words, Mr. Beaseley?"

"Not that kind of four-letter words, Mr. Harris. Oh, you know what I mean. Mr. Harris, I assure you, I don't take my responsibilities lightly. Running a radio station is a very serious mission and I approach it with a great deal of humility. Sometimes when I think of the untold, uncountable millions I may be influencing, I get very humble. Well, Mrs. Beaseley and I both felt when we acquired the station and the license to operate that we wanted our call letters to mean something. We wanted to give our audience a message of hope and cheer every fifteen minutes or every half hour when the announcer made his station break. We didn't just pull our call letters out of mid-air, out of the blue, Mr. Harris. We thought about it and thought about it and finally decided on WGH–P. Do you know what WGH–P stands for?"

"No, what does it stand for?"

"With God's help—Peace. We have our announcers pause between the H and the P. It isn't much, but it is something to remind people regularly that we are all mortal and that there is a higher being to whom we owe a debt. Don't you think so, Mr. Harris?"

"It sounds like a very sincere thing, Mr. Beaseley."

"Oh, it is. Very sincere. Now . . . we are, of course, only a local station. Your broadcast on Friday night will be on the entire Amalgamated network. I can't help thinking how much good it might do if you were to mention our call letters and tell what they stand for."

"I'll certainly try, Mr. Beaseley. Of course, you're in the business yourself. You know how it is. It might be impossible to get it in or we might have to cut it for time. But I promise you that I'll try to get it into the show."

"Thank you, Mr. Harris. I know you will."

Ginny came in with the minitape and put it on the desk. Mr. Beaseley smiled at her but kind of edged away as she passed.

"This is a minitape, Mr. Beaseley. I don't know whether you've ever seen one or not."

"No, I haven't."

He bent over and picked up a burned match on the carpet, got up, put it in the ash tray and bent over the minitape on the desk.

"It's very compact."

"We find it a very helpful little gadget," I said. "It only weighs thirty pounds, carries its own battery supply and records up to a half hour on a small reel of tape. I've been using it to get my tapes for the memorial show."

"Is it very expensive?"

"About two hundred and fifty."

"My, that is very expensive, isn't it? Well, maybe someday we'll be able to afford one at WGH–P."

"Now, about Fuller, Mr. Beaseley. When did you first meet him?"

I started the minitape and held the mike between us.

Mr. Beaseley put his hand over the mike.

"Before we start talking on the record, perhaps you'd better listen to something first."

"Of course, Mr. Beaseley," I said. But I kept the minitape running.

"Some of the things I have to say to you might not be exactly what you're expecting."

"Amalgamated has lots of tape. It doesn't matter if we waste a little."

"You don't understand, Mr. Harris," he said.

"What don't I understand?"

"You don't understand that I wasn't fond of Herbert. Except maybe at first. Mrs. Beaseley was, but I must admit that I really didn't approve of him."

"Mr. Beaseley, it really doesn't matter one way or the other whether you approved of Herb Fuller. What I want is for you to remember some of the things he did when you knew him in Worcester."

"Oh my goodness! Some of the things he did! I certainly wouldn't want to tell your audience about them."

"Why not?"

"Well. After all, there must be a lot of children listening to the radio."

"At ten o'clock on a Friday night?"

"No, I suppose there aren't many children up at that time. But this is a network program, isn't it?"

"Yes, it is."

"Well, there you are. It's three hours earlier on the West Coast. There are bound to be some children up at seven o'clock out there."

"That's true, Mr. Beaseley. Now suppose you forget about Fuller for a couple of minutes. Tell me something about yourself."

"My name is Paul Beaseley."

"I know that."

"I know you know it, Mr. Harris." There was just the slightest hint of impatience in Mr. Beaseley's voice. "I was stating it for the record. It might help you identify this tape recording. Of course, I suppose you could identify my voice, but this way there is no chance for an error."

"All right. You're Paul Beaseley."

"That's right."

"And?"

"And what?"

"What else?"

"You want my height and my weight? Mrs. Beaseley thinks I've been putting on a little too much weight lately. Actually, a certain stoutness runs in my family. I remember my father . . . do you know that when he was eighty-four, he weighed over two hundred——"

I cut in. I had to. This way we'd have gone right on through the rest of his family and missed Friday completely.

"Suppose I just ask you questions, Mr. Beaseley? And suppose you just answer them? Just the questions I ask. All right?"

"That will be fine."

"Where were you born?"

"In Worcester. Do you want the street address?"

"No. That won't be necessary."

"Fine."

"How did you happen to buy the radio station in Worcester?"

"I was in the wholesale grocery business in Worcester. You might say I was born into it. My father founded the business and I went to work with him right after I got out of school. I just sort of took over and when he retired he signed it over to me."

"Was it successful?"

"Oh yes. Very successful."

"And how did you get interested in the radio business?"

"That happened in a rather unusual manner. Ed Oakes

was the one that built the radio station . . . got the license and opened it up for business. You don't know Ed, of course, but he was one of those fellows, you know, too much money for his own good. He got interested in all sorts of crackpot foolishness. One year it would be racing cars, those fancy kinds with the big twisted pipes coming out from under the hood. Another year, I remember he bought a Pullman car. Said he always wanted to own one. Anyway, don't misunderstand me. I liked Ed very much. He was just a sort of foolish young man. Too much money."

"But he bought the radio station in Worcester?"

"He built it. We laughed at it at first. Thought it was just another one of Ed's foolish notions. We thought he'd get tired of it in a year or so, like he had with the racing cars or the Pullman. But then the more we thought about it, the more interested we were. Worcester, as I'm sure you know, Mr. Harris, isn't Boston. It isn't even Providence. It was quite a feather in our cap to have our own radio station. I was the president of the Worcester Chamber of Commerce that year and we all got behind Ed. The merchants advertised on the radio station and the first thing Ed knew what had happened to him, he had a successful business on his hand."

"In that case, how did you happen to buy it?"

"He got bored with it. I'd been working with our local church dramatic group. Mrs. Beaseley and I are both interested in dramatics and bit by bit I began to take the programing part of the station over. Finally Ed said he wanted to sell it, I made him an offer, he accepted it and the station was mine. That's when Mrs. Beaseley and I changed its call letters."

"When was that, Mr. Beaseley?"

"In 1931."

"And what happened to your wholesale grocery business?"

"Oh, I ran that too for a while, but finally I decided I couldn't do both jobs. My brother Henry took it over. Of course, I still own it, but Henry runs it for me."

"So you found yourself in the radio business?"

"That's right."

"And you liked it?"

"Oh yes. We both liked it. Mrs. Beaseley, I mean."

"And then you met Herb Fuller?"

"Oh no. I didn't meet him. He came in to audition for one of our programs. It was a sort of Amateur Hour, but it had an extra, added ingredient. You see, Mr. Harris, Mrs. Beaseley and I both felt a great sense of our responsibilities running a radio station. The contestants on our amateur program also had to deliver a two-minute sermon. Our listeners voted by phone and the content of the sermon counted as much as the talent the performer displayed. Herbert was in the Navy then and one night he came down from Boston to audition for the program. We had a twenty-five-dollar first prize and his shipmates thought he could win easily. You see, our programs were heard in Boston. It wasn't as if we were just a little, small local station. All of New England was aware of Worcester, thanks to WGH–P."

"What did Herb do?"

"He sang."

"When was this, Mr. Beaseley?"

"Oh, I really couldn't tell you the exact date. Perhaps sometime in 1933. I could look up our employment records and give you the date if you're interested."

"That's close enough. He sang. Well?"

"Not very well. About the way he's always done it. Of course, now that so many people are so used to hearing him, you think he does it well. Actually, as I was telling Mrs. Beaseley the other night, Herbert really doesn't have any talent at all until you get used to him."

"How did he make out in the amateur contest?"

"He won. First prize."

"How do you explain that? The audience must have liked his singing that night."

"Oh no. His sermon won the contest for him."

"He had a sermon prepared?"

"No, he didn't have one prepared. He was rather taken aback when he was told that in addition to performing he had to deliver a two-minute sermon. He just got on and made one up as he went along."

"It was good?"

"It was more than just good, Mr. Harris. It was thrilling. It won him the contest. We got over five hundred requests for it. Fortunately we'd made a record of that particular program and we were able to have it mimeographed and sent out to the people who'd requested it."

"Do you remember what it was like?"

Mr. Beaseley reached into his pocket and took out a folded piece of paper.

"That's what decided me about this trip. When I read about Herbert's death I remembered that sermon of his and I looked through the old files of the station in the basement storeroom and found a copy of it. I thought you might like to have it. I thought you might have some use for it."

"I do indeed. May I see it?"

Mr. Beaseley handed me the paper.

As I read it, I could almost hear Fuller's fruity voice reading it. It went like this:

"I don't know anything about sermons. Like the rest of you, I've heard maybe two thousand of them in my life and right now I can't remember a single word of one of them. I'll bet you can't, either. And yet, the best sermon I know has no words at all. None at all. I hear it at night when my ship is out at sea . . . cut off from the land . . . out under the lonely stars, separated from the world by a limitless void of water. It's like . . . well, it's like there was no other world. Like there were no other people. Just me . . . standing there on that iron deck under the stars. And one night I got to wondering out under those stars what God was really like. What He looked like. How I'd know Him if I ever saw Him. And you know the answer I got? I got it from the silence of the night, from the lapping of the water against the side of the boat, from the light of the stars . . . up there out of reach. And the answer was so simple, my friends. So simple. The answer was that they were all God. The stars, and the night, the silence and the lapping of the water. And me too. Above all, me. I was God too. And I wouldn't have any trouble recognizing Him when I saw Him because He was everywhere around me. In everything I heard, everything I said; everything I saw. Everyone I met. God was the sum total of all of us. It was a mighty pretty sermon. Mighty pretty. And it makes you wonder. It really does. How can Man be so small and so insignificant and at the same time be so Great and so Wonderful!"

He thought I might be able to use it!

The next thought was one that I was almost afraid to voice. I crossed my fingers and said, very casually,

"By the way, Mr. Beaseley. You don't still happen to have the recording of that show, do you?"

"It's funny that you should ask me that, Mr. Harris. The same thought occurred to me when I found this sheet of paper. I wondered if we still had the recording around somewhere."

"And do you?"

"I really don't know. Something came up and I didn't have the time to look through the storeroom. Mrs. Beaseley is funny about things like that. She just can't throw anything away. I'm sure it's there somewhere in that storeroom."

"Mr. Beaseley, I want you to do something for me. I want you to take the next train back to Worcester. And when you get there, I want you to go down into that storeroom. Take enough food for two days and stay there until you find that recording. And when you do, take the first train down to New York and give it to me. After you get here, sit yourself down and write out a bill for your services and a bill for your train fare and your expenses."

"Why, thank you very much, Mr. Harris. That's very nice of you."

My mind was racing around, writing the script around that sermon. I could use it as the motif of the whole show. Open cold with it. Build my show from there and use it as the pay-off punch with music underneath coming up to a Paramount finish. It was the greatest find since radium.

"The next train to Worcester," said Mr. Beaseley, "isn't until three-thirty this afternoon. I will, of course, travel coach."

"Mr. Beaseley, you travel first class. Get yourself a compartment. Buy yourself a Pullman if you want to, but get that recording into my hands by Friday morning."

"Oh, I think I can promise you that, Mr. Harris. And you will try to work in the call letters of my station?"

"I promise you that I will work them in, Mr. Beaseley."

"Well, perhaps I'd better let you get some work done. I'm in your way."

"No, you're not, Mr. Beaseley. Sit there. Make yourself comfortable. I'd like to ask you some more questions if I may."

"Certainly."

"What happened after Fuller won your amateur contest?"

"A great many things. I already told you that we got over five hundred requests for copies of the sermon. Our local paper reprinted it and he was quite a celebrity in Worcester."

Mr. Beaseley lowered his voice momentarily.

"Quite frankly, Mr. Harris," he said, "I never did quite understand what the sermon really meant. It sounded very good and there's no doubt that it moved a great many people, but when you take it word by word . . . just for the sense of it . . . it doesn't really add up to very much, does it?"

"It doesn't have to, Mr. Beaseley. You were part of a very historic moment. It must have been a little like the moment Hercules first discovered that he was strong. Or the moment Rembrandt discovered he could paint. You were the midwife at the birth of a legend."

"Oh come now, Mr. Harris. Aren't you exaggerating a trifle?"

"Not a goddamned trifle. I beg your pardon. Not a bit. You said it yourself. He couldn't sing. But he won your amateur contest. Why? Because he could take words, roll them over those cockeyed tonsils of his and make people believe that they were listening to something important or profound. He could move people. That was the beginning of the legend. Sure, you only got five hundred requests. But the same talent, developed, refined, perfected, worked just as well on five thousand, five million and finally a hundred and fifty million. He didn't sing any better than he did in 1933, but that became an asset. That became part of the legend."

"I'm afraid you're being carried away, Mr. Harris. You obviously didn't know Herbert very well. In a great many ways he was not a very nice person. In a great many ways, he was a very bad person."

"What do you mean by that, Mr. Beaseley?"

He said nothing for a full minute.

"Mr. Harris," he said, finally, "I realize that in the eyes of a lot of people, I'm a faintly ridiculous person. I can't help that. I don't think I am ridiculous. My friends don't think so. Mrs. Beaseley doesn't think so. But all my life, people who didn't know me well thought I was ridiculous. It hurt me at first. Particularly when I was a child. But I soon learned to accept it. The way you accept the fact that you limp or stutter. I don't mind the slight smile that people always have around their mouths when they talk to me. I truly don't. I noticed it on you, Mr. Harris."

"I'm sorry."

"Oh, don't apologize. It's not your fault. That, unfortunately, is the way I impress most people. It's a handicap and I'm used to it. I suppose, in some ways, I am ridiculous. To some people. If they don't know me. But there is one thing I do mind, Mr. Harris. Mind very much. I don't like to be taken advantage of."

"None of us do, Mr. Beaseley."

"Herbert took advantage of me."

"How?"

"After he won that amateur contest he was the talk of Worcester. That sounds silly, doesn't it? The talk of Worcester. Anyway, I tried to find him. All I knew about him was his name and the fact that he was a sailor on a ship that had been in the Navy Yard at Boston. In those days the Navy wasn't very cooperative with radio stations. They were no help at all. I wasn't able to find him. Finally about six months later he walked into my office, with no warning at all. He was in civilian clothes. He'd been discharged from the Navy. He was looking for a job."

"And you hired him?"

"Of course I hired him. I gave him a two-hour program of his own in the morning, from seven to nine o'clock."

"Did he know the effect of his sermon on the good citizens of Worcester?"

"Not at first. He discovered how famous he was almost immediately, however, and he started including a little sermon in his broadcast every morning. Mrs. Beaseley and I were delighted. Mrs. Beaseley is a very religious woman. She has been all her life. She is the president of the woman's society in our church. And in a way, I'm religious too. I take part in a great many of the church activities. We were both delighted that Herbert was interested in spiritual things."

"What were these sermons like, Mr. Beaseley?"

"Oh, very much like that first one. Of course, it's simple to use hindsight now and realize that Herbert just figured if that was what they wanted, he could certainly give it to them. At the time, both Mrs. Beaseley and I were convinced of his sincerity. He also always opened his program in the morning with a little prayer."

"He'd found a good thing."

"Yes, I think that's very true. I think he thought he had found a good thing. He was auditioning it in Worcester."

"An out-of-town tryout?"

"Trying it on the dog, Mr. Harris."

"Mr. Beaseley, I don't find you the slightest bit ridiculous."

"People don't after a while. It's that first impression that's so awful. Anyway, Herbert branched out a little. He began including hymns in his program every day. He was very successful. We had more sponsors on his program than we had on all the other programs on the station."

"He was a big hit?"

"A very big hit."

"How did he get along with the people of Worcester socially?"

"He was in great demand at social functions. He was the life of the party everywhere he went. Aside from all that, however, Mrs. Beaseley and I were very fond of him. He lived with us in those days and Mrs. Beaseley used to fuss over him; you know how women are. And I must admit, he was a very appealing youngster. I suppose his basic appeal was that he reminded everybody of their kid brother, whether they ever had one or not. Everything was just fine for a year."

"And then?"

"And then he started to change."

"How?"

"Not all at once. Not overnight. Not completely. He still sang his hymns, still did a daily sermon, but every once in a while he'd slip in a dirty joke. Oh, he'd clean it up, take the dirty words out of it, but if you'd ever heard it in its original form, you'd recognize it immediately."

"And people started complaining?"

"Oh no. That was the funny part of the whole thing. They liked it. They found nothing contradictory in the combination of smut and piety."

"Was he making a lot of money by this time?"

"Not in comparison to what he made later. In terms of Worcester, in terms of 1935, quite a lot. About two hundred and fifty dollars a week. He spent most of it. He had to work hard at that. Worcester in 1935 wasn't the kind of a town where you could get rid of two hundred and fifty dollars a week easily. But he did it. He picked up checks everywhere he went. It was a deadly serious game with him. When you were with Herbert you were forbidden to spend money for anything. He bought a lot of clothes. And he bought a Chrysler convertible. A red one. Like most towns, we have a tenderloin section . . . a . . ."

"A red-light district?"

"Yes, I suppose that's one way of putting it. Cheap bars, questionable cabarets and houses of prostitution. Herbert became a well-known figure in the district. I found out about it almost immediately, but I didn't do much about it. At first, I thought I'd sit down and have a talk with him. At that time, I used to think of him, I suppose, sort of like a father. He was living in my house and you know you fall into habits. Then I thought I'd let it pass. He was sowing a few wild oats. I didn't think it was very serious. It would pass. It was something he had to get out of his system."

"Did he?"

"No. Never. Not then. Not later. Not even the day he died. He never got it out of his system."

"So he started sowing some wild oats? Then what?"

"He didn't just sow them in the bars and the houses of prostitution. Bit by bit he got smuttier and smuttier on the air. And strangely enough the same people that loved him for the hymns and the sermons loved him for this too. You see, he had already wormed his way into their consciousness. They knew him. They liked him and they were tolerant with him. Oh yes, once in a while he was a dirty little boy but deep down underneath he was a good person. But deep down underneath, Mr. Harris, he wasn't. Mrs. Beaseley and I finally had to accept that."

"When did you first begin to realize it, Mr. Beaseley?"

"There wasn't any one thing that made it obvious. We were very fond of Herbert. You have to remember that. We had no children of our own. You have to remember that too. He was a very appealing, persuasive boy when he wanted to be. It was very hard for us to realize what he had really become."

"Or was from the beginning."

"Or was from the beginning. I realized it a little when I discovered that most of the time he was dead drunk on the air. When I discovered that the water pitcher he drank out of during his broadcasts was really filled with gin. That was bad enough. I'm not a Puritan. Mr. Harris, but I do believe a man has a certain obligation to his job and the people he works for."

"But you said yourself he was a big hit on the air. Why should it matter to you if he did it drunk, sober or standing on his head?"

"It did matter to me, Mr. Harris, because Herbert still meant something to me. As a person, as a human being."

"You didn't tell your wife about this?"

"No. One morning . . . Could I have a drink of water, Mr. Harris?"

I poured him a glass of water out of the carafe on my desk. He drank it slowly. He put the glass back on the desk and didn't say anything for a full minute.

"This is rather embarrassing. It's a small station, Mr. Harris. It's not like here. . . . It's . . ."

"I know, Mr. Beaseley. I've worked at a few of them in my time."

"Well, then . . . you know what it was like. We all had extra jobs to do. One morning a week, Wednesdays, I opened the station up at four-thirty in the morning. It gave my one engineer a morning off. I ran the board until he came in at noon. Well . . . this particular morning when I came in, I knew something was wrong the minute I opened the outer door. The place smelled funny. We have a sort of vestibule before you're in the station proper, with a tiled floor, and the minute I stepped in the vestibule, I could smell something. I didn't know what. I found out when I opened the inner door. The waiting room was in disgraceful condition. We only had two studios, Mr. Harris. They were on opposite sides of the waiting room and between them was the control room, connecting them. From the waiting room you can see into both studios and the control room. Anyway, the cigarette urns were overturned and the sand was spilled on the rug. The seat was torn out of one of the canvas chairs. The water cooler had been tipped over and the bottle was smashed in the opposite corner as if someone had thrown it across the room. A large section of the stair carpeting leading up to the offices upstairs was burned. I was appalled."

"I'll bet you were."

"I thought somebody had broken in. I started climbing the stairs and halfway up I found . . . I don't know what you call them . . . panties, I guess."

"A lady's unmentionables."

"Yes. Upstairs was in a worse condition. Chairs were smashed, a file cabinet was overturned and its contents spilled on the floor, somebody had torn a window shade into small pieces and set fire to them in the middle of the room. Fortunately the fire had evidently gone out of its own volition. I was sick to my stomach at the senseless destruction, and then I opened the door to my office."

"And found Fuller dead drunk on the floor."

"On the sofa. Dead drunk, with his arms wrapped around a woman. There was also a half-empty bottle of liquor on the floor. The top was broken off and had jagged edges. It was obvious that in his drunken stupor he'd been unable to open it and had smashed the top on the desk. The glass top was smashed to pieces."

"And you fired him?"

"No. No, I didn't, Mr. Harris."

"Why not?"

"My first impulse was to hit him with anything I could lay my hands on. My first impulse was to destroy him, to tear him apart with my bare hands. But I didn't. I cleaned the place up, got rid of the woman, sobered him up and kept Mrs. Beaseley away from the station until the damage was repaired. I took fifty dollars a week out of his salary until it was all paid for. But I couldn't fire him. Not without telling Mrs. Beaseley why, and I couldn't tell her that."

"You did nothing about it?"

"I didn't have to. Worcester did it for me. Suddenly he was finished in Worcester. Nobody listened to him any more. Suddenly he was no longer sought after by the Rotary Club, the Boy Scouts or the Chamber of Commerce. Suddenly the sponsors dropped off. One by one. Suddenly he was back to thirty-eight dollars a week again. Don't ask me why. Maybe he'd gone too far. Maybe he was a fad that came full circle and ended. Suddenly he was just another very small frog in the puddle."

"Did it straighten him out?"

"Yes. It straightened him out. For a while. He dropped the dirty jokes. He went back to the hymns. It was strange watching him during that period in his life. It was like watching somebody who'd lost his way in the woods. He was retracing his steps. He found the familiar landmarks he knew. Somewhere past there he'd lost his way and he was retracing his steps carefully. Mrs. Beaseley used to say, 'See, I told you it was just a phase he was going through. I told you he was just sowing some wild oats. I told you he was a good boy at heart.' We hardly spoke to each other, except around Mrs. Beaseley."

"Did he get back his popularity?"

"Not right away. Not all at once. But before the year was out he was right back at the top again. He was more careful this time. He was feeling his way, trying to find out how far he could go and still get away with it. He added a little smut here . . . a dirty joke there . . . and finally he stopped just short of the border line. He had the mixture right finally. He became a sort of Peck's Bad Choir Boy."

"Was he behaving himself off the air too?"

"He was a little more careful there too. He was still drinking heavily. He and I no longer made any pretense of our feelings for each other. He thought I was ridiculous. I despised him. But because of Mrs. Beaseley, because of the sponsors, because of his success, I kept him around. Until, finally, a colleague of yours happened to be in Worcester one day, happened to hear him and happened to offer him a contract."

"Sid Moore?"

"Yes, I think that was his name. I never saw him again. I've heard him. Many times. He never varied the mixture after that. He'd learned the formula and he stuck to it. And I'm afraid that's all I really know about Herb Fuller. I'm afraid it won't be of much use to you."

"That original sermon will, if you can find the record."

"I'll find the record, Mr. Harris."

Mr. Beaseley took a large handkerchief out of his pocket and blew his nose.

He looked at me.

"Why do you suppose we do it, you and I?" he asked.

"Do what, Mr. Beaseley?"

"Why do you suppose I'm going back to Worcester to find that record? Why do you suppose you're going on the air Friday night to tell the world what a great man he was? Why do you suppose neither of us won't just get up in front of a microphone and tell the truth about him?"

"I don't know the answer to that, Mr. Beaseley. Why did you come to see me in the first place?"

"Because, quite frankly, Mrs. Beaseley wanted me to. Mrs. Beaseley is a very sick woman. Mrs. Beaseley has a very strong maternal feeling, Mr. Harris, and we don't have any children of our own. I try not to destroy it. What's your excuse?"

"A very simple one. It's a job. The most important job I've ever had."

"Your excuse is no better than mine, is it?"

I tried to think of how to answer him. I wanted to tell him that I didn't give a good goddamn what kind of a human being Herb Fuller was. I wanted to tell him that after Friday night there wouldn't be any Herb Fuller. We'd bury the legend with full military honors and let it go at that. I didn't tell him anything. Ginny saved me by buzzing on the local phone.

"I knew you were recording," she said. "So I didn't interrupt you. Mr. Moore called to remind you to get up to Studio 41 this morning."

"Right," I said.

"I won't take up any more of your time, Mr. Harris."

"I'm sorry, Mr. Beaseley. I have to get up to Studio 41. That's where they have Fuller's body. Would you like to come along with me?"

"No, thank you, Mr. Harris. I've seen his body. I'll go up and chat with Mr. Cutler for a few minutes and get that afternoon train to Worcester."

We shook hands.

"Thank you, Mr. Beaseley."

"Don't worry, Mr. Harris," he said. "You'll get that transcription in plenty of time."

Holy God!

I felt a blush start in the pit of my stomach and work its way up to my ears. I was remembering the comedy bit Ginny and I had done when he walked in.

"Mr. Beaseley," I said, "I'm sorry."

"About what?"

"When you came in. That silly business with my secretary on the couch. We just . . . we clown around a lot. It doesn't mean anything."

He smiled again.

There was nothing tentative about it this time.

"If you ever get up to Worcester, I wish you'd drop in on us. I'd like you to meet Mrs. Beaseley."

"I'd love to," I said.

We shook hands again and he left.

I turned off the minitape. I was sure collecting a lot of tapes that weren't going to be heard on anybody's airwaves any Friday night. I put the Beaseley roll in my top drawer. On the way out I stopped at Ginny's desk.

"I'm going up to 41. I'll be back sometime early this afternoon. Call Rickie Tyler at the Astor and find out when we can get together. And if we don't get a transcript of the Fran Fuller tapes by three o'clock, goose Sid Moore on it."

"For eighty dollars a week?"

"Complain to the union."

For once I had no trouble getting a cab. Evidently I'd slipped noiselessly into a new groove at Amalgamated like a Cadillac with an automatic shift. I was getting to be brass. Peter spotted me coming out of the elevator and by the time I got through the lobby he had a cab waiting at the curb with its door open and its motor running.

"Don't have an accident with the Crown Prince in your jalopy," he said to the cab driver.

I flipped him a quarter.

What the hell!

Noblesse oblige.

The cabbie was very unimpressed.

"Where to?" he asked.

"Eighty-first and First."

"Oh brother!" he said.

"What's the matter? Your license won't cover you above Seventy-ninth?"

"You wouldn't like to do me a favor? You wouldn't like to get out and take yourself another cab?"

"I wouldn't. I'd have to give Peter another two bits. What have you got against Eighty-first and First?"

"You're going to Studio 41?"

"Right."

"Maybe you are and then again maybe you ain't."

"Look, let's go. Tell your story in third."

He put in the clutch and we headed north.

"Mister," he said, over his shoulder, "I'll do the best I can. I don't know how close I'll be able to get. The last haul up there, the closest I got was Seventy-ninth and Park."

"Crowds?" I asked.

"Crowds! I should have such crowds at my wake. Crosstown traffic on Seventy-ninth is fouled up and they won't let you stop within four blocks of the place."

"Let's make a try at it, anyway."

"Mister, I'm not trying to tout you off a cab," he said, over his shoulder again. "My advice would be I head for First Avenue and you take a bus uptown. The buses get through."

"No buses. Let's go."

"O.K. I got all day and that clock keeps ticking the nickels away. It's your expense account, Mister."

He wasn't exaggerating much. I started noticing the people from Fifth and Seventy-fifth on. At first it was just fifty or sixty people to a block strolling aimlessly westward through the side streets. Seventy-ninth Street was really a mess. You know how it looks around Baker Field of a Saturday afternoon just after a Columbia game's broken up? The pedestrians had overflowed onto the street and there was one thin line of traffic inching its way through. The cabbie put the heel of his hand down on the horn and we pushed our way slowly through the crowd. I got out at Seventy-ninth and Third and walked the rest of the way. I got hell from a cop on the corner of Second Avenue after fighting my way upstream like a salmon.

"This street is one-way traffic today," he barked at me.

"For people too?"

"You're damned right for people. You want to go east you should take Eightieth—that goes east—pedestrians and cars."

I showed him my press card.

"I don't give a damn you're William Randolph Hearst," he

said. "Today you're just a pedestrian. Pedestrians going east take Eightieth Street."

I walked north on Second and took Eightieth.

It was a lot easier until we got to the corner of First Avenue. It was a mob. You just caught yourself in the middle of it, put your hands at your side and shuffled along in one big mass movement. It was a funny kind of a crowd too. Women mostly and lots of kids. The men looked a little seedy, the kind you see coming out of the grind houses on Forty-second Street in the afternoon. It was a noisy crowd. A happy crowd. Like they were on their way to some ward heeler's May Day Party in Central Park. The bottleneck was at the corner of Eighty-first. The Amalgamated ushers in their sterile gray and blue monkey suits were helping out the cops and they had a system. Everything funneled across the street and the line going into Studio 41 extended east down Eighty-first Street. The people coming out were shuttled across the street and headed west on Eighty-first. Fortunately one of the ushers knew me and he and a couple of others formed a sort of flying wedge in front of me that got me to the stage door.

When I opened the stage door and stepped out of the noisy mob on the street the change was sudden and stunning. The silence was like an immediate deafness as the heavy soundproof door swung shut behind me. As my ears adjusted themselves, I could hear the low rumble of an organ and the sweet cloying smell of flowers came at me like a wave. The doorman touched the frayed brim of the old felt hat he had pulled down on his head and I noticed that the curtain had been pulled across the stage, which was completely empty. The doorman pointed to a door at the bottom of a short flight of stairs.

"Out that way," he said. "Watch your step."

I opened the door and went through a passage that led me up the left aisle of the theater.

Studio 41 used to be an old movie grind house. The kind that runs a triple feature, charges twenty-eight cents, has a big popcorn machine in the lobby and smells faintly of cat urine. Amalgamated had done quite a face-lifting job inside. There were new rugs on the floor, the seats had been replaced, the stage had been rebuilt and platforms had been constructed to hold the cameras and the dollies. After they'd bought it, when TV became big business and all the networks had run out of space, they'd spent over fifty thousand dollars making it socially acceptable to the freeloaders that came to watch their shows. It was tastefully decorated in the Amalgamated Gray and Blue.

It still smelled faintly of cat urine.

I stood at the rear of the house for a couple of minutes looking around.

They'd done another hell of a job of remodeling. All the seats had been ripped out. The floor had been painted black and there was a thick blue carpet running from the doors to the outer lobby, down the center of the theater, around the coffin and out the rear exit door on the other side. The coffin itself was red maple with silver handles and was set smack in the middle of the theater with two white pinpoints of light hitting it from the ceiling. The rest of the room was in complete darkness with heavy black drapes hung over the balcony seats and along the side walls. The only light in the room with the exception of the spotlights came from two huge stained glass windows on the apron of the stage, which were dimly lit from behind. The stage itself was banked with flowers and the organ music came out of speakers placed strategically around the auditorium. Off to the left, just below the stage, were folding chairs and a pulpit, evidently for the nightly sermons and choir program. At the rear of the theater, on each side, were two TV cameras, painted black. It was one hell of a setup.

Beautiful.

If it was a Roman holiday outside, the atmosphere was properly funereal in here. The ushers had worked some sort of a miracle in the outer lobby. A double line filed quietly past the coffin with its honor guard of two soldiers, two sailors and two marines. The line never stopped, never jammed up and there was no talking, no laughter, no whispers. The stage setting, the lighting on the coffin and the semidarkness had its effect. The crowds moved along quietly and the only sound, except for the organ, was the steady shuffle of hundreds of pairs of feet across the rug. I felt somebody touching my arm, and I turned. It was Nick Cellantano.

"I was wondering when you'd get here. Sid said you'd be here this morning."

"I got held up at the office with some tapes for the show."

What the hell was I doing explaining and apologizing to Nick for?

"Good job," Nick said, nodding his head toward the coffin. "If you're going to do something like this, this is the way to do it. Look how awed they are. How do you like the stained glass windows?"

"Lovely."

"We've been clocking the crowd. We're averaging at about two hundred and fifty an hour. This keeps up and he'll be the highest rated corpse in the world. Originally we planned to shut down at ten o'clock, but we got word from downtown to keep the joint open until midnight. I got some booze in the manager's office for the newspaper boys if you'd like a shot."

"I'd better wait until I do my tapes. The crown prince can't smell of booze at the royal wake."

"I shoulda thought of that. Me, I have faith in chlorophyll.

I've got the photographer backstage sitting on his prat. We can take the shot any time you're ready."

"Let's get it over with."

We started walking down the side aisle, into the passage and backstage.

"What did you have in mind?" I asked.

"A stock shot. You standing at the coffin looking down soberly. You think you can keep from laughing in his face until we get the shot?"

"Sure."

Nick looked me over.

"Mind if I make a suggestion?" he asked.

"Go ahead."

"Maybe we'd better trade ties. Let's keep Countess Mara out of the papers this time."

"If you say so."

I took off my tie and handed it to Nick. He handed me the black knitted one he was wearing. I put it on.

"Maybe I'd better have a quick shot and a chlorophyll chaser."

"You're the boss."

"After Friday I am. Now I'm just a talented vulture in a borrowed black tie."

"The booze is through here."

We went into a little cubbyhole backstage. This was the theater manager's office. They'd done a hell of a job with the rest of the theater but progress and sanitation had stopped at the threshold of this room.

It was filthy.

Pipes ran across the ceiling, and the walls, which had once been yellow, had rust streaks from floor to ceiling. One wall had a sliding panel that gave the manager a full view of the stage from his desk. Except for that desk, a battered, scarred monstrosity with cigarette burns along its edges, the only other piece of furniture in the room was a moth-eaten couch that looked as if it would raise a choking cloud of dust if you were foolish enough to sit in it. The other three walls were decorated with pictures dating back to the days when Studio 41 was still the Alhambra.

There were lithographs of Jack Hoxie and Hoot Gibson.

Karl Dane and George K. Arthur.

Bessie Love and Ramon Navarro.

Wallace Beery and Raymond Hatton.

Nils Asther and Colleen Moore.

One whole side of a wall was taken up by a gaudy three-sheet showing a guy dressed in a blood-spattered surgical gown cutting a woman in half with a buzz saw. It was a doozer. "The Great Edwardo! He defies description! Final Week!"

Nick saw me looking at it.

"Ever see that act?" he asked me.

"No."

"Great act. Went big here and up in the Puerto Rican section. This guy used to put the dame through his buzz saw, stop halfway and invite the audience up on stage to look. Bloody? They used to rope off the first four rows and cover them with brown butcher's paper. Bloodiest goddamned thing you ever saw."

"Good trick."

"Yeah. I saw it six nights running. Examined hell out of the equipment. Never could figure out how the bastard did it. No kidding, when you came up onstage that assistant of his was chewed up plenty by the buzz saw."

"Maybe it wasn't a trick. Maybe he really cut them in half."

"At the end of the act, he used to chuck the two halves in a wicker basket and carry it offstage. But it was always the same dame, show after show. Beats me how he did it."

"Whatever happened to him?"

"Haven't the faintest idea. He'd be great for color TV."

"How are those drinks coming?"

"Right with you."

Nick poured us two big hookers, straight.

I gulped mine down.

It was terrible booze.

I looked at the label. It was a brand I'd never heard of.

"Where the hell did you get this stuff?" I asked. "You must have found it in the desk when you moved in."

"Isn't it terrible?"

"Yes, it is. Terrible. Lousy. Unbelievable."

"What a goddamned stupid company. I wouldn't tell you how much they're spending for that setup outside. You wouldn't believe me. A coronation's cheaper. I ask them for some dough for booze for the newspaper guys and they hit the ceiling. I tell them some of the facts of life. Wedding, wake or circumcision you gotta set up booze for the newspaper guys. They finally kick in. Yeah. They deliver me a case of this poison. It makes sense to them. 'You got your story made,' they say. 'What are they going to do, put the rap on Fuller because you serve lousy booze? For once in their lives they have to do a puff piece without a payoff.' So we got lousy booze."

I took three quick gulps of the lousy booze.

Nick had something on his mind. He kept taking short little puffs out of his cigarette and kept looking at me in quick, short, little glances. He hadn't touched his drink.

"You on the wagon?" I asked him.

"No. No. I'm not on the wagon."

He took a big gulp.

"Before I'm finished," he said, "this booze may put me on the wagon."

"Something on your mind, Nick?"

"It can wait."

"No, go ahead. What's the matter?"

"Nothing. Nothing the matter, Ed."

I put down my glass. I'd been leaning against the desk and my pants were spotted with dust. I brushed them off with my hands.

"O.K., I'm set," I said. "Let's get outside and get it over with. Who did Hymie send up to take the pictures?"

"Karl. Karl Backlund."

I whistled quietly. Karl Backlund. No passport pictures this time. Karl Backlund was the only Amalgamated photographer who got a credit line on his pictures when they were sent out to the papers. The rest of them were just mechanics. They aimed, they focused and they shot. Their pictures had about as much individuality as a bag full of clothespins. But Backlund, he was something else again. Maybe you've seen some of his prints in *U.S. Camera* or at the Museum of Modern Art. I was a little ashamed of the boot it gave me that they'd sent Backlund up to take my picture.

"So Hymie sent Backlund up to take the shots?"

"Sent him up?"

"Yeah. Sid said he asked Hymie to send someone up to take the pictures of me at the bier."

"Oh. Well . . . Hymie didn't send him up. He's been here. He's assigned to Operation Formaldehyde permanently. Hymie called up a half hour ago and told him he had clearance to take a couple of shots of you at the coffin."

It was my turn to say, "Oh."

I said it.

"Oh."

"At least they'll be able to recognize you in the pictures."

Nick handed me a stick of gum.

"I'm ready," I said. "Let's get it over with."

I flipped the gum wrapper in the corner and walked to the door.

"Did you bring the minitape?"

Great!

"I forgot it. I left it on Ginny's desk."

"That's all right. We have a couple of extras here. You can use one of those. I'll have one of the ushers load it up and bring it out front for you."

He picked up the phone, dialed a number and made the arrangements. When he finished he walked over to where I was standing.

"Ed, before we go, I'd like to ask you something."

"Sure, Nick. What?"

"It's none of my business and maybe you haven't even thought about it. What I mean is maybe I'm a little early with this . . ."

"With what?"

"Well . . . after Friday night things are going to be a lot different for you. What I mean is . . . Oh balls, I'm asking for a job."

"You've got one, Nick."

"A job with you."

"I don't have a job to give you, Nick. As of now, I have one crummy little local radio show. I'm a big wheel anywhere within a radius of thirty miles of the George Washington Bridge. Once in a while, when Marge Kelloway thinks of it, she puts an anecdote out in the bundle of eyewash she sends out every morning. Once in a while my name turns up in the highlight columns. Once in a while. It depends on how much of her expense money Marge spends getting some slob on a paper drunk. Or it depends on how nasty I've been to Marge on a given day. I don't have a job to give you, Nick."

"Come off it, Ed. That was last week."

"Sure, that was last week. Look, if I dropped dead on Times Square with the H-Bomb secret in my back pocket, with a little luck and a little pull, Marge Kelloway might just possibly get a mention of the suit I was wearing at the time in *Women's Wear Daily.*"

I was stalling. We both knew it.

"I don't know what you heard about me, Ed."

I took the gum out of my mouth and parked it on the underside of the desk. I sat down and poured myself another drink.

"O.K., Nick. Go ahead."

Nick poured himself a drink and sat down. He had the look people get when they've been debating with themselves a long time and have finally decided to get something over with. He took another long gulp and wiped his mouth with the back of his hand. He took his handkerchief out and blew his nose.

"Lousy booze," he said.

I had the feeling that if I said, Let's forget it for now, Nick, he'd have grabbed at the chance. I didn't say it.

"O.K., Nick, shoot."

"Yeah. Let me recap first, O.K.?"

"O.K."

"I was Fuller's press agent. Big deal. Big laugh. Getting publicity for him was tough. He needed a press agent like Marilyn Monroe needs falsies. How many times you think I heard that? How many times you think I heard the rest of those bastards in Press Info laughing behind my back? They figured I was pensioned off. Great job, they used to say. Press agent for Herb Fuller. How can you possibly manage to get his name in the paper so often, they used to say. I've got a skinful of holes from the needles they used to put in me."

"So?"

"So, Saturday morning when I throw my handful of dirt and take the black ribbon off my sleeve, I don't have a job. Oh, sure, they'd make a place for me back in Press Info. Sure, they'd love to make a place for me. How old do you figure I am, Ed?"

"I don't know, Nick. Forty, maybe . . . forty-two or three."

"Thanks. Save it for the memorial show. I'm fifty-three. I'm a little too old to start trying to get the inane remarks of a couple of fifth-rate Congressmen who appear on a debate show on the front page of the *Times*. Not to mention the salary that pulls down. Not mentioning permanent possession of the dirty end of the stick. Not to mention the needles and the knives."

"They won't send you back to that, Nick."

"No?"

I didn't know. Maybe they would.

"I get fourteen five a year, Ed. You'll be making more than that a week, but to me that's good dough. And I figure I'm worth it. To you, I mean. Sure, it was easy to keep Fuller in the papers the last couple of years. Easy. But remember something else. I been with him more than just the last couple of years. Once upon a time he was just another disk jockey, spinning records, talking about the weather and waking some poor slob up that had to go out and break his tail making a living at six in the morning. I stole a lot of space for him then. I've been in this business a long time, Ed. I know my way around. The last couple of years it was easy. In a way it was easy. A lot of people have it in for me because they figure I had a breeze. A lot of people can't keep their mouth off a guy if they're jealous. Especially if they're knocking themselves out for eighty-five, a hundred bucks a week writing releases on religious programs or trying to make a whodunit sound like the logical contender for the Pulitzer Prize. Space comes hard to those guys and they hated the way it came easy to me. A press agent has a funny perspective on life. Two or three inches of type can be the difference between success and failure. It's a crazy standard, but it can make the difference between fourteen five a year and eighty bucks a week."

"I can see that."

"Well?"

"Well, what?"

I was getting real good at this. An old technique Sid Moore taught me. Answer a question with another question. It never commits you.

Nick came back at me.

"How about the job?"

I shot my wad. I had questions I hadn't even used.

"Nick, don't you think it's a little too soon to worry about that? How do we know the show will be any good? How do we know I won't lay a big bomb Friday night?"

"Who's gonna rap it?"

Seven questions. Not an answer among them. Nick took another slug at his drink.

"You've got it made. Like I had it made with Fuller the last couple of years. All I want from you now, Ed, is a promise that you'll consider me when you get around to getting yourself a press agent. You're gonna need one for a while. A good one. For a couple of weeks, after you take over Fuller's shows, it'll come easy. Everybody loves Bonnie Prince Charlie, but after a couple of weeks, he'd better do more than just gurgle, burp and look cute. You know what I mean, don't you? Don't take it wrong, Ed. It has nothing to do with you personally. All I mean is, after a couple of weeks it's not news any more that you've replaced Fuller. Your news value decreases every day on the other side of the funeral. What I mean is, you gotta stop being Fuller's heir and become Ed Harris. I think I can help you there."

"Why didn't you like Fuller?"

"What's that got to do with it?"

"Nothing. I'm just curious."

"Can I tell you my way?"

"Sure."

"You never knew my old man. He had a kind of clerk's job down at City Hall. Nothing much. He wasn't any hot shot. I don't think he ever made fifty dollars a week in his whole life. But he had one thing. He had a knack of sizing people up and pinning them down with words. Well, in our neighborhood—we lived in one of those suburban developments out on the Island, you know, attached houses, a six-foot backyard and a garage under the house—well in our neighborhood there was an old man—a lawyer—a real bastard. He was always calling the cops to break up stick-ball games or complaining about the noise if somebody had a party. Everybody hated his guts, but everybody tipped their hats to him and never told him off. Somehow, I never figured out how, he had it over everybody. I remember something my old man said about him. He said, 'Mr. Smith'—Mr. Jones, whatever the hell his name was, he said, 'Mr. Smith doesn't drink. It isn't that he doesn't like to drink or because he has any moral scruples against it. It's just that he figures if you've been drinking and he hasn't, that gives him an edge over you and Mr. Smith is a great one for having that edge over everybody.' You follow me?"

"I'm following but not very close behind."

"All right. Fuller. Specific. Fuller was a Smith. My old man would have pegged that right away. Fuller always had to have that edge on you. On everybody. He had to have a hold . . . a zinger in his back pocket. He had it with me."

"How?"

"You'd think I'd be the happiest press agent in the world. I had one client and if he burped on the air, it made the papers. You'd figure I had it made. Wouldn't you? Wouldn't you figure that?"

"You'd figure it."

"But I didn't. Fuller didn't let me. He hit me over the head with it every day. Big deal. Wasn't I wonderful getting his name in the paper so often? How did I ever manage to do it? He figured he didn't need me any more and I knew it. Fine. Except for one thing. He had the edge. For a lousy fourteen five a year he had a whale of an edge."

"If you knew that, he didn't have much of an edge. You knew he wouldn't fire you because of that so that took his edge away, didn't it?"

"You're trying to make it simple. It isn't simple. He'd never fire me. He just liked to keep me worrying about it. Never being quite sure he wouldn't."

"Couldn't you quit? As Fuller's press agent you had a pretty good reputation. It should have been worth a lot more than fourteen five in the open market."

"Sure. Quit. Like that. And have the Great Man lose an edge? Sure. Quit. Look, when you make the kind of money he made, you don't have to buy toys to play with. You play with people. He was the Great Man and nobody gave his toys away until they stopped amusing him. And my sweat—my fifty-three-year-old sweat—amused him. He wasn't going to lose that."

"What makes you think I won't be like that?"

Nick looked at me. He was considering the question.

So was I.

"That's the chance I take. You take the chance that maybe I've forgotten how to be a good press agent."

"That starts us off even," I said.

"Just think it over, Ed. From what I can see, you've been bitten by the Fuller bug bad. I figured I'd make my little contribution to your understanding of America's beloved humorist."

"You have. Let me think about what you've said."

"O.K. Think about it."

"Now let's get the pictures over with."

"Sure, you go ahead out. I'll call Backlund."

I walked out of the office, down the corridor and back into the theater. The crowd hadn't thinned out any. They were still filing past the coffin. The only difference was that the little red lights on the front of the television cameras were lit. We were on the air. I looked at my watch. It was ten after twelve. Amalgamated Television was picking up its regular half hour at noon.

On the stage was a choir in black robes. They were singing a hymn.

Nick came up behind me.

"I forgot about the time," he whispered. "We'll have to wait until twelve-thirty to take the shots, they rang in an extra minister on us—want to come back and have another drink?"

I was already feeling my drinks.

"No, I'd better not," I said. "If you can hunt up the kid with the minitape I'll knock off the tapes before we take the pictures."

"I'll get you set up in the corner of the lobby. Things are pretty well under control out there now. Do you want a mike stand set up?"

"No, I think it would be better to use one of the lapel mikes. I can sling the minitape over my shoulder and just go down the line, grabbing likely-looking subjects."

"The place is crawling with likely-looking subjects. I'll hunt up the kid with your minitape."

He headed for the rear of the theater.

I stood watching and listening for a while. I had to give it to them. Again. They were really doing it right. After the choir finished, the lights dimmed down and the camera swung around for a pan of the shuffling crowd, filing in and out of the theater. When the lights went back up again, the spot was on a guy in a black suit standing at a lectern just in front of the stained glass windows. I recognized him as a very fashionable minister of a very fashionable church. The names of both escaped me at the moment.

He was a real pro. Or maybe it was just the atmosphere and the droning, professionally monotonous voice that kept me riveted to the spot. I stood and listened to the sonorous voice, batting out the rolling phrases.

"What we are seeing here today, what we are honoring here today with our presence and our sorrow, is, in a large sense, the victory of Man over Death. Before me now are the last earthly remains of the man they called Herb Fuller. His body is there in that coffin.

"He is dead.

"We know that. Our eyes tell us so. The verdict on the death certificate tells us so. Logic tells us so, and yet you people deny those things. You make liars out of the logic. You make liars out of the certificates. You make liars of your eyes . . . liars of the doctors. Every man, woman and child within sound of my amplified voice who has ever laughed at a Fuller joke or felt the warmth of his personality—if you will, his humanity—knows that these qualities are not dead. For a little period of time, Herb Fuller was a part of our lives. For a little period of time, he made those lives of ours more entertaining, more interesting—in some cases, more bearable. And those little periods of time—each unimportant in itself, but in toto so very important—those little periods of time cannot be destroyed, cannot be suddenly wiped out in the wreckage of a car on a hillside in Connecticut. I say to you that Herb Fuller is not dead. Look at that coffin with me and disbelieve your eyes. Distrust your senses. I say to you that each of us carries with us a piece of him inside us and while we live, while we remember, he is not dead. He is alive. Gloriously alive."

A real pro.

I pushed my way into the outer lobby and over to a corner where Nick Cellantano was standing with a page boy who held a minitape in his arms. Things were a little more hectic out here. The ushers had the crowds in hand, barely, but in hand. I could see through the outer door of the lobby that the street outside the theater was just as confused, just as congested, just as choked with people as it had been when I'd come in.

"They'll be off the air in ten minutes," Nick said. "If you want to wait until then, we can get the pictures over with fast. Backlund is inside and ready for us."

"Is the machine loaded?"

Nick asked the page boy.

He visibly snapped to attention.

"Yes, sir," he said. "Yes, sir. I put a clean reel on myself."

Who could ask for anything more?

I took the minitape out of his hand, attached the small black lapel mike, the kind that fits into the palm of your hand, to the outside connection on the front of the box and slung the whole thing over my shoulder by the strap.

"I'll see you later, Nick," I said. "I think I'll just wander around the lobby and pick them up as they come in and go out." I waved my hand and walked away. I walked over to one of the outer doors that was admitting people one by one and stopped a stout woman in a shapeless black coat. She had a boy of six or seven by the hand. I moved both of them out of the main stream of American life.

"May I ask your name?"

"You have to have my name? Why did you stop just me?"

"I don't have to have your name if you don't want to give it. If you'd rather not . . ."

"My name is Mrs. Rieber. Helen Rieber. I live at——"

"I don't need your address, Mrs. Rieber."

"I don't mind giving it. You know, if you want it, I don't mind——"

"That won't be necessary, Mrs. Rieber. I just want to ask you a few questions. This is a recording machine——"

"You mean we're on now? On the radio? Me and you? Now?"

"It's a recording, Mrs. Rieber. It isn't on the air now. It will be later in the week. Now, would you mind telling me why you're here today?"

"Here? Well, I came down with a group of women. We have a club and we came down together."

"Why?"

"What do you mean why? Would you mind repeating the question? I mean, we came down together, a group of women. My club. We go lots of places together. We got separated outside in the crowd."

"But why did you decide to come here today?"

"Oh, I see what you mean. I told you. We go places together. We decided this was a place to go. Together. We used to go to Herb Fuller's broadcasts together. My friend knows somebody in the ticket bureau at Amalgamated and we used to get sixteen, eighteen, twenty tickets at a time. Depended on how many women wanted to go. Together."

"How often did you go to the broadcast?"

"Together, you mean?"

"Yes, together."

"Oh . . . let me think. It's hard to think when you shove that thing in my face. Oh, every month. Every six weeks. Like that. In my club we take turns who should be what you might call the entertainment chairman. The entertainment chairman is like the person who decides where we should go together and when my friend, the one who knows the person in the ticket bureau, was chairman, she used to get tickets for us all to go to the Herb Fuller show. Sometimes sixteen, eighteen, twenty. Like that. Every month, maybe. Every six weeks. Like that."

"Then you were Herb Fuller fans?"

"The club, you mean?"

"The club—or you personally?"

"He used to keep us in stitches."

"You thought he was funny?"

"He used to keep us in stitches."

"Why?"

"I beg your pardon?"

"You want me to repeat the question, right?"

"Please."

"Why?"

"Why what?"

"Why did you think he was funny?"

"He was always doing things, like. Always saying things. And the way he used to do things. Well, believe me, he kept us in stitches."

"And what will your club do now, every six weeks, now that he's dead? What will happen when your friend is entertainment chairman again?"

"My friend can still get tickets from her friend in the ticket bureau. On the whole Amalgamated Broadcasting Company I'm sure they have other programs my friend can get tickets for from her friend in the ticket bureau. The only thing is, with the Fuller show you used to get things."

"Get things?"

"Like he had a spaghetti sponsor, when you came in you got a couple cans spaghetti—or celery or olives or what have you, you know? Like a box lunch they used to give you, so heavy you could hardly carry it. Only you didn't eat it there, you took it home. Maybe you'd come home with eight, ten cans. I don't think anybody else treated his studio audience like that."

"Did you feel that Herb Fuller was your friend?"

"My what?"

"Your friend."

"No, I didn't know him. Never met him in my life. I told you, this friend of mine got tickets to his program. We never met him or anything like that. Once we stood around outside after the show, to see him when he came out. But we didn't meet him or talk to him, or get an autograph or like that."

"May I talk to your little boy? What's his name?"

"Ronnie. Ronnie, the man wants to talk to you."

Ronnie looked at me suspiciously and moved closer to his mother. I bent down and put my hand on his shoulder.

He shrugged it off.

"Ronnie," I said in my gentlest tone, "do you know who Herb Fuller was?"

Ronnie said nothing. He moved closer to his mother. I expected to see him disappear under her skirt any minute. His mother yanked away from him like he was a mustard plaster that was due to come off.

"Ronnie," she said sharply, "the man asked you something." Her voice got softer, a little on the wheedling side. "You know who Herb Fuller was, dear. The man Daddy liked so much." She turned to me again. "He's shy," she said.

Ronnie spoke.

Loud.

And clear.

"I'm hungry," he said. "You said we were going to eat. When are we going to eat?"

He got another yank. "Enough!" It was a command.

"That's enough. I told you we'd eat later. Now, answer the

man." She gave him just the slightest pinch. I hoped to God he'd talk before she wound up de-arming him.

"Why are you here, son?" I asked him.

"Mommie wanted to come. She said we'd see a funny man. She said we could eat in the Automat when we saw the funny man."

"Thank you very much, Mrs. Rieber," I said, "And thank you, Ronnie."

I walked across the lobby to another open outer door. This was the door feeding the line coming out of the theater back into the street. I stopped an old lady.

"Did you just come out of the theater, Madam?"

"Yes I did."

"May I ask why you came here today?"

"I came to see him, rest his soul."

"You were a fan of his?"

"I should say I was. I never missed him when he was on radio or the television. Night or day. I should say I was a fan of his. My heart goes out to his poor wife and those dear children of his."

"Did you feel that he was a friend of yours?"

"Friend? A member of the family, you should say. My son used to chide me about that. If he would come to visit me when Mr. Fuller was on the TV, I used to shush him and he used to say, 'Mother, I do believe you think more of him than you do of me.' I almost did, too."

"Why?"

"Because he was always there with something cheery or something funny to say when you needed him. If your arthritis was bothering you or you had some other kind of trouble, you just had to turn that dial and there he was and before you knew it, you forgot about your arthritis or whatever was bothering you. He'll be missed, believe me. By a good many."

I thanked her and turned away. Two teen-age girls came out of the inner door, giggling. One of them caught sight of the microphone, nudged the other and they came over to me.

The bold one smiled tentatively.

"That's a funny-looking microphone," she said. "It's a microphone, isn't it?"

"Yes," I admitted.

"Funny-looking one. So small."

Her friend hung back.

"You broadcasting now?" the bold one asked.

"Recording," I said. "The mike is hooked up to a recording machine."

"Tape?" she asked. "Or wire?"

"You're pretty bright."

"We have both in school. Tape and wire. Which is this?"

"Tape."

"Seven and a half or fifteen?"

"Seven and a half. How would you and your friend like to go on the air?"

"Sure," she said. "Sure, we'd like it."

"What's your name?"

"Mary Crothers. Mount Saint Michael High School. My friend and I are juniors."

Her friend was still hanging back and Mary Crothers, Mount Saint Michael High School, junior, tried grabbing her classmate by her loose fitting sweater to drag her forward to immortality on a seven and a half inches per second tape recorder. Her friend wasn't being dragged.

"My friend is shy."

"Did you promise to take her to the Automat?"

"What?"

"Nothing. Private joke."

"Very private, I guess."

"What's your friend's name?"

"Helen Clardy. We're in the same class at Mount Saint Michael."

"Are you girls off from school today?"

"Regents. We have the day off because it's Regents."

"And why are you here?"

"We flipped a coin. My friend wanted to go to the Paramount. We flipped a coin. A quarter. I won."

"You were inside?"

"We just came out."

"And?"

"And what? Oh, you mean what was it like? It was nice. All those flowers and the music and that preacher up there talking. It gave me a kind of spooky feeling."

"A spooky feeling."

"Yeah. Spooky. You know, like someone was dead."

"Someone is dead."

"I know that."

"Did you go past the coffin?"

"Sure. What do you think we went in there for?"

"And?"

"And what? Oh, you mean what did we think? My friend thought it was terrible they didn't have him in a tuxedo. She thought it wasn't dignified enough, he wasn't in a tuxedo. I told her what difference did it make but she thought it wasn't dignified enough. She said everybody she ever heard of died was buried in a tuxedo."

"Were you fans of Herb Fuller? You and your friend?"

"Not what you'd really call fans maybe. Not like, for instance, real fans. We used to see him on the television once in a while. My friend said how could you miss seeing him? He was O.K., but we weren't what you could call fans of his. Not like, for instance, you'd be a fan for a singer, like Eddie Fisher or Frank Sinatra or somebody like that. My mother and father thought he was wonderful. I guess you could say they were fans of his."

"You say you weren't really fans of his. Why not?"

"Well, we weren't. We didn't dislike him or anything like that, but it's like we couldn't be fans of—like—Edward Arnold, or Edmund Gwenn or somebody like that . . . you know, middle-aged men. Not that he wasn't funny or nice or so forth . . . but . . ."

"But you couldn't feel romantic about him? Is that it?"

"You could say that. He was like he was your father, if your father was funny. Which mine isn't. You could like him and all that, but you couldn't be a fan of his. You see the difference?"

"I see the difference. But if that's true, why are you and your friend here today?"

"Well, this is like a prem-eer or something like that. An event, you could say. My friend didn't want to come. She hates funerals and things like that and I tried to tell her this wasn't like a funeral . . . this was like an event. She still wanted to go to the Paramount. I told you. We flipped a coin. A quarter. And I won."

"Thank you very much. And thank your friend for me."

"She didn't say anything."

"Thank her anyway."

"Sure."

Across the lobby I could see Nick Cellantano looking around over the head of the crowd. I figured he was looking for me, but before I could raise my hand to attract his attention I felt a pull at my sleeve. It was Mary Crothers of Mount Saint Michael High School.

"You forgot to turn your machine off. You're wasting tape."

She was right. I turned it off.

"Thanks," I said. "You want a job in radio sometime, try

Amalgamated. We can always use a Mount Saint Michael girl who knows her tape."

"Just don't edit me out of the broadcast," she said.

"Cross my heart."

"When is it going to be on the air?"

"Friday night, ten o'clock."

"Local or the full network?"

"The full network."

"Big deal," she said. "Good-by."

I said good-by and raised my hand to catch Nick's attention. He saw me, nodded his head and motioned for me to come back inside the theater. I pushed my way through the crowd and joined him just inside the door. I was struck again by the silence and the heaviness of the atmosphere.

"They're just going off the air," Nick whispered. We were back to whispering.

"We can take the pictures in a minute or two."

"Is Backlund ready?" I asked.

"Standing by. How did you make out with the slobs?"

"One old lady thought he was wonderful. Cured her arthritis. I heard a dastardly rumor outside that the corpse is not wearing the traditional black tie. What did they put on him, a ski suit? It shocked hell out of a very silent little girl from Mount Saint Michael's High School."

"The corpse is wearing a blue serge suit. That was a Command Decision. I hear there was a big hassle. One faction maintained that if he wasn't planted in a tuxedo, he'd be kicked back by Saint Peter for being out of uniform."

"And the blue serge faction?"

"The blue serge faction prevailed. The simple dignity of the blue serge suit as proper for all occasions is a rock-ribbed American tradition. The clincher was, as I understand it, the simple statement, 'Herb would have wanted it that way.' "

"There was no plaid jock-strop faction?"

"No articulate plaid jock-strop faction."

There was a burst of sound from the pipe organ on the stage. The whole theater rumbled with "Rock of Ages."

Nick smiled weakly and held up five fingers.

"They'll make a hit out of it yet," he said.

The TV cameraman in front of us tilted his camera up toward the ceiling and covered it with a black, silk cloth. He blew his nose and walked to the side aisle that led backstage.

Nick nodded his head toward the disappearing cameraman.

"Bad booze has no discernible effect on TV cameramen," he said.

It was a great truth. Will probably be in all the school books some day.

"There's Backlund over there by the coffin," said Nick. "Are you ready?"

"Ready."

We walked down the center aisle, or where the center aisle used to be, between the two lines feeding in and out of the theater. I wet the palm of my hand with spit and brushed back the hair around my ears. Unless I do that, every picture I take looks like my hair grows horizontal.

When we got to the coffin, I nodded at Karl Backlund. He nodded back. Nick spoke to the usher standing beside the Marine Guard and the incoming line was stopped. People in the rear started griping and an usher quieted them down. The people up front near the coffin were delighted. They'd hit the mortuary jackpot. They didn't have to hustle past, take a quick look and leave. They had the wonderful opportunity of standing there and staring at the man in the coffin. I stared too. I made a little mental check list:

Item: One blue serge suit.

Item: White shirt.

Item: White handkerchief in pocket on jacket.

Item: Black four-in-hand tie.

Item: Mortician's smile.

Item: Slight suggestion of rouge on cheeks.

Item: Slight smudge of dirt under right eye.

Item: One peanut shell, adjacent to right shoulder, almost unnoticed against the sterile undertaker silk that lined the inside of the coffin.

He looked dead. Good and dead.

Nick nudged me.

If I'd known there was going to be so goddamned much nudging at this wake, I'd have worn a vest in self-protection.

"We'd better get it over with," Nick said, "Stopping the line like this, we probably have traffic backed up clear down to Twenty-third Street by now."

He turned to Karl Backlund.

"Any ideas, Karl?"

"I was told to take a couple of shots of Mr. Harris and the deceased. I wasn't told anything about what the shots would be."

Backlund had a look on his face as if he was about to commite Leica blasphemy and hoped everybody understood he was acting under orders.

I adjusted Nick's black tie and suggested we just take a simple shot of me standing, looking down at the coffin.

Everybody thought that was a wonderful idea.

I felt another nudge. I turned around. The guy who was now at the head of the stalled line leaned forward.

"You want we should wave when he shoots the picture?"

I told him I didn't think we wanted that.

He looked disappointed.

I suddenly realized I still had the minitape hanging from my shoulder by the strap, so I took it off and slipped it under the casket. I looked down at Herb Fuller. I looked grim and Backlund shot off his flash. I looked grim again. Another flash went off. Backlund nodded again, put the two used flash bulbs in his pocket and walked away before anyone could tell him to turn in his exposure meter, he was through. Nick and I went over to the side and the line started moving forward again. When we got into the manager's office he poured us two more drinks. I was a little worried. They were beginning to taste pretty good.

"Anything else?" he asked.

"I don't think so."

"You want to do any more recording?"

"Christ! I left the minitape under the coffin."

"On or off?"

"Off."

"Don't worry about it. I'll get it later. You finished with it?"

"I think so. Yeah, I'm finished with it. I don't think I'm going to get any more usable stuff here. I think I'll head back for the office. I'd better pick up the minitape. The reel of tape is still on the machine. I'll need it later for my editing session."

Nick rubbed the glass around his hand.

"Got any idea yet about what you're going to do? On the show?"

"Vaguely. I'm playing it by ear."

"You haven't put wheels on it yet?"

"It's still on the drawing board."

"But you're letting it harden in the mold?"

"It's only second down. I'm not about to punt yet."

"I'll quit if you will," said Nick.

"Agreed."

I downed the whisky.

"This," I said, "is lousy booze."

"Agreed," said Nick. "Come again and bring a bottle."

"You coming out?"

"No. I think I'll sit for awhile and look at Jack Hoxie or Colleen Moore. Or maybe I'll pull a big switch and look at George K. Arthur."

"Nice little fellow, George K. Arthur."

"Sweetest little fellow anybody knows."

"Have fun," I said.

That was another ritual.

I was touching base on all of them today.

My sharp curve was breaking fast.

Nobody in radio who earned over sixty bucks a week ever said good-by or so long, or it's been nice seeing you.

"Have fun," I repeated.

"Likewise."

The countersign. Now I was free to go.

I got the minitape out from under the coffin. Not, however, without some difficulty. One fat woman was under the impression that I was trying to hijack the corpse and summoned the Army guard. He summoned the Marine. He recognized me and I was allowed to retrieve the machine, duck through the lines and go out of the theater through the double doors in the rear. Things hadn't improved any on the street. I joined the phalanx of people moving in a general westerly direction and eventually wound up on the corner of Lexington Avenue and Eighty-first Street where it again became possible to move under my own power and of my own volition. A taxi was out of the question so I headed downtown toward the IRT station on Seventy-seventh Street. On the corner of Seventy-ninth Street, a hawker was doing a big business in black crepe paper armbands at fifteen cents a throw. He also had celluloid buttons with Fuller's picture on them, rimmed with black silk. These cost two bits. He hadn't sold many of these.

I stopped in a drugstore on the corner of Seventy-ninth Street and phoned Nicole at her hotel.

Her room didn't answer.

I'd have been surprised if it had.

I went back to the cigar counter and got a half a buck changed into dimes. I figured it was a worth-while investment of time and money to renew an option on my French property.

The first dime got me through to Bud Reed's office at Warner's. Nicole was in town doing personals, radio interviews and TV guest shots for the greater glory of the epic she'd made at Warner's last year, so it figured that she was with Bud, turning on the charm and exposing the Bosom to any newspaper or radio freeloaders Bud could round up for lunch. If England's wars were won on the playing fields of Eton, Sunday Supplement picture spreads are won on the damask linen of an expensive restaurant.

Bud's secretary said she was sure Mr. Reed was with Miss Duval. She didn't know where except that they were having lunch with some movie editors.

I could make a pretty good guess.

Bud had more expensive expense account tastes than most movie press agents. If they weren't at Henri's or Twenty-One, they had to be at the Harwyn.

They were.

Nicole sounded petulant in a peasant sort of way and right away I started appeasing.

I told her how busy I was and how important the work I was doing was.

I told her how much I loved her and how impossible it was to see her until after Friday night.

I told her how hard it was to fight the almost overpowering desire to rush right over to the Harwyn Club and take her away from it all for a mad ride through the countryside in a yellow convertible.

I gave her quite a snow job

And I agreed to pick her up at the hotel for a quiet dinner at six-thirty.

I left the drugstore and headed south again. I fought my way into the subway and finally into a train. It was twenty to two when I walked into the office. Ginny was out to lunch and there were a couple of notes on my desk.

I took the reel of tape off the machine, called Schrafft's, ordered lunch and picked up the afternoon papers, which were stacked on my desk.

The *Journal-American* had a full page of pictures of the festivities at Studio 41. There were the usual shots.

Two dirty-faced little boys looking up at the Marine Guard beside the casket.

An old lady twisting a handkerchief in her hand as she looked down at the coffin.

A shot of Carol at the bier with Eddie Brown supporting her elbow.

An outside shot of the crowds.

A shot of the coffin seen through the view finder of a TV camera.

I read the latest installment of Bob Considine's biography, which began on page one and jumped over to page thirty-nine. Page thirty-nine had a two shot of Herb Fuller and Sid Moore in army uniform about to board a plane. The caption said, "Listeners will remember one of Herb Fuller's most memorable series of broadcasts. In 1945, in company with Amalgamated executive Sid Moore, Fuller followed a pint of blood donated by a fan from the New York blood bank to an actual transfusion on the battlefield of Europe. In the above picture, Moore and Fuller are about to take off on that historic errand."

The *World-Telegram* had a feature story on page three. It was an interview with an usher at Studio 41. It was very moving.

The *Post* picked up the straight AP story and ran it on page 14. Earl Wilson devoted his column to a collection of the cleaner Fuller quips. The column was illustrated with a Murray Korman picture of Nicole's bosoms.

I turned to the back of the paper and started reading Jimmy Cannon. Cannon ignored the whole thing. His column was about Rocky Graziano.

It was a refreshing note.

The *Journal-American* had given a cartoonist his head on the editorial page. There was a full-page cartoon of Fuller somewhere above the clouds smiling down on the world.

The Schrafft delivery boy picked this particular moment to walk in with my lunch. I wasn't sure I'd be able to down it.

Just as I got the last bite of my ham sandwich down, Ginny walked in.

"Long lunch hour," I said.

"I was shopping."

"Fine."

"For you."

"Great. What did you buy me?"

She opened a bag and put four black ties on the desk.

"Nylon," she said. "That way you can just go ahead and cry all you want and they won't wrinkle or shrink."

"How much do I owe you?"

"I signed your name to a petty cash slip."

"For how much?"

"Twenty-five dollars."

I picked up the four ties.

"Twenty-five bucks! For four ties?"

"I didn't know whether you'd be taking me to the funeral. Just in case you did, I bought a black hat and a pair of black shoes."

"On petty cash?"

"Certainly. You don't think I'd wear a black hat or black

shoes on my own time? I think it's a perfectly justifiable company expense."

"You're a dear, sweet animal."

"You too. How was the wake?"

"Gay mad fun. Anything happen here while I was gone?"

"The tape from Fran and the kids came in. I had them make a dub of it, piped it to Ediphone and set up a tape room for you for the afternoon."

"Good."

"Red Connors called."

"Who he?"

"Red Connors of the Editing Department. He said he heard you were going to use some of Fuller's old shows Friday night and he wanted to be sure that you didn't use anything that might be in bad taste. He wants to talk to you."

"Get him for me."

Ginny dialed his number. Editing Department was the Amalgamated euphemism for Censorship.

Ginny handed me the phone.

"Hello, Red," I said. "Ed Harris."

"Ed, about this Friday night show. I understand you're using some old Fuller tapes. Is that right?"

"That's right."

"I know I can trust your judgment on that, but I wanted to remind you of something."

"Go ahead."

"Well, you know Fuller. I had a great deal of trouble with him. There was never anything in his scripts that I could take exception to and I had no control over his ad libs. The result was that I'd pass his scripts and then he'd throw in something on the air that brought down a flood of objections and I was left holding the bag. He said some very dirty things on the air, you know."

"I know. Off the air too."

"Off the air it wasn't my problem."

"No, but it's mine."

"What is?"

"Skip it, Red. What can I do for you?"

"Those tapes of his you're using Friday night . . . could I have a transcript of them?"

"I haven't picked them out yet, Red. Actually, all I'm going to do is run them in, once in a while . . . you know . . . short hunks . . . to give something of the flavor of Fuller."

"That's what worries me. The flavor of Fuller. Did you hear the last show he did? The morning he was killed?"

"No, I didn't."

"A typical example of what I went through with him. He had an ad lib interview with Carol before she sang and they started kidding around about being absent-minded. She just remembered that she'd left her wrist watch at home in her top drawer and she was afraid the maid would put something heavy in the drawer on top of it. You follow me?"

"Right on your heels, Red."

"Well, he said, 'that's easy to fix, kid; tell the maid to look for it and put it in a safe place . . . the maid always listens to the show while she's working around your place, doesn't she?' I'm quoting now, Ed, from the transcript of the broadcast. That was only three days ago but the mail is flooding in. Like somebody took a finger out of the dike. Anyway, Carol says—and I'm quoting now, 'Sarah, look in the top drawer of the dresser in my bedroom.' 'Sure, Sarah,' says Fuller. 'You won't have any trouble finding it. Everybody knows how easy it is to get into Carol's drawers.' "

There was a pause while Red clucked his tongue.

"Ed, that isn't even a *double-entendre*. That's just plain dirty. That's only one example of the kind of thing I've had to deal with for the past couple of years. Every white hair in my head is named Herb Fuller."

"What do you want me to do, Red?"

"Just don't get carried away with the Fuller flavor Friday night. The people that like that kind of filth and that side of Fuller's character won't have to be reminded of it and, with him dead, I think the excerpts you use should be of the inspirational kind. There are plenty of those."

"There are indeed."

"I knew you'd understand. By the way, Ed, I've heard that you're taking over the Fuller spots. Congratulations."

"Thanks."

"I know I won't have any trouble with you."

"Not with me, Red. I'm the good, clean, wholesome American-boy type. As soon as I pick out the tapes I'm using on the show, I'll let you know."

"Fine, Ed. Thanks. It'll be a pleasure to work with you."

"So long, Red."

I hung up the phone.

"Want me to send him copies of the tapes you're using?" asked Ginny.

"Hell, no. I'm not going to start out with that little bastard in my hair. How was the tape from Fran?"

"The world has lost an entertainer but she has lost a husband and a friend. It's all bearable because it isn't her loss alone. The whole world shares it with her and makes it easier to bear."

"You're kidding."

"So help me, Guglielmo Marconi. It's all right. She does it very well. She has the nicest little catch in her throat. That reminds me. Smitty called."

"Who is Smitty?"

"Fuller's secretary. She wanted to know if you could drop in to see her sometime today."

"What for?"

"She didn't say. Maybe she wants to audition for you."

"What's Smitty like?"

"Nice-looking. Kinda crinoline and old lace with a pony-tail hair-do. Nice legs. Nice complexion. Mind like a French movie."

"What does that mean?"

"All of a sudden it has to mean something?"

"Getting back to Fran, what kind of a marriage did they have?"

"You want facts or toilet gossip?"

"Toilet gossip."

"She couldn't stand the sight of him. But she liked being Mrs. Herb Fuller. The way I heard it, she didn't give a damn how much playing around he did or who he did it with as long as he didn't do it around her and didn't get into the papers. But she liked being Mrs. Herb Fuller and she wouldn't give him a divorce. Ever. No matter what he did."

"Did she do any playing around?"

"The toilet gossip doesn't say. Probably not, or the toilet gossip would have known about it."

"What time is my tape room this afternoon?"

"Three o'clock."

It was ten to.

"I'll go up and see what Smitty wants and I'll be in the tape room all afternoon."

"Oh, I almost forgot. Today was Carbo's day off. They had to give you another engineer."

That annoyed hell out of me. A good tape engineer is as important as a good script. He can make or break your show. Carbo was tops and I wasn't going to be able to wet-nurse a new engineer through the tapes. I had to work with somebody I knew and trusted, somebody I could throw a script at and come back and find the tapes edited and in shape for air. Carbo was that kind of engineer.

"Who did they give me?"

"Relax," said Ginny. "I raised hell with them about not getting Carbo. He was out all night on a special for the newsroom. He was too pooped out to be much use to you anyway. They're giving you Mike Jackson. It's his day off, too, but I made them bring him in on double time."

"Good. Mike's almost as fast as Carbo and just as good on matching levels. O.K. I'm going up to see Smitty."

"Don't get any ideas. You already got a secretary, remember."

"Sure. Twenty-five bucks for four black ties."

"You talk like it's your money."

"You act like it's yours."

"Funny. Funny dialogue we got. You're a regular Herb Fuller."

"I'm going to see Smitty and I'll go to the tape room from there."

I got big smiles all the way out to the elevator. It was like I was the Queen of England, going down a receiving line. As I passed a secretary, her typewriter would stop, she'd look up and dazzle me with her molars. I patted Lillian on the back.

"Hello, Sexy," I said.

She stuck her tongue out at me. Slowly. With that tongue bit, the speed of exposure makes all the difference in the world. I was given a look at the slowest tongue bit in the history of American Radio Broadcasting. I admired its brand new coat and walked out into the reception room. The receptionist fluffed her hair at me and smiled the mechanical smile.

"How are you today, Mr. Harris?"

"I'm just fine. And how are you?"

"Just fine."

Like Ginny said, funny dialogue.

She was wearing a blue man's button-down shirt that was

at least two sizes too small for her around the chest. I pressed the button for the up elevator.

The elevator stopped, the door opened slowly and I pushed my way in. I'd drawn the singing operator. The car started upward with a jerk . . . stopped and started again. John was in his usual form. Riding four stories with him was like coming into La Guardia on instruments in the middle of a snow storm. You knew you were going to make it but you weren't quite sure.

We made it. I got off at the nineteenth floor.

I walked over to a guy in overalls who was working on the little black and white floor directory opposite the elevators.

"Which way is Herb Fuller's office?" I asked him.

"To the left," he said. "Funny thing you should ask, I was just taking his name off the directory."

"*Sic transit gloria,*" I said.

"Yeah."

I turned left and walked into a corridor that led to a series of offices. Once out of the corridor the atmosphere changed. There were heavy rugs on the floor. Not carpeting. Carpeting was for brass. Rugs were for deities. An inner reception room was furnished like a living room with a fireplace, upholstered sofa and foam rubber easy chairs. The room was empty and I walked through another door marked "Herb Fuller—Private." Private, hell! He was a four-star general if I ever saw one. Inside the door was another inner reception room. More rugs. More period furniture. Seated at a kidney-shaped desk was a girl. It had to be Smitty. She was talking on the phone so I gave her a good going over.

Nice-looking. Very nice-looking.

Crinoline and old lace. Check.

Pony-tail hair-do. Check.

Nice legs.

Very nice legs. God bless the kidney-shaped desks with no false front to obscure very nice legs.

Nice complexion. Peaches and homogenized.

She put the phone back on its cradle and looked up at me. "You're Ed Harris," she said.

The way she said it, I wouldn't have denied it even if I weren't.

"Yes," I said.

"Mr. Harris," she said, "I didn't mean for you to take time out to come up here. It wasn't that important. Ginny must have misunderstood my message. I just wanted to talk to you."

"I wouldn't miss talking to you for the world."

"Why don't we go into his office and be comfortable?"

This was a girl it would be very easy to be comfortable with. I felt a little like a pet nephew who was just going through his dead uncle's attic. I was beginning to realize some of the wonders of my legacy. I followed Smitty into the inner office. This was obviously Fuller's sanctum sanctorum. The walls were lined with framed testimonials from the Veterans Administration, the American Legion, the Air Corps, the Army, the Navy, the United Nations, the National Association of Manufacturers, the Safety Council and God knows who else attesting to the fact that he was an important cog in their particular wheel. There were pictures of him, autographed, of course, with his arms around Presidents, Cabinet members, movie stars and dogs. There was a huge couch against one wall and the ceiling was a blown-up map of France. Indirect lighting. Drapes of camouflaged parachute silk and against one wall a huge bookcase. There was a switch here. Instead of books, the shelves were bulging with boxes, cartons and cans . . . all the products he advertised on the air.

Smitty sat down on one end of the couch and didn't say anything while I looked around.

I sat down. On the other end of the couch.

"The reason I wanted to talk to you, Mr. Harris," she said, "was to find out if there were any changes you wanted made while I was still here. I understand you'll be moving in here next week and I guess there's nothing worse than moving in somewhere and living with somebody else's personal belongings."

Some of them wouldn't be too hard to take.

I tried a different tack.

"What do you mean, while you're still here?"

"Well, I won't be here after Friday. You have a secretary."

"That doesn't mean you're going to be fired."

"Oh no. I'm quitting."

"You're quitting?"

"Look, Mr. Harris. You have a secretary. I was Herb Fuller's secretary. They offered to give me a very nice job as executive secretary to a vice-president. I'm not interested in that."

"What are you interested in?"

"Something I can't have. You already have a secretary. If you think it will be helpful, I'll stay on for a week with Ginny. I know a great deal about the programs you'll be doing. I might be of some use to you, until Ginny catches on to the routine. I'm sure she will. Ginny's a very smart girl."

So is Smitty. I could have guessed this was the time to give me a good close-up look at her. I was right. She crossed her legs. Slowly. I was close. Her skirt went up. Briefly.

"It's a very nice office," I said. "A little blue skyish for my taste, but very nice. What happened to the desk?"

"There is no desk. Mr. Fuller used to do a great deal of his work stretched out on the couch."

I'll bet he did.

I had a mental picture again of Ray Milland in the "Lost Weekend" stashing bottles away wherever he was so he'd never be without a supply. Fuller seemed to do the same thing with women.

"I'd need a desk."

"I'll put a memo through this afternoon."

"And could you send those testimonials down to the museum and get rid of that junk in the bookcase? Let's try a really revolutionary thing. Let's put some books in the bookcases."

"I'll take care of it, Mr. Harris."

"Just an ordinary desk."

She smiled and recrossed her legs. High.

"It would be very nice working with you, Mr. Harris."

"Why won't you?"

"I told you. You have a secretary."

"I'm a big wheel, starting Monday. Big wheels sometimes have two secretaries. One for the routine work. The second for special assignments."

"Would you like a drink, Mr. Harris?"

"I would love a drink, Miss Smitty."

"Smith. Louella Smith. Smitty."

She walked over to the bookcase, moved a large can of spaghetti and took out a bottle of Scotch from behind it.

She moved aside a huge Marine testimonial, revealing a wall-safe-type refrigerator. She pulled out a tray of ice cubes and produced two glasses from a wall cabinet that I had supposed was a file. She poured two healthy drinks, put the cubes in the glass and passed me one of them.

"I hope you like it on the rocks."

She smiled again.

"We'll get along fine," she said.

"For that week you're here. While you're familiarizing Ginny with the operation."

"Cheers," she said and waggled her pony tail at me while she swallowed most of her drink.

I sipped at mine tentatively. This was good booze.

The phone rang. She picked it up off an end table.

"Mr. Fuller's office. . . . Just a minute."

She handed me the receiver.

"It's for you. Ginny."

"Yes, Ginny?"

"I just wanted to tell you I gave the tapes to Mike and he's going ahead without you. I gave him the transcripts and the cuts you'd made on paper. He's going to make up a show reel for you."

"Fine."

"How are you doing?"

"Fine. Just fine."

"Toilet room gossip. Her shorthand is lousy."

"I hadn't noticed."

"If I'm lucky you'll never find out."

"Good-by, Ginny."

"Good-by, Mr. Harris. Call me if you need help."

I handed the phone back to Smitty.

"Was Ginny afraid I was going to vamp you out of her job?"

"Not afraid. She recognized the possibility."

"She can relax. I told you. I'm quitting."

"Suppose I asked you not to?"

"Suppose you did?"

"Suppose I did?"

"Are you?"

"Suppose I am?"

"You're very fond of Ginny? She's a good secretary? She's a nice girl? Quit while you're ahead, Mr. Harris. I don't want the job. More important than that, I don't need the job."

"Why not?"

"You wouldn't believe it."

"Sure I would. I'm a very gullible guy."

"I've been working for Herb Fuller for the past two years. That means two things. Number one, I made enough money to go off by myself somewhere for a while. Maybe on a cruise. It will be nice to smile at somebody just because I want to. To please somebody just because I want to."

"I can assume then that you gave me the crossed leg business just because you wanted to?"

"Put it down as reflex action. Besides, I hadn't made up my mind then not to put the bite on you for the job."

"What made you decide not to?"

"You. You look like a nice guy. It would be much tougher working with you if you were a nice guy."

"I'm really a bastard."

"I'm all full up on bastards."

"O.K. What's reason number two?"

"I'm a nice girl. I'd like to go back to being one."

"You've got all the equipment for it."

"You're not married, are you?"

"No."

"Good. Sometime just call me up and take me out to dinner. On a social basis . . . not a business basis. O.K.?"

"O.K."

"You'll like the office when they get it fixed up the way you want it. Did you ever hear about his desk?"

"No."

"He had a great idea. Who was more American than Herb Fuller? Nobody. And shouldn't he have some kind of symbol of his unique quality? Sure. And how about a desk? Not just any old desk but a very special one. He had a great idea. He would have a desk made up of all the wood that America produces. Herb Fuller, the great symbol of the average American, would sit behind this desk that had in it every kind of wood there is in America. How about that? Symbolic? You bet, brother."

"Did he have the desk made?"

"He sure did. He called in a cabinetmaker. And not just any cabinetmaker, either. You remember that guy that had the big show at the Armory a couple of years ago? No? Well, anyway, this guy was the greatest. He told him exactly what he wanted and right away he had trouble. The carpenter told him such a desk was impossible. The carpenter explained that certain woods had certain stresses, or something like that. I don't know the technical end of it but anyway this carpenter told him it would be impossible to put all those different kinds of wood together into a desk. They just wouldn't work together. Or stay together. Or something. Anyway, it couldn't be done. Herb wasn't buying that. He got another cabinetmaker. He told him the same thing. It couldn't be done. The more he heard that the more determined he was to have the desk. He finally got a guy over on Third Avenue who said sure it could be done. But it was going to be expensive. The guy got a potful of money and made the desk and it was a beauty. It was gorgeous. For a while we had a parade of celebrities through here looking at the desk. He was delighted with it. It was unique. He used to pound it with his fist and say, 'This is America I'm pounding . . . all of it right under my hand and nobody else in the world has anything like it.' One day, without any warning at all, the desk started making noises."

"Noises?"

"Creaks. Snap, crackle and pop. He had carpenters, cabinetmakers through here every hour on the hour. Somebody told him maybe it was termites, so we had the whole office deloused . . . what do you call it?"

"Fumigated?"

"Yes, fumigated. That's right. But the desk went right on

creaking. Finally one day it got noisier than ever. I was in here at the time and all of a sudden the whole thing just collapsed into a pile of sticks. I made the mistake of laughing. God! Was he mad! The cabinetmakers started parading through here again and they all told him the same thing. That certain woods didn't go with other woods. He could have a desk made of woods that were compatible, but not with all the woods in one piece. That was one of the few times I ever saw him defeated. The trouble was, everybody knew about the desk and knew what had happened to it. He thought they were all laughing at him behind his back. From then on, we never had a desk in his office."

"What was the setup like around here?"

"I don't know what you mean."

"The outer office is empty. I thought he had a big staff working with him."

"He did. Five writers, a couple of legmen, eight or ten others to work on music clearance, contacts, talent contracts, not to mention the staff that did nothing but handle the fan mail. It was quite a little kingdom."

"Where are they now?"

Smitty laughed. I repeated the question.

"Where are they now?"

"Vacation. Leave of absence. In mourning. Take your pick. To tell you the truth, they're all out looking for jobs."

"Why?"

"The King is dead."

"Sure, but the kingdom is still alive. Long live the new King."

"You?"

"Me."

"Look. Did you ever have a job that you couldn't quit?"

"Sure."

"There wasn't anybody that worked with him that didn't

make up his mind three mornings a week to quit. But nobody ever did."

"Why not?"

"Two reasons. One, money. Two, he didn't like people to quit on him."

"How could he stop you from quitting?"

Smitty laughed again.

"You didn't know him."

"I know him pretty damn well by now. I've spent the last two days finding out about him. Forgive me if I sound a little naive. I'm still discovering Herb Fuller and I haven't discovered a goddamn thing I can use Friday night."

"I don't envy you."

"Why not?"

"Because you're not going to discover anything you can use Friday night. You're either a very stupid or a very sincere guy."

"What does that mean?"

"Let's take stupid first. Stupid because you're offered the world on a platter and you're looking at the hallmark on the platter. What the hell do you care what kind of a guy Herb Fuller really was? What business is that of yours? Suppose you find out all about him? Suppose you do? So what? Can you use it on the air? You don't even have the excuse that you're looking for material for your memorial show. You won't find that kind of material talking to people who knew him. Then why are you bothering? Why are you confusing yourself about the show you're going to do Friday? You know the kind of show you're going to do Friday. And you can sit down and write that this afternoon—right out of the press clippings."

"I won't argue that with you."

"Why are you doing it then?"

"Fascination. Didn't you ever get fascinated with somebody?"

"Sure. Same guy you're fascinated with. For a different reason."

"Then you should be able to understand it."

"All right, so you're not stupid. Maybe at the beginning you thought you would gain something by digging into his life. Maybe you were trying to find one trace in his private life of the commodity he sold on the air. Maybe you wanted to be a con man with a little integrity left . . . all you wanted to find was a little gold in the gold brick you were peddling."

"And there isn't any?"

"You know there isn't. Not now. Maybe there never was. Whatever else they say about Herb Fuller, they have to admit that he was one of the great actors of his time. Every time the television camera went on or the microphone was opened, he was giving a performance. It's not his fault that everybody on the other end of the TV set or the radio set accepted the performance for reality. And when you come right down to it, what difference did it make to anybody that listened to him that he wasn't what they thought he was? He was while they were listening. What he did when the mike went dead was his own business and didn't affect them."

"You're a pretty cynical little girl. It doesn't go with your pony tail."

Smitty poured us two more drinks. I was beginning to feel a little lightheaded.

"I wouldn't be talking like this if I hadn't made up my mind to walk out. I'd be vamping hell out of you and playing the King is dead, long live the King. Look, Harris, let me be blunt with you."

"Go ahead."

"Maybe sincere was the wrong word. Maybe scared is a better word."

"Why scared?"

"Scared for a lot of reasons. Scared first of all because you've had the chance of the century dropped in your lap. God knows why. Scared because you're afraid to boot it. Scared because you don't know whether you have that kind of talent. And don't kid yourself about Fuller's talent. He was able to fool fifteen million people a week and that's a talent."

Maybe it was the drinks or maybe I was getting a little sick of the needling, but I found myself getting mad.

"What makes you so smart? Who put in the couch and made you an analyst?"

"O.K., Mr. Harris, forget it."

"Forget it, hell. You want to play Freud, we'll play Freud. I'm scared because I don't think I can step into Fuller's shoes and so I'm digging around in his life to find out what a bastard he was, so that I won't figure it's so hard to follow him, is that it?"

"No, that's not it."

"What is? Go ahead, make your nice little pony-tailed point."

"My point is simple. Think of some of the things you've found out about Fuller and admit that you haven't even scratched the surface. Admit that every lousy thing you find out about him doesn't surprise you. After a while it won't even shock you. And admit that you're scared silly that it's going to be awfully easy for you to step into his shoes. Not just on the air. You're scared because it's going to be even easier to step into his shoes off the air. You've found out a little what that's like, haven't you?"

"A little."

"Now tell me about the historical perspective. Tell me how after all Fuller was a kind of a king. Or the closest we come in twentieth-century America to a king. And tell me it doesn't scare you a little to realize that starting next Monday you're going to have control of the lives of a lot of people. If you want to sleep with them, they'll sleep with you. If you want to torture them a little for kicks, they'll hold still for it. If you want to play Potsy with their lives, that's O.K. too. And tell me it doesn't scare you a little because you know that the idea intrigues you a little. That's why I say you're scared, Mr. Harris."

"You mean there's a certain amount of bastard in all of us and I'm being given the chance to let it develop."

"Something like that. You asked about the other people and I told you they were out looking for jobs. And you're about to say the same thing you said to me: 'Why do they have to look for jobs; don't they think I can use them?' "

"Something like that."

"That's why they're out looking for jobs. They can't take a chance on you. Just as I can't take a chance on you. They have a chance now to get out. The King is dead and they don't want to find out what the new regime is like. While he was still alive, they couldn't leave. You think that sounds melodramatic. It isn't. One phone call from Fuller and they'd find every network, every local station, every agency with its door closed when they came around to call. Did you ever hear of Fuller's black list, Mr. Harris?"

"You mean a real black list?"

"Ask Carol Carson about the announcer she fell in love with."

"I know about that."

"Then you know about Carol too."

"I know about Carol too. What about you?"

"Sure, look me over, Mr. Harris. Why not? You've been

spending the week getting acquainted with your harem. I'm sure my name has come up."

"What about you?"

"Secretary in residence. My shorthand is lousy but I'm stacked like a brick warehouse. I cleaned that up a little. Four-letter words don't go with my pony tail."

I looked at my watch.

It was twenty to four. I had to get out of here soon and get down to the tape room.

Smitty got up and went back to the bar. I suddenly realized she was a little drunk. I took the drink she poured for me and put it on the table next to the couch. I had to start laying off for a while.

"My advice to you," said Smitty, "is to keep the bar in the office."

"Right."

"Were you in the army?"

"Navy."

"You remember how you felt when the war ended?"

"Yeah. I remember."

"Me. Same way. Now. For two years I've been waiting for the war to end. Now it's over. It ended on a hill in Connecticut. Did you feel happy and sad about it all at the same time?"

"I guess everybody did. Glad it was over and glad I was still alive and yet kind of sorry that the excitement was finished."

"Me. Same way. Now. I got drafted two years ago. Out of the typists' pool. Temporary fill-in. Lots of excitement. Glamor. Bright-eyed. Bushy-tailed. God, that was a long time ago."

"You stayed on."

"Sure. Two years. I'll show you my purple heart. Loaded with clusters. Did you know he used to give me twenty-five bucks a week extra? Christ, I was naive. He told me it was because he didn't like the people who worked for him to be underpaid and Amalgamated had to stick to a wage scale to keep out of trouble with the union, so he always gave his people a little extra."

"But you earned it?"

"What's it to you? Sure. I earned it. Bright-eyed and pony-tailed. I earned hell out of it. That's why I'm not going to stay on with you. That other time I didn't know I was earning it. I thought it was because Amalgamated would get in trouble with the union and he liked the people who worked for him to be well paid."

I sneaked another look at my watch.

"If I stayed with you, I'd know I was earning it. What was there about him that made it necessary for him to sleep with all the women he had around him and beat hell out of the ego of the men?"

"Maybe he was scared too?"

"Come off it, Mr. Harris. Don't try to understand his motives or give him credit for any human misgivings."

"Smitty, I have to go. I have an engineer waiting in a tape room. Can we talk some other time about your staying or leaving?"

"I'm leaving."

"Can we have a drink anyway?"

"Sure. Right now."

She finished what was left of her drink and poured another one. I sat down again. Drunken women don't like to be walked out on. Not that she was drunk. Not drunk. Loaded . . . just pony-tailed tight.

She picked up my drink off the table.

"What's the matter? You driving?"

"Editing."

"That's another thing you'll have to learn if you're going

to be the Great Man. I've seen him go on the air cockeyed and nobody ever suspected it. Better get in practice."

She freshed up my drink and I took a sip out of it. Smitty sat down again beside me.

"How much extra a week would you give me? Thirty-five? He paid twenty-five, but he had to break me in. Right now I'm a trained secretary. I know my place."

She pointed to the couch and started to laugh. It turned into a cough and I found myself pounding her on the back.

"Smitty, why don't you knock off for the day and go home?"

"You're not my boss. Not yet. I don't know if I'll accept the job or not."

She stopped and suddenly she got very serious. I could feel a crying jag coming on.

"Don't let me take the job," she said. "You want to make me, do it on your own time. Take me out to dinner. Buy me flowers. Flatter hell out of me. Give me a line. Seduce me."

"Come on, Smitty. I'll put you in a cab."

"Don't want to be put in a cab. I'm all right. You want to hear something funny?"

"What?"

"I was in love with him. Isn't that funny? I'll bet I'm the only one in the harem was in love with him. How about that? The harem girl that's in love with the Sultan. How silly can you get?"

"A lot of people were in love with him."

"He could do that if he wanted to. It was like homework to him. He could be the meanest, lowest bastard that ever lived and then all of a sudden he'd turn it on. He'd have you eating out of his hand. Maybe he was just keeping in practice for the microphones and the cameras. Maybe it was just another gimmick . . . another expression of the power he had to have over people. For a while it would be enough that you were afraid of him or dependent on him, but suddenly you had to love him too. And you used to grit your teeth and say, like hell I love you, but he always made you do it, only for a while, but you couldn't stand up to him . . . anyway . . . not any way at all."

"What are you going to do now?"

"You mean right now, or after Friday?"

"After Friday."

"I told you. I'm going to take a cruise or something. I'm going to be a nice girl for a while. For a while, hell. I'm going to be a nice girl. I'm going to go out on dates. Hold hands in the movies . . . get sent corsages. The war is over."

"Good-by, Smitty. Let me know if you change your mind and want the job."

I got up and started toward the door.

"Sure, Mr. Harris," said Smitty. "Sure. Likewise. You let me know if you change your mind and don't want the job."

"What the hell are you talking about?" I was mad again. The only trouble was I didn't really know if I was mad or just going through the motions because I thought I should.

"I'm Ed Harris. I've been Ed Harris for a long time. You think all of a sudden, starting next Monday, I'm going to be Little Herb Fuller."

"Sure. And then you'll be not so little Herb Fuller and you'll wind up being Big Ed Harris . . . the Great Man. Don't think you can avoid it."

"What you're saying is that it has to be that way. It doesn't."

"Tell that to Faust."

I smiled. I couldn't help myself.

She smiled back.

"Don't pay any attention to me," she said. "No attention at all."

"O.K. I've got to go down to the tape room. You'll be around until Friday?"

"Longer than that. I'm going to break Ginny into my duties, remember?"

"Yeah, I forgot."

"Just one question, Mr. Harris."

"O.K. One question."

"Why you?"

"I don't know, Smitty. I honest to God don't know. Maybe because they pulled my name out of a hat. Or maybe just because Sid Moore wanted it that way."

"You're Sid's boy?"

"I am now. I signed a contract with him."

"That might be the reason. He has something on them. He had something on Fuller too. I don't know what, but he threw a lot of weight around . . . even up here . . . for a local big shot. Were you uptown at that grind house where they have the body?"

"I just came back from there."

"It makes you want to laugh, doesn't it? So solemn, so serious. For keeps. They're like a bunch of kids with a pet squirrel that died. Crying and keeping a straight face, making believe they're burying the King of England when all it is, is a dead squirrel in a biscuit box."

I stood at the door. I was halfway out. I didn't dare come into the room and sit down. That way I'd never get down to the tape room. I hoped to God Mike had sense enough to go ahead without me. Smitty killed another drink. That was four since I'd been there. She got up again and started making another one.

"Join me?" she asked.

"No, thanks. Why don't you knock off for a while?"

"Herb Fuller would have liked it this way."

She poured another drink and sat down again. She wasn't

finished talking yet so I leaned against the door and waited.

"You know something?" she asked. "This sounds cockeyed to you, but I wouldn't be surprised somebody fixed that car so it smacked into the side of that hill."

"Who?"

"Anybody. Carol maybe. Nick Cellantano. Me. Maybe even Philip Carleton himself."

"Sure. Carleton was going to kill off the one guy that kept his network out of the red."

"See. You're an ignorant little guy. Just like I said you were. Simple. Simple-minded. You're damn right Carleton would have killed him if he could. Figure it out yourself. You're president of a big radio and television network. You get honorary degrees from universities. You got Cadillacs you haven't even used. But a little bastard with a trick voice and the ability to twist people around his finger is responsible for getting you those Cadillacs and those honorary degrees. He happens to be the one that keeps that network together and in business. At first you get down on your knees and thank the Good Lawd for sending you his pal Herb Fuller. For a while. But then Herb Fuller gets delusions of Godship. All of a sudden it isn't your network any more. It's Herb Fuller's. And he does anything he goddamn well wants to and if you don't like it, you can lump it. He makes a point of letting you know about the offers he's gotten from NBC and CBS. And if he gets a little bored with running people's lives to the extent of telling them which toothpaste to use or which cigarette to smoke and starts telling them which political candidate to vote for—there isn't much you can do about it, except apologize, give equal time and ask him please not to do that again. And when he tells you, on and off the air, to go take a flying fling for yourself, you gotta smile and say, 'Ain't that Herb Fuller a card!' and you gotta remember that doing that gives him an even greater hold on the Great Unwashed because here he is telling off his boss in public just like every one of them would like to do. You get the picture?"

"I get the picture."

"Wouldn't you maybe loosen the brake or something? Wouldn't you find a nice little guy like Ed Harris who does a nice little local program and who will know who's the boss right from the start? Wouldn't you figure it would be a calculated risk to build him into the same draw but keep him under your thumb in the process? You are so goddamned right you would."

"My, you use a lot of profanity!"

"I once knew a girl who was aide to General Sherman. You know, when she came back from the Civil War, she had the goddamnedest southern drawl you ever heard."

"But the war's over, Smitty. You said so yourself."

"Can't a girl make her own adjustment to civilian life?"

"It's a shame to waste you on a cruise, holding hands in the movies and waiting for the delivery boy to show up with a corsage."

"Go on down to your tape room. I'll be listening to your show Friday night."

"You may get a surprise."

What did I mean by that?

"Then again I may not."

This was an exit line and I took advantage of it. I waved, turned and walked into the outer office, through the waiting room, down the corridor and out to the elevators. It was five after four. I pressed the down button and got off at the eighth floor.

The tape rooms at Amalgamated were the best in the world. The Ampex tape machines at Amalgamated were the best money could buy and the engineers who worked them were artists. Mike Jackson was one of the best.

When I walked in he was dubbing off the tape I'd recorded that morning up at Studio 41.

"Good stuff," he said. "Some of the levels were pretty bad so I dubbed them, stuck a filter on them and cleaned them up for you."

"Fine."

"When you didn't show up, I figured rather than waste time I'd make up a show reel on it for you. If you like it, fine. If not, I have the original here and we can start over."

"Let's hear what you did."

Jackson picked a large aluminum reel off the wall where it had been hanging from a wooden peg. He put it on the machine and threaded it through the playback head. He pressed the start button on the machine and watched a volume indicator on the machine. He adjusted the volume and ran it back to the beginning.

"All set," he said and pressed the start button.

The tape started with the sound of shuffling feet over the strains of an organ playing "Rock of Ages."

"I figured," said Jackson, "you could run this under narration . . . something setting the scene, fans paying their last homage to their beloved radio and TV friend, that kind of crap. I got two minutes of it on the front of the reel here. You won't need all that, probably, but in the final dub I can make a loop for you and run it as long as you need."

"Right," I said. "Run it in to the beginning of the interviews."

Jackson pushed the fast forward button and the fast gibberish that sounds like Donald Duck came out of the speaker.

"It should be about here," he said and stopped the machine. He started it again at normal speed. He'd hit the spot right on the head. Tape engineers have fantastic ears. They can make sense of that fast gibberish because they've been working around it so much.

"Let's hear it," I said and Mike Jackson plugged in the speaker over the door.

"I figured after you set the scene with the shuffling and the organ in the background you'd go into a bit about talking to the people . . . and that would lead us right into the tape. Like this." The tape started.

"May I ask why you came here today?"

"I came to see him, rest his soul. My heart goes out to his poor wife and those dear children of his. He was always there with something cheery or something funny to say when you needed him. He'll be missed, believe me. By a good many."

Jackson stopped the tape.

"That was an easy one. I just had to blend a little and cut you out in between. That high school kid was a bitch of a job. I had to build her piece word by word. Listen to this." He started the tape machine again.

"And why are you here?"

"My friend wanted to. It was nice. All those flowers and the music and that preacher up there talking. It gave me a kind of—feeling. We used to see him on the television. He was like he was your father."

He stopped the machine.

"That was a bitch of a job," he said. "You remember in the original the kid says, 'My friend wanted to go to the Paramount.' I clipped it after 'wanted to' and stuck your question up front so it made sense. I had a hell of a job matching the inflection. Then the next part in that sentence, 'It gave me a kind of—feeling.' She said, 'It gave me a kind of spooky feeling.' I clipped out the word 'feeling' but it didn't work. I cut ahead in the tape and found another sentence with the words 'kind of' in it and I lifted those and put them in there. Sound all right to you?"

"Sounds fine to me, Mike."

"I was working on the dame with the kid when you came in. I don't know if we can save any of that."

"Don't worry about it. I'm just going to use a little bit of that. I think the old lady and the girl are enough."

"O.K. You want to hear the piece from Fuller's wife?"

"Yeah."

Jackson rewound the tape we'd been listening to and put another reel on the machine. This was Fran's piece that had been piped down.

Like Ginny had said, it was great. Catch in the throat and all.

"You've got a problem," Mike Jackson said after he'd taken the tape off the machine.

"What kind of a problem?"

"You're going to do narration, right?"

"Right."

"Narration . . . then some tape . . . then some more narration. You're going to do the narration yourself?"

"Yeah."

"That's your problem. How are you going to keep from laughing out loud? When you didn't show up at three, I started playing some of the tapes, making optional cuts. You sure get some beauts."

"I sure do."

"I particularly like that one from Eddie Brown, the flower of the musical world. Did you know I used to be Fuller's engineer?"

"No."

"Two years. How about I order some coffee?"

"Fine."

Jackson dialed the Rose Room's extension and ordered two coffees and cigarettes.

"Two years I was his engineer. It was a liberal education. I used to love coming to work because there was always that element of risk involved."

"What do you mean, risk?"

"You know the way Fuller used to talk. Filthy. I've never known him to use a sentence that didn't have at least three filthy words in it. It used to amaze me that he could talk so foul and never forget himself on the air. You know, it was a kind of speech pattern with him, like a lisp or a stutter. He couldn't talk without the dirty words and I used to think it would be impossible for him to turn it off when the mike was on. Most of the time he did."

"Sometimes he didn't."

"It was a liberal education."

Jackson laughed.

"He was a funny bastard. No kidding. Once in a while I used to get the feeling I was head keeper in a nut house. He'd get on the air with one of those soupy God bits he did all the time. Out of his mouth would be flowing all those words that had every old lady listening in, in the last stages of ecstasy. This serious stuff would be flowing out of him—that voice of his would be in high gear and all the time he was talking he'd be making filthy gestures with his hands . . . No kidding. I used to sit there and watch and wonder how a guy could be using his hands one way and his voice another without ever getting them mixed up, you know what I mean?"

"I know what you mean."

"He was great."

The delivery boy showed up with the coffee and the cigarettes.

"You take it," said Jackson. "You have an expense account."

I took it. We sat down and drank the coffee.

"You certainly got some beauts. This should be the greatest comedy show of the year. That Eddie Brown tape will have the Brill Building in hysterics."

"Why?"

"Eddie was robbing him deaf, dumb and blind. He was on the payroll of every song plugger in town. Every time you heard a song on Fuller's program, you could chalk up another twenty-five bucks in Eddie's pocket. Eddie got twenty-five bucks a plug. Of course everybody on the show was on the take, including Fuller. He did it big. He stole big, but the rest of them regularly did the Buck Grayson bit."

"What's that?"

"You'll find out damn quick. You've been doing a local show, so Buck Grayson hasn't come into your life yet. He will as soon as that mike of yours is hooked up to a network. Buck Grayson is a guy hired by big national sponsors to get their product mentioned on the air. Not a commercial but slipped into the script. Grayson used to listen to shows all day long, monitoring them for plugs. He'd sit with a list of his clients in his hand and every time one of them was mentioned he'd make an X next to it and put down the name of the performer that said it on the air. The company paid Grayson a hundred and fifty for every free network plug and he passed part of it along. The regulars who worked with Grayson on this had a choice—they could either take a case of Scotch or seventy-five bucks cash. Of course you had to be careful, the agencies and the regular sponsors used to bitch like hell about the free plugs, but most of the Fuller Family were past masters at slipping it past. You know, it's simple. It's a hot day, so it's natural to say you spent the morning with your head in the ice box. If you say ice box or refrigerator, it's just a piece of copy. Clean. But if you mention a brand name—it's a case of Scotch."

"Fuller knew this was going on?"

"Sure. He pulled a lulu one morning. The sponsors had been on his tail about the free plugs being slipped in so he called the Family together and told them they'd have to cut it out for a while. Even Carleton had sent one of those red memos of his about it. Fuller told them he'd take care of their Scotch supply for a while and then they'd have to lay off for a couple of weeks. Anyway, he got on the air that morning and went into a bit about what lousy janitors they had at Amalgamated. 'Look at this studio,' he said. 'Did you ever see such junk in your life? Let's get it cleaned up. My Lord, look at all this stuff.' And then he went right through about fifteen different products at seventy-five bucks or a case of Scotch apiece. That's still considered the high-water mark in the mooching league."

"He got away with it?"

"Sure. He'd get a generous impulse once in a while. As long as it didn't cost him anything he'd get generous once in a while. Like when Nick had a baby. He had the writers dish up one of those sentimental hunks of copy about what you see in a new baby's eyes—you know the kind of thing. Anyway, he followed it with a funny bit about how poor Nick was going to have to start shelling out for things like washing machines, driers, and so forth. He mentioned all the things by their brand names and each manufacturer, to show his gratitude, sent one along. He passed all the loot on to Nick."

"You're giving me a liberal education, Mike."

"I heard you were supposed to be a pretty smart guy. I'm surprised you don't know some of the crummy back alleys of the business. I guarantee you, you'll know them all a week after you take over from Fuller. You'll be a past master at larceny just like he was. Are you keeping Smitty on for inspiration?"

"She wants to leave."

"She must have calluses on her can by now. Not to mention a full set of Fuller fingerprints. I see you got to know our Carol."

Jesus Christ! I'd forgotten that the Carol tape was on the pile with the rest. Ginny must have handed it to Jackson along with the others. I was embarrassed.

"You heard the tape?" I asked.

"I heard it. It was in a box without any label on it."

We drank our coffee silently. Jackson wiped his mouth on the back of his hand and went back to his tape machine.

"I don't think there's anything in it that you can use on the air," he said.

"I don't think so either."

We didn't say anything else for quite a while. I made some meaningless pencil marks on the transcripts and Jackson fiddled with pots on the console. We were both startled by the sound of the clock. Every hour on the hour, the electric clocks that Amalgamated uses adjust themselves with the Naval Observatory. Occasionally they are a couple of seconds fast or slow and with a lot of whirling of gears and sprockets they jump ahead or fall back to align themselves with the official, accurate observatory time.

Ginny walked in with seven or eight boxes of tape in her arms.

"I didn't expect to see you here. I thought you'd still be up in the office with Smitty."

"I'm here."

"Good for you."

"Did you buy any more ties for me?"

"Stop already."

"Anything happen while I was out? Any phone calls? Anything?"

"There's a meeting in Mr. Carleton's office at ten in the morning. His secretary said that Mr. Carleton would like you to bring the rough draft of the script with you."

"O.K."

"Rickie Tyler wasn't in. I left a message that you called."

"Right."

"You want me to stay around tonight? Can I help you on the typing or the editing?"

"No thanks, Ginny. Oh God, I'm supposed to have dinner with Nicole at six-thirty. Get her on the phone for me, will you?"

Ginny put the tapes down on the table.

"These are the Fuller tapes you wanted. I figured you'd need them now for the editing session."

"Fine. Which ones do you have?"

"The four on the top are the blood plasma story. The others are just miscellaneous stuff . . . jokes and odds and ends. A guy from Cerebral Palsy called and wanted to know if you'd make an appearance on their telethon tomorrow night. Nick Cellantano called for an up-to-date bio on you and wants to set up an appointment for you with the Photo Department for some pictures. *TV Guide* called and wanted to make a date for a reporter to interview you. They said they were considering putting you on the cover the week you take over Fuller's TV shows. The Accounting Department called again, bitching about your expense account last week. Two insurance men called for appointments. And that's about it."

"Busy day."

"Are you hitching me up to the plow beside Smitty?"

"Smitty is retiring."

"Undefeated?"

"Practically."

Ginny had been working for me for almost three years. I suddenly realized, in the tape room, that she was a very pretty girl. She was wearing a silk print dress and her breasts poked out. They were round and full. As a matter of cold fact, she was quite a dish and I found myself looking at her with something new in mind. Herb Fuller was really getting to me, in more ways than one. I must have been staring because I noticed a flush on her cheek. Honest to God, she was blushing. I wouldn't have believed it possible. She looked up and her eyes caught mine.

"Forget it," she said.

"Forget what?"

"I'll get Nicole for you."

She picked up the phone, dialed nine to get an outside line and then dialed the hotel.

Mike Jackson had been leaning against the Ampex machine, smoking a cigarette, looking at both of us.

He picked up the tapes, took them out of the box and stacked them on top of the machine.

"Any particular order you want to hear these in?" he asked.

"Let's start with the European ones."

"The blood plasma thing?"

"Right."

Ginny handed me the phone. Nicole was on the other end. She was using her late afternoon voice which sounded the way subtle perfume smells. Nicole talked for three full minutes telling me nothing in a very provocative way. When she paused for breath I slipped in the information that I wouldn't be able to have dinner with her after all.

There was nothing subtle or perfumed about her reaction to the news. She was mad. Good and goddamned mad.

Ginny and Mike had a wonderful time listening to my end of the conversation. It must have sounded great.

"Darling, listen. There's nothing in the world I'd rather do than have dinner with you, you know that. Dinner, lunch and breakfast and I swear to God when this week is over and this show is out of the way, you'll see so much of me that you'll be sick of the sight of me."

Long pause.

"I know that, darling. Believe me, I know that."

Another long pause.

"Darling, you know I do."

Short pause.

"You bet I'll prove it to you. As soon as this show is over."

Longer pause.

"Darling, I can't. Not even for ten minutes. I have to do a script and edit tapes. I have to have a script for a meeting with Carleton tomorrow morning at ten."

Very short pause.

"He's president of Amalgamated."

Pause.

"I know you do."

Pause.

"I know you are."

Pause.

"I am too. Darling, don't make it any more difficult for me. I can't see you later. I have to go up to Sid Moore's apartment with the script."

Short pause.

"He's the program director. I told you about him."

Short pause.

"No, you can't. It's a business conference."

Pause.

"I can't, darling. We won't finish up until very late and I have to get some sleep. I told you I have a meeting with

Carleton in the morning. Darling, believe me, there's nothing I can do about it. And please don't take that attitude about it. Do I get sore when you have to run over to Brooklyn to make a personal appearance at some movie house?"

Long pause.

"All right, darling. I promise. I'll call you when I leave Sid's house. I swear it."

Short pause.

"Of course I do. . . . You know that. . . . More than ever. . . . I promise, darling. The minute I finish with Sid."

Long pause

"Good-by, darling."

I hung up the phone and turned and faced my audience.

"I should have your troubles," Jackson said.

"All right, let's get to work," I said. "You can read all about my love life in *TV Guide,* if I live through this week. Ginny, go on home. I'll see you in the morning."

After she left, Jackson and I got to work on the Fuller tapes.

What we had were evidently the raw tapes, the originals, rather than edited dubs. There were repetitions, false starts and occasional off-speed pieces. The audio quality on them was very good.

Jackson was amazed at the quality.

"These must have been recorded on wire," he said. "Nobody was using tape in those days . . . except maybe the Germans. Fuller must have had a wire recorder and then had the original wire stuff re-recorded on these tapes. The quality is amazing."

It was indeed. We listened to all four reels of the stuff and finally edited down the hunk we wanted. It was a very effective piece. It was strange sitting there in the tape room listening to the Fuller voice. The more I got involved with his life the more I felt as if he had never died, or never existed. The voice itself, reproduced mechanically, had a reality of its own. Listening to it fill the room as we ran the volume up for editing purposes, it was almost an entity by itself. It was as if the voice lived in a vacuum and it wasn't important that it came out of a body and that that body had an existence, a reality and a frame of reference in real life. The quality of suppressed and controlled emotion, real or phony, it wasn't important which, made you believe what the voice was saying, made you feel the emotion the voice wanted you to feel. After we had cut out the false starts, edited out the pauses and pasted it all together, Jackson and I sat back with a stop watch in our hands timing the piece and listening to it as an entity.

"I'm speaking to you now from a small town in Germany. The name of it isn't important, even if the Army would permit me to tell it to you. It's a pretty beat-up town. Pretty beat-up. As I stand here on the main street and look at the rubble on either side, there is no characteristic to tell you that it is one specific town anywhere. In a way it is any town in any war. Any town that has been caught between artillery barrages and small-arms fire. A few hours ago this town was held by the Germans. Your sons and brothers, your husbands and your nephews stormed it, with their M-1 rifles and that peculiar heroism that distinguishes the American G.I. in combat. They advanced, from gatepost to gatepost, from ditch to ditch and wrenched it bodily from the trained killers of Adolf Hitler. It has fallen. It has been captured. For this one rifle company, an objective has been taken. But in the big picture of a war, one rifle company, one objective, one battered German town is unimportant. You won't find it mentioned in the communiques or find it in any of your history books. But some of you will remember the name of this town forever. Remember it because this is where your boy, your husband, your nephew was killed. The Graves

Registration crews have already carried the dead away. There is nothing left in this small town now except the living and the wounded. And I'm standing now at a Battalion Aid Station where those wounded are being cared for until the ambulance arrives to take them back to the Division clearing station. Some of the boys I can see from where I am standing won't live through the night. But some of them will because of something I am holding in my hand. It isn't much to look at, my friends, nothing much at all, just a bottle with some tubing attached to it. But it's one of the great links between you and your loved one . . . a blood line . . . because what I'm holding is a bottle of plasma. I've carried it halfway across the world with me. From the blood bank in New York where it was extracted from the arm of somebody listening to my voice right now. It has come to the end of its journey, here on this dusty main street in this battered German town. It has come to the end of its journey. And because it has, one of the boys lying here will live through the night and his family will never have to remember the obscure name of a battered German town forever."

Jackson turned off the tape machine and we lit cigarettes.

"You know something?" I said.

"What?"

"That's the first thing of Fuller's I've listened to since he died that I believe."

"Hooray for him," said Jackson. "Guys are dying in front of him and you're proud of him because he felt something."

"I know, but look, Mike. I've been poking around in his life. I've been living with the feeling that this wasn't a man at all . . . this was some kind of a monster, who hated people, who lied, cheated . . . a sort of glorified con man with his voice amplified, and I couldn't find one normal, human emotion of love, gratitude or decency. I've found one, and don't slough it off on me."

"O.K., so it was a good piece."

"Were you around when this went on the air originally?"

"No, I was lying in some Battalion Aid Station myself."

"Play the transfusion tape."

Jackson started the machine again and we listened to the tape that had been recorded originally on wire in a Battalion Aid Station during the transfusion. It was a beautiful two and a half minutes of drama and reality. We had patched Fuller's cut piece onto the end of it.

"I hope you were listening carefully to that," said Fuller, "I hope you were listening. I was watching. You couldn't see the sweat standing out on the face of the Medics captain and the corporal that assisted him. You couldn't see that blood flowing quietly into his veins . . . giving him back a fighting chance of staying alive. I could see all that. And more. I could see a hundred million of us, an ocean away from this battered German town, not being shot at, not lying on our backs on a canvas stretcher, suspended between life and death . . . not knowing that those hundred million have a great power of life flowing through their veins. Ask your doctor, he'll tell you you have a lot of extra blood flowing through your veins . . . you can spare some of it . . . Just a pint is enough . . . enough to keep some other young American, in some other battered town, alive. I remember an old vaudeville joke now. That may seem strange to you, my good friends, to remember a joke now . . . but it's pertinent. It means something important. Remember the way one character used to say to another . . . 'What do you want . . . blood?' Well, my dear friends, that's what we do want. Blood. Yours. To replace the blood kids all over the world are spilling in the dusty roads of towns with unpronouncable names to keep you safe. Can you turn them down? Can you?"

We stopped the machine again.

"O.K., Mike," I said. "Stick it on the show reel."

"You don't know the order of the cuts yet, do you?"

"No. I'll know later when I get more of a script. I want to get to work on that right now. I'll tell you what. You go ahead and isolate hunks out of those other tapes while I start batting out some narration for the blood spot and the stuff I got up at Studio 41 today. When you finish give me a ring in my office and we can listen to them together and decide which ones to keep."

I left the tape room and went back to my office. It was twenty-five to seven and I felt hungry. I also had the beginning of a headache. The liquor I'd been drinking at Studio 41 and with Smitty was wearing away into a quiet hangover in the making. I resisted the temptation to have some food sent in. I was getting sick of eating out of a cardboard container and felt I could afford the luxury of spending an hour sitting in a restaurant with real linen napkins eating real, expensive food. I also resisted the temptation of calling Nicole.

The office was deserted. The typewriters were covered with their rubber-smelling covers and all the lights were obediently turned off. We were in the middle of our regular yearly economy wave with memos flying around about turning lights off when you leave the office and don't throw a piece of carbon paper away until it's completely useless.

My desk was covered with phone messages.

I hadn't really thought about the show all day. And it had been quite a day. I sat at my desk, pulled the light switch over my head and turned around in the darkened room to look at the RCA Building. I sat and thought of some of the things Smitty had said to me. I stopped counting the figures on my future salary checks and thought about myself. Me. A human being named Ed Harris. I knew myself pretty well. Somewhere between the snotty little punk of Sid Moore and the Galahad of my high-school year book was the truth I knew about myself. A guy out of the navy who found himself in the radio business as a performer. A guy who had taken on a certain amount of the protective coloration necessary for survival in that kind of a jungle. A guy who maybe drank a little too much. A guy who maybe slept around a little too much. A guy who posed as a cynic because it was a way of keeping people at arm's length. A guy who knew that after the trial balance was run up he came off on the good side of the ledger. Basically a pretty decent guy. A guy who was willing to make reasonable compromises for his greater comfort, greater bank balance and greater pleasure. But how much longer would the compromises be reasonable? The last time a corporal had become a Chancellor, the world had almost fallen apart. The time before that when a corporal had become an Emperor, it took half of Europe to get things right side up again.

Balls.

Delusions of grandeur are easy in a dark room with a window view of the RCA Building.

Serious, now, you bastard. What's eating you?

Fuller is eating me.

The Fuller yet to come is eating me. I can hear Marley rapping on my chamber door this minute. I can hear the Raven.

Balls.

So a loaded broad in a pigtail says you're scared and all of a sudden you're scared.

Broads.

And how about that Ginny?

Scared? Of what? Of making all the money in the world? Of being a celebrity? Of being the Great Man?

You're damned right. Of being the Great Man.

My stomach growled.

You're not the reincarnation of Fuller. You don't have to

be a carbon copy on or off the air. You're just Ed Harris and they're going to make you a national figure.

Are they?

And why you? Whose Hooper did you ever top?

Who ever heard of you in Great Falls, Montana?

And why would they be interested in you now or forever?

And how long will it be before you start playing the Carol tape at your parties, for laughs?

Jackson was nice about it. Never cracked a smile. Never said a word. And you were a little disappointed he didn't. You were ready to leer with him and strut a little, weren't you?

You oughta go and eat.

You oughta write that script.

And what the hell does Carleton want with that meeting in his office tomorrow morning?

Why don't you just chuck it and go climb into bed with Nicole?

Or Carol.

Or Smitty.

Cut it out. Go out and eat.

I went out and ate.

I got back to the office a little after nine. I checked in first at the tape room. Mike Jackson had done most of the hard editing. He'd pulled out the junk and had a collection of pieces that made up a show reel. We were in good shape. With about another hour of work we'd be right up-to-date with what material we had. I listened to all the tapes he'd worked on, made a couple of minor changes and went back to the office to bat out some more of the script.

I don't know how most radio writers work. I like to write a script in isolated hunks and then put it all together, adding, subtracting and joining up. At the moment I was interested primarily in doing the blood bank spot. It was funny the hold that piece had on me. Maybe it was a kind of talisman for me. It was important. It was the only evidence I'd been able to find that Fuller wasn't All Bastard . . . the only evidence that there was a little Human Being left in him. That was becoming important to me. Damned important. Anybody who saw a piece of the shooting war got so he could spot a phony piece of copy a mile off. I'd seen my share of correspondent commandos who sat on their tails in a rear echelon bar and wrote about life in the foxholes. You got so you could spot the phonies. You could also spot the honest copy, and that piece of tape of Fuller's was honest. It was important to me that it was.

I sat down at the typewriter and started to bat out some narration for the spot.

"If you're looking through the official files of the Army, the Navy or the Marine Corps, you won't find the name of Herb Fuller. You won't find him mentioned by the Ernie Pyles or the Hal Boyles. Herb Fuller tried to be a part of that war. He tried at least three times. They were very nice to him but they told him to go back home, go back to his microphones. They told him he was more valuable there than he would be lugging an M-1 rifie through the swamps of Anzio or the sands of Iwo Jima. He didn't like that."

I stopped for a minute and lit a cigarette.

I always reach a kind of saturation point when I'm writing crap. I find it helps to sit quietly and light a cigarette and start over. I started over, using the short sentence approach.

"Herb Fuller wasn't a hero.

Not in the accepted sense, he wasn't.

He didn't have a string of medals across his chest.

He never stormed a pillbox.

Or captured a German machine-gun nest single-handed.

And yet . . .

And yet . . .

He was more important than an infantry division.

Or a whole Medical Corps.

No, you won't find his name in the roster of heroic marines who died on atolls strung across the Pacific.

No, you won't find his name on a morning report on the Anzio beachhead. . . .

Or in the water-logged records of the Arizona under the waters of Pearl Harbor.

Where were you on the morning of . . . (Check date of blood broadcast) . . . Like a couple of million other Americans you were sitting by your radio listening to Herb Fuller. But if you expected jokes or wisecracks, to take your mind off the black headlines on the front page of your newspaper, you were in for a disappointment. This is what you heard:

FULLER TAPE CUT ONE:

STARTS: I'M SPEAKING TO YOU NOW FROM A SMALL TOWN

ENDS: . . . NAME OF A BATTERED GERMAN TOWN FOREVER

TIME: 1:45

Remember that? Sure you remember it. You remember it because suddenly out of the cold metal of a loudspeaker in the harsh tones of a man you knew and trusted . . . a war came alive. Suddenly you knew that there was something you could do.

Something important.

As important as sighting a mortar.

Or pulling the lanyard of an artillery piece.

Something vital.

Life or death.

You.

Suddenly you were no longer an isolated civilian sitting in a kitchen in the Bronx, a front parlor in Iowa or a porch in Mississippi. Suddenly you were in a Battalion Aid Station, within small arms range of the enemy.

TRANSFUSION TAPE: CUT TWO
STARTS: HOLD THAT A LITTLE . . .
ENDS: . . . WITH THE END OF THAT STRETCHER
TIME: 2:35

You didn't pay any attention to the baby crying upstairs in the bedroom, you forgot about the ironing you'd been about to do. You listened . . . with all your attention.

FULLER TAPE CUT THREE
STARTS: I HOPE YOU WERE LISTENING CAREFULLY
ENDS: . . . TURN THEM DOWN . . . CAN YOU?
TIME: 1:20

Could you? Could you turn them down? Could you look at the large vein throbbing in your arm and weigh the loss of some of that extra blood of yours against the lives of those anonymous young Americans lying in other field hospitals on other battlefields?

You couldn't. Could you? ——— million of you couldn't. (CHECK NICK CELLANTANO FOR FIGURES ON BLOOD DONATIONS AS RESULT OF THIS PITCH) ——— pints of blood flowed out of ——— arms. ——— Americans lived instead of dying.

No. . . . Herb Fuller was no hero.

He didn't storm any pillboxes.

Or capture any German machine-gun nests.

Or wear five rows of fruit salad across his chest.

But with the help of an army of his listeners who were willing to roll up their sleeves, he formed a blood line between the Home Front and the Battle Front. And you . . . you there in Kansas . . . or you in Florida . . . or you, young fellow in Maine . . . may be listening to my voice now because some of that blood he enlisted in Freedom's battle is coursing through your veins now."

Wow!

I do get off a fruity one now and then.

I pulled the pages out of the typewriter, clipped them together with a paper clip and shoved them into the folder with the rest of the script.

I was ready for Sid Moore. He'd love that bit about storming the pillboxes and capturing the machine-gun nests.

I pulled the string on the light, closed the office door and walked around the corner into the tape room.

Mike was just getting ready to leave.

"You got enough here right now for a five-hour show," he said.

"I know. I'm awful heavy on narration too. It will need a lot of pruning."

"You figured out what you're gonna do afterward?"

"What do you mean afterward?"

"After Friday. After you take over the Fuller spots."

"Sure," I said. "I got it all figured out. I'm going to make a lot of money."

"You can't possibly avoid it, can you?"

"I don't see how I can possibly avoid it, Mike."

"What I meant was, have you figured out what kind of show you might be doing? You know, are you just going to continue doing the Fuller stuff or are you going to do something of your own? Some special gimmick, you know what I mean?"

"I don't know, Mike. I honest to God don't know."

"I just thought I'd ask. I have a couple of package ideas I'd like to show you. You know, maybe you might be able to use one of them."

"Fine, Mike. I'd like to see them. You all finished up?"

"Yeah. I coulda screwed you, you know . . . double time. You know, some of the other engineers, as soon as they get an overtime or double time, they slow down to a walk, make the job last twice as long. I don't work that way."

"I know you don't, Mike. Why don't you just add an hour to your time?"

"Thanks."

"It's not my money."

"This time next year it will be. You'll be Mr. Amalgamated."

"Don't make any bets on it. You like the tapes?"

"I told you. I think they're great. Crap, but great. That blood bit is something. Phony as a nine dollar bill but something."

"What do you mean phony? Don't kid yourself he was that good."

"Don't kid yourself he wasn't."

"You don't think he honestly was moved while he was doing the tape?"

"How do I know? And what difference does it make? It worked. It got blood. Look, Edison is screwing around in his laboratory. All of a sudden a hunk of glass lights up. Who cares whether he was thinking, 'Now I'll invent the 75-watt bulb.' Who gives a damn? It works."

"I give a damn."

"That'll pass, brother."

"Why?"

"I'm warning you all this talk is costing Amalgamated double time. You want to hold a panel discussion at double time I'm willing."

"No, I'm serious. What do you mean . . . that'll pass?"

"I mean right now you're up to your ears in Fuller. You been spending every waking minute of your life this week thinking about him. Am I right?"

"Right."

"So everything he does is important to you. You worry about his motives, his feelings. Why? Because starting next week you start living his life. Or at least you start living his public life. So right now he's the most important guy in the world to you. Even more important than yourself. . . . After a while you'll discover that it's your name that's on the salary check and all this interest in Fuller will pass."

"Maybe you're right."

"Listen, at these prices I'm either right or you're a damn fool standing here listening to me. Why don't you knock off on Fuller for a while and go back to being Ed Harris for a while? You're in great shape on the tapes. You've still got two days for the script. Go out and get drunk or laid."

"Or both."

"Or both."

Mike turned off the tape machines and put the light out. We closed the door of the tape room behind us.

"You want a lift?" he asked. "I have the Studebaker outside."

"Thanks. I have to go to Sid Moore's. That's right around the corner."

"Strategy meeting?"

"Something like that."

"All right," said Mike. "So I'm an engineer. I make my hundred and seventy-five. I never get my name in the paper, or go to Portugal on my vacation. I won't even get an obit in the paper when I die unless the family pays for it. But you'd be surprised how many bastards I don't have to be nice to."

"Like Sid Moore?"

"You said it, brother, not me. Just count your fingers after you leave him."

"I promise."

Mike waved and headed for the elevator. I stopped off at the reception desk and dialed Sid's number. The phone rang six times. I was about to hang up when he answered.

"Sid?"

"Yeah?"

"Ed Harris."

"Hiya, Coach? Where are you?"

"I'm just leaving the tape room. Like you said, I'm calling to give you a warning. Get that woman out of your room."

"When are you coming over?"

"In about fifteen minutes."

"Good. I'll have a tall cool one for you."

"See you in about fifteen minutes, Sid."

I hung up.

I walked down to the corner and picked up the early editions of the *News* and the *Mirror.* I stopped at the drugstore for a cup of coffee and opened the *News.* Ben Gross had a picture of me in his column, cheek by jowl with Godfrey and Gracie Allen. It was the old picture that Amalgamated had shot when I started "Metropolitan Memo" before I put the pounds back on that the Navy had taken off. The justification for the picture was a short take headed "Radio Row Is Talking About . . . Ed Harris and the Fuller Memorial Show this Friday Night. Both CBS and NBC have tried luring him away from Amalgamated, but he's not listening." I turned to Ed Sullivan.

Nothing.

A "Listen Kids" column.

The *Mirror* pulled out all the stops on the editorial page. Take equal parts of Herb Fuller's face, the American flag, an eagle and a pair of angels and you have the general idea. Centered in the middle of this was a poem.

It went like this:

"We may not see his like again,
I hear a million say.
We may not see his like again,
Now that he's gone away.

His friendly smile, his sunny grin
Have left this Vale of Care.
And God has called his angels in
To welcome him up there.

The laughter of a little boy
Won't seem as warm and gay.
For all of us have lost some joy.
Herb Fuller's gone away."

I left the papers on the next stool, flipped a quarter across the greasy counter and walked out into the street. It was a beautiful night as I headed east toward Sid Moore's place. It was twenty-five after ten. A wonderful time of the night in New York. The people who use the town as a workshop have all gone back to their bedrooms in Queens, Westchester and Connecticut. The theaters haven't emptied out yet and the café society crowd haven't started their nightly rounds. There's a wonderful kind of casualness to the people on the street at twenty-five after ten. Nobody is hurrying anywhere. It's too early for assignations and too late for appointments. It's a wonderful time of night in New York.

I crossed Park and walked into the lobby of Sid's building. Sid lived in that New York institution, the remodeled brownstone. To a New York big wheel living in a brownstone had several virtues. A good address. High ceilings and big rooms. The high rent was counterbalanced by a janitor who was on the ball and polished hell out of the brass knocker, doorknob and mail slot that was standard equipment on the front door. The inner lobby of the building wasn't really a lobby in the accepted, or hotel, sense of the word. It wasn't quite a vestibule, either. It was more like an oblong screening room. The front door was open, but when you walked through it you found yourself in an oblong room with another door closed in your face. This was where you pressed the appropriate button and identified yourself into a shiny brass speaking tube. If you were acceptable to the owner of the button you pressed, he in turn pressed a button in his apartment which unlatched the inner door. If you were of a sufficiently sentimental frame of mind or had had sufficient martinis, it saddened you to reflect that this was all that modern civilization had left of the principle of the drawbridge.

I pressed the appropriate button and without being challenged by the speaking tube, heard the inner door click in welcome. I pushed through it and climbed the carpeted stairs to the second floor. Sid was standing in his doorway. He was dresed in a silk dressing gown, wore a leopard ascot and held a tall glass in his hand. He clapped me on the shoulder and stepped aside to let me in. I'd never been to his apartment before and I gave it a quick once-over while he asked me whether I wanted a gin and tonic or bourbon on the rocks. The walls were painted a kind of mocha brown and there was a closely woven straw rug on the floor. The furniture was modern. There were a couple of modern paintings on the wall and the bookcases against one wall were filled with French paper-back books. It looked about as warm and personal as the men's room in Radio City Music Hall.

Sid was in a little kitchenette off to the right of the living room. I couldn't see him but I could hear him emptying an ice tray.

"How do you like the place?" he asked.

"Very interesting," I said. "Very clean."

"I think it stinks. I had that fairy interior decorator fix it up for me while I was out in Chicago and I just haven't gotten around to fixing it up my way yet."

"Which fairy decorator?"

"The one Donna Adams had on her show for a couple of weeks last summer. When I moved in here, I figured I'd need some furniture, so I called him up and made a deal with him. I told him if he'd fix the place up for me I'd see that he got some mentions on some of our shows. Brother, did that son of a bitch throw me an incurve. Looks like a goddamned fairy flophouse."

Sid came into the room and handed me a gin and tonic.

"Look at these goddamned paintings. What the hell, I'm only here a couple of nights a week. It didn't cost me anything."

"I think it's very interesting, Sid. Lousy but interesting."

"Did you bring the script with you?"

"Some of it."

"Good. I thought we'd just throw it on the floor and walk around it."

I took a healthy slug out of the gin and tonic.

"I'll show you the rest of the place later. The can is right in there past the kitchenette and off to the right is the bedroom and down the hall I have a kind of sitting room in the back."

"Sounds fine. A hell of a lot better than my one room."

"I meant to talk to you about that, Ed. You gotta move out of there."

"Why? I like it."

"To hell with what you like, kid. You gotta follow your interference, kid."

"And where is my interference going?"

"Straight into the Waldorf until we can find you a place with a good address."

"And a brass knocker?"

"A what?"

"Skip it, Sid. O.K. I'll move out. I'll get a good address. But no fairy decorator."

"No fairy decorator."

"I got some good tapes."

"You better have some good tapes. You know we've had four clients begging to let them sponsor the memorial show? I had to call Carleton on it, but I was all set to make a rhubarb out of it if he didn't see it my way."

Sid poked me with his drink.

"Right from the start, kid, we have to let Carleton know he can't push us around. Anyway, he saw it my way. Sponsors for the memorial show? Who needs them? It'd be like sponsoring the Coronation. Public service is what it is. Besides, let them sit on their cans awhile and get real anxious. We'll be happy to let them in later on the Ed Harris show."

"What did Carleton say?"

"Same thing I'm saying. Only he used more words and took longer. What it boils down to, kid, getting it all formed up in one ball of wax, is that we're too close to the green to use a five iron."

"By God, I wish I'd said that."

"What?"

"Sid, can I have the 'Toward a More Picturesque Speech' rights to your conversation?"

"I thought you weren't going to be your usual snotty self tonight, Coach. I thought we were going to have a nice quiet talk and read your script."

At this point the toilet flushed.

A minute later I heard the door to what Sid had told me was the bathroom open and a girl walked into the room. She had two bobby pins in her mouth and was combing her hair. The two top buttons on her shirt were open. It was the receptionist.

"Hello, Mr. Harris," she said. Just the way she said it in the office.

I was surprised to see her.

Sid patted the seat next to him on the couch and she sat down.

"You get one drink and cab fare, honey. Ed and I have business to talk over."

"I'll leave in a few minutes, Mr. Moore. I would like one drink, if I may."

Mr. Moore yet.

Sid got up, made a motion for me to finish up my drink, which I did, and then disappeared into the kitchenette again. The receptionist and I sat looking at each other. I wished to hell she'd button those goddamned buttons and what the hell was her name. I couldn't call her Miss Receptionist, or could I?

"Miss Receptionist, how do you like your job?"

"My name is Marcia. Marcia Miller."

We shook hands. Her palm was moist.

"How do you like your work, Marcia?"

"Very much."

"Your hours are pretty long though, aren't they?"

"Is that a crack?"

"Marcia, honey. Of course it isn't. Why should I make a crack about you? You're very important in my life. Every morning, from now on, when I get off that elevator there you'll be—smiling at me. And how could I be mad at anybody all day long after starting my day off with you smiling at me? You're a kind of disposition insurance to me, Marcia, and I wouldn't want you to be mad at me for anything. Not even for this whole big wonderful apartment of Sid's, even. Not even for that would I take that chance with you, Marcia, honey."

Marcia honey wasn't amused. She picked up a pack of

cigarettes from the collection of plumbers' pipes and chrome that passed for a coffee table in Sid's apartment. I struck a match and lit her cigarette. She blew the smoke smack in my face. I inhaled some of it and blew it back in her face. She quit.

There was a lull in the conversation.

Sid broke the silence by appearing with three drinks.

"You and Marcia getting acquainted?" he asked.

"Sure," I said. "We smoke the same brand of cigarettes."

He sat down and Marcia entwined her fingers in his.

He disentangled them. "Not now, honey," he said.

Marcia put her fingers in her lap.

There was an awkward silence.

Sid broke it.

"Been working hard?" he asked.

"Yeah."

"Good. We're definitely cleated on this show. It's got to be the greatest. By the way, Ed, did you know that Marcia used to be on the radio?"

"No, I didn't," I said.

"Sure. Where was it, honey?"

"Bennington."

"That's right," said Sid. "Bennington. How about that?"

We all drank. Quietly. Marcia put her drink on the coffee table and got up. Sid patted her fanny as she passed in front of him. She disappeared into the bedroom and came out a minute later carrying her purse.

"Don't get up," she said.

Nobody had moved.

"I'll get a cab."

"You do that, honey," said Sid. "I'd take you home, but Ed and I have a big skull session coming up. Gotta run over the signals."

Marcia extended her hand. I shook it. Gently.

Sid patted her on the fanny again and she left, closing the door quietly behind her.

"I'm beginning to understand the fast turnover in receptionists, Sid."

"Good kid," he said. "She wants to get on the air. Wants to get on the air real bad. I might let her fill in for Donna Adams for a couple of weeks this summer while Donna's on vacation."

"Sid, when was the last time you paid for anything? Your drinks and meals wind up on the expense account at the station. You get your apartment decorated by a fairy decorator who settles for a couple of free plugs on the air that don't cost you a dime. The colleges are filled with receptionists who are just dying to get on the radio. What the hell use is your salary? What do you spend it on? Clothes?"

"I haven't paid for a suit in ten years. I have a deal with a manufacturer. Plugs."

"How about rent?"

"Rent I pay. But I put it on the expense account under entertainment. I have to entertain clients, don't I?"

"Yeah."

"You talk like this is brand new to you, kid. Don't tell me you haven't been using 'Metropolitan Memo' to promote yourself some of the niceties of life. Skipper, I believe in live and let live. I never checked you on any cuffos you handed out on the air, did I?"

"Sid, you have a strange kind of ethics, don't you?"

"Sure. I get mine. I let you get yours. When you're in the bucket under the basket I feed you the ball. I expect you to do the same for me."

"How about that tour of the apartment you promised me?"

"Follow the fullback."

I followed the fullback. Our next stop was the bathroom, which was covered with black tiles. There were pink fish imbedded in the tiles and the toilet seat itself was chartreuse. It was something.

"Seems a shame to do something as dirty as go to the can in here, doesn't it?" he said.

I agreed.

We walked back into the living room and out into the long hall. A door off the hall opened into a bedroom which was dominated by a large circular bed. It was mussed.

"My workshop," said Sid.

We walked through the bedroom into a front sitting room which was furnished in white. There was a wall-to-wall white shaggy rug on the floor, a long white couch, three white overstuffed chairs and a white grand piano. Sid pushed the light switch and pressed another button next to it. The room went dark and slowly flushed blue.

Sid moved over to the long couch. I followed him.

He pointed behind the couch.

"Blue flood lights with the kind of dimmer they have in movie houses. You can control the intensity of the color. How about that?"

"I'm surprised we didn't hold the Fuller wake here. Seems a shame to waste this."

"Believe me, Coach, this isn't wasted. This is like a decompression chamber. Greatest little seduction decompression chamber you ever saw. I guarantee you, ten minutes in here with that goddamned blue spotlight dimming and the Seduction Suite coming out of the phonograph and you're on your way into the bedroom."

"Is that what the decorator had in mind?"

"Who knows what he had in mind?"

"How was she?"

"Marcia?"

"Yeah."

"Athletic. Never seen a college girl wasn't athletic. Must be all that field hockey they play. She has a mole the size of a fifty-cent piece."

"Let's go back to the living room. This place depresses me."

Sid was over at the side of the room. He pulled a drawer out of a cabinet. It turned out to be a phonograph.

"This is something Herb Fuller taught me."

"Anything Herb Fuller taught you, I have to see."

"He got on a psychologist kick one time. Paid this guy a lot of money to build a Seduction Suite for him. Records. It's all in the sequence. Without the dame even being aware of it, the music is slowly working on her. Moving her along mood by mood until she's panting."

"You mean you play six or eight records in the proper sequence and you can't miss?"

"Something like that. The records vary with the different types. For instance, here are the ones I used tonight."

He picked six records off the turntable. I looked them over casually. The first record was a Chopin prelude. The last one was Ravel's "Bolero."

"That Bolero," said Sid. "Greatest closing piece of music ever written. On all the lists . . . with all the different types, that's the closing number. When you get your place I'll give you the list. It cost Fuller a couple of hundred bucks."

"Thanks," I said. "Now let's get the hell out of here. I feel like a blue baby."

"Fuller had the goddamnedest collection of lists. I told you he was on this psychologist kick. He had one list of records, you played them in sequence you had anybody crying his eyes out. He had another list used to almost drive you out of your mind. None of them had any effect on him, but he used to invite people into this room he had at his place and start the phonograph and sit around and talk and get his kicks just watching their reactions."

"Let's go back to the living room."

"O.K."

We walked through the bedroom again.

"Smells like a locker room," said Sid.

It did, too. There's a special smell a bedroom has on certain occasions. Sid's just reeked of it. That may have been what had my head spinning. Or maybe it was just the gin and tonics I'd been gulping down on top of Smitty's Scotch and Studio 41's bad booze. I could feel myself getting quietly loaded.

When we got back into the living room, Sid refilled our glasses and I made a mental note to take it easy for a while. The trouble with gin and tonic is that it's deceptive. It doesn't taste like liquor. I figured I was about four drinks this side of a boom-lowering and knew it. That was half the battle. Knowing.

"Let's see the script," Sid said.

I passed him the folder.

He held it in his hands.

He weighed it.

He shifted it from one hand to the other.

"Ed," he said. I waited for him to continue. He didn't.

"Yes, Sid? What's on your mind?"

"Ed," he said. "Ed, I never had a son."

"You sure?" I asked.

He ignored that.

"I never had a son," he said, "I never will, I guess. Ed, boy," he said.

Suddenly I realized something. He was cockeyed. Holy Mother of God! He's a maudlin drunk. Who'd have suspected it? Who, indeed!

"I'm older than you, Ed, and you have a rough time of it ahead of you, Ed. A rough time. You're gonna be in a sand trap a lot of the time, Ed. A lot of the time."

I sat waiting for the commercial. It didn't take long to arrive.

"You're gonna hear a lot of crummy bastards in this lousy business putting the rap on old Sid. A lot of them. A lot of them will tell you Sid's always out for number one. To them I'm the cleanup hitter in the bastard line-up. I'm not saying I haven't burned one down the middle on some of them. I'm not saying I haven't crossed them up with my change-up pitch. They don't take a toehold at the plate when old Sid's on the mound. But just the same, Ed, I want you to know something. I don't have a son . . . but if I did, boy, I'd want him to be just like you."

I was getting embarrassed. It bothers me when people step out of character. And Sid was way out. And I wasn't quite sure whether he was just cockeyed, whether it was a rib or whether the wheels were turning on something important.

"I just want you to know old Sid's gonna protect you in the clinches, kid. Nobody's gonna do any holding and hitting on you. Not while old Sid's the third man in the ring, they're not."

"You just being sentimental Old Sid Moore or do you have something specific on your mind?"

"You're goddamned right I've got something specific on my mind. You're gonna be big, kid. The biggest. And they're gonna start getting to you about Sid. All the way from Carleton on down."

"Look, Sid, forget it. I signed a contract. I couldn't dump you if I wanted to."

"That's what Fuller said. He used to call me his mentor—his Svengali. I had a contract with him too. You didn't know that, did you? Sure. But they got to him. He dumped old Sid. You wouldn't dump old Sid, would you, kid?"

It had a familiar ring. Sure. Carol. The same bit.

Sid reached over and put the script on the floor. By God, I thought, he really is going to throw it on the floor and walk around it. I wasn't sure he'd be able to.

"You think Sid's an old tough bastard, don't you? I loved that no-good-son-of-a-bitch Fuller. Loved him. Like he was my kid. I dug him out of that station in Worcester. I stuffed him down their throats. Buddies. Fuller and Moore. I had a contract. He was mine. I made him. But he dumped me. They got to him."

"Who's they, Sid?"

"They. What's the difference who they are? They got to him. I'm warning you, kid, they better not get to you about Sid."

He sat quietly for a minute. We both digested that piece of information in silence. We both drank.

"Let's look at your script," he said and picked it up off the floor.

He opened the folder . . . stared at the front page for a minute and then closed it again and put it down on the coffee table.

"Did you go through a lot of Fuller tapes?"

"Miles of them."

"Did you listen to any Monday shows . . . say a couple of years ago?"

"I don't know. Why?"

"Funniest goddamned things you ever heard in your life. I mean back when he was shacking up with Carol regularly. They used to go at it all week end long. On the Monday show when she'd come up to sing he'd say to her, 'How did you spend your week end, Carol?' 'Oh,' she'd say, 'I didn't do anything much. Just relaxed, washed my hair, things like that.' 'Is that so?' he'd ask. 'You didn't play any games?' 'No,' she'd say. 'Didn't get any exercise?' he'd ask. Like that. Funniest goddamned thing you ever heard."

"Pretty hilarious, Sid."

"You don't think it's funny, do you, Ed boy?"

"Sure. I think Herb Fuller was the funniest living American. At least."

"I didn't think he'd dump me, Ed. I didn't think he'd take a dive. I didn't think he'd go into the tank just because Carleton told him to. Not after what I did for him."

"Couldn't you sue them? You had a contract, Sid."

"Sure. I had a contract. Sure, I coulda sued them. Sure. They'd a dragged it through the courts as long as they wanted to. Meanwhile they'd have had old Sid hung over the barrel. Who was gonna hire old Sid, if the word got around that he had a case of ex-employment smallpox? I compromised. I let them break the contract. In return they let me continue eating. They let me keep my job. They gave Sid the well-known reaming job."

"What makes you think they'll let you hang onto me this time?"

"They have to. I have them fighting my fight now. They know I could blow their Herb Fuller sky-high right now. They know if I open my mouth, he's really dead."

"What the hell could you tell them about Herb Fuller that I haven't found out in the last two days? Anybody who wants to ask a couple of questions of a couple of people can find out what a no-good bastard he really was. You think this is a great secret?"

"Come on, Ed. Don't talk like a bonus pitcher who hasn't even been down to the Three I League. What can you tell anybody that's gonna make them hate Fuller? That he screwed everything that didn't bite? That he drank? That he pushed people around? That he wasn't Will Rogers or Abe Lincoln? Is that gonna destroy the legend? Is that gonna kill him with the fat slob in Nebraska who cured her nasal drip laughing at him? You know goddamned well that won't bother her a bit, even if you could tell it to her. Even if you could. Even if somebody would print it. Which they won't."

"And what can you tell them, Sid?"

"I can tell them. Don't forget it. I can tell them."

"What?"

"None of your goddamned business."

He suddenly swept his glass off the coffee table. It went spinning across the room and crashed against the wall.

"None of your goddamned business," he said.

"Take it easy, Sid."

He turned the violence off as fast as he'd turned it on.

"Sure, Skipper. I'll take it easy. Only when they start getting to you, tell them Sid Moore doesn't give a goddamn for their black lists anymore. Tell them Sid Moore isn't going to be any goddamned shuttlecock this time. This time Sid Moore has his contract and he keeps it or he starts talking."

"I'll tell them, Sid. Nobody's gonna dump you, Sid. Why would I want to dump you? You gave me my job at Amalgamated, didn't you? You got me this chance to step into Fuller's place. Sid, I owe you more than I'll ever be able to repay."

"O.K., kid. You're a good kid. If I had a son I'd want him to be like you."

I picked up the pieces of glass off the floor.

"Leave it, kid. Make me another drink."

"Why don't you sit it out awhile, Sid?"

"Who's driving? I'm home. I don't have to go anywhere. Neither do you, kid. I can put you up for the night. Take your shoes off and get good and loaded with Sid. We both have it coming to us."

"Why not?"

I finished off my drink and made us two more. I was getting good and loaded and I knew I shouldn't. I was a little frightened of what I'd just been through. And a little curious. Maybe a little more curious than frightened. I wanted to know what Sid knew. The key to it was in the bottle on the shelf in the kitchenette. It was the best excuse for getting drunk that I ever had.

When I got back into the living room with the drinks, Sid was reading the script. I set the drinks down and read over his shoulder.

It was suddenly very important to me that he liked it.

I found myself breaking in every other page, saying, "This is all rough, first draft, you understand. It'll need some tightening and some cleaning up."

When he finished Sid put the folder back on the coffee table.

"The greatest," he said. "There won't be a dry eye in the house."

"Thanks."

"Are you sure you're getting that recording out of that guy in Worcester?"

"I had a wire from him this evening. The record is on its way by Air Express."

"How'd you like the blood tapes? How'd you like them? How were they? The greatest?"

"The greatest. The quality was wonderful. Mike and I were surprised at the quality you got out of a field wire recorder."

"Mike who?"

"Mike Jackson. The engineer. He worked on the tapes with me."

"He liked the quality? You wouldn't believe you could get quality like that out of a wire recorder, would you?"

"They were great, Sid."

"The greatest."

Sid was smiling. I had a feeling. A hunch. I knew it was important to keep him talking.

"How come you went along with him on that job? That was after you split up with Fuller, wasn't it?"

"Yeah. Right after. Maybe you could say even Fuller had a little sentimental streak in him. Not much, but a little. I dreamed the blood bit up, just to show there was no hard feelings. Maybe they let me go along to show they didn't have any hard feelings. They didn't know how the whole thing was going to turn out."

"You mean they didn't know you were going to come back with great tapes like that?"

"You keep calling them tapes. It was wire, remember?"

"I'm so used to saying tape, I just automatically say it. You recorded it in the field on wire, right, Sid?"

"Right."

"How'd you get such good quality on them, Sid?"

Sid was smiling again. He punched me on the knee.

"Secret process," he said. "Sid Moore's V-2 rocket. My secret weapon."

"They're great."

"How's your French dame? What's her name?"

"Nicole."

"How is she?"

"I don't know. I haven't seen her lately."

"Tough, kid. Tough. Don't worry, it won't get rusty on you."

"That must have been quite an experience, Sid. That trip with Fuller."

"Experience? You bet your ass it was an experience. You bet. Experience!"

"What was it like?"

"Like? An experience. First we went to—what's the name of it? You know, that fancy uniform place? Sid Moore and Herb Fuller got fitted out for the classiest uniforms you ever saw. Had great big patch on the sleeve. Official War Correspondent, it said. That was his idea. Nobody said anything about it. He just ordered two big patches for the shoulders. Biggest goddamn patches you ever saw. About the size of a Ford hubcap. Official War Correspondent. The guy from the Army PRO that set the whole thing up told us we had the simulated rank of colonels. Old Herb wanted to wear eagles on his shoulders. Said if he was a goddamned colonel, he wanted everybody to know it. We talked him out of that. He settled for this goddamn hubcap on the shoulder."

"How did you go over?"

"In a bomber. The Army set it up for us."

"You rode a bucket seat?"

"Bucket seat hell. They put in two cots with air mattresses. We were VIP's. The V'est goddamned IP's you ever saw."

"Where did you land?"

"Orly."

"Did you stay in Paris long, Sid?"

"We were at the California. You been to Paris, Ed?"

"Yes, I've been to Paris."

"You know the California Hotel. Right across the street from the Herald and the Shell Building. What the hell's the name of that street?"

"The Rue de Berri."

"Yeah. Fuller used to call it the Rue de Cherry. That Paris! Ed, that town is like the World Series of Sex. You ever seen so many beautiful women in your life? And they all ride bicycles. It's a real pleasure to walk down that Champs Élysées and watch all those cute French cans riding up and down on a bicycle seat. Never saw one though that had a mole the size of a fifty cent piece."

"Never saw a fifty cent piece either."

"If I was Mr. Hershey or Mr. Nestles, I coulda come over there and set up a harem. I never had so much respect for a chocolate bar in my life."

"How did Fuller like Paris?"

"Fuller? Paris? The way Jimmy Walker liked New York. The way John McGraw liked the Polo Grounds. Excuse me a minute, kid. I'll be right back."

Sid lurched to his feet and disappeared into the bathroom. I finished my drink and mixed myself another. Sid came out and made himself another drink.

"When did the big bust-up come with you and Fuller, Sid? Before the Paris trip or after?"

"I told you. Before. Before. Before. After trying to shove him down their throat for a couple of years, they finally saw the goddamned light. They told me to go ahead. Go ahead, they told me, come up with a format for him and we'll put him on the network and try it for size. You know what happened. It was a hit all the way. A clean line drive over the pitcher's box. That's when they gave old Sid the heave-ho. They didn't throw Sid out right away. They gave me a piece of Fuller, a small piece, and they kept whittling it down. Nobody knew about it. Everybody thought I was collecting plenty. I figured if we pulled off this blood bank thing, it would make all the difference. They'd stop cutting away at my piece. I figured wrong."

"What makes you think they won't do the same thing to you this time, Sid?"

"The last time I was running scared. I was making a lot, but I was blowing it all in. If they tied me up in the courts, cut off my salary, kept me permanently unemployed, I stopped eating. Not any more, Coach. Sid's been socking it away. You were snotty a couple of minutes ago about my freeloading. You bet your tail I've been freeloading. I've been socking the dough away. I got enough now. Enough to start talking unless they invite me in and keep talking until I blow their whole goddamned network three miles high. They can't starve me out this time."

"You've just been waiting for something like this to happen, right?"

"Like what? Something like what?"

"Something like the accident."

"Sure. You lose a lot of ball games yanking your pitcher for a pinch hitter too early. I figure now is the time to send up the biggest goddamned hitter on my bench."

"What does that mean?"

"None of your goddamned business, kid. You just finish your little script, read it into an open mike and you and me are gonna be in the chips for the rest of our lives."

I walked back to the couch and sat down. Sid followed me.

"This trip to Europe wasn't a junket to me," said Sid. "It was the most important thing I ever did, in my whole life. In my whole life. The most important thing I ever did. You know that? How the hell would you know it?"

"Sure it was important, Sid. Why?"

"See? You don't know. You're such a wise guy, but you don't know all the answers. The most important goddamned thing in my life. They had me on the ropes. I'd been whopped in the solar plexus, but I figured I could ride with the punches. I figured one big thing like this, pulled off right, and I'd be back in the fight. What a jerk I was. Figuring that would make any difference to them."

"Carleton?"

"Sure. Carleton. You been to Paris, kid?"

"Yes, Sid. I've been to Paris."

"During the war?"

"During the war."

"You ever see anything like it? A man didn't get himself laid four times before breakfast wasn't trying. And believe me, kid . . . Fuller was trying. He told me, it was like he'd died and gone to heaven. That was where his whole French kick started. That's why his programs were always lousy with French singers and dancers."

I felt myself getting sick. The room was spinning and I was fighting to keep from throwing up. I got up and headed for the bathroom. I made it in time. I washed my face with cold water, put some water on the back of my head and let the faucet drip on my wrists for a couple of minutes. I sat down on the toilet seat until my head cleared. It was important that I straighten myself out. Sid Moore was talking his head off and these were things I had to know. I had to keep him drinking and talking and keep from passing out before he'd finished. I came out of the bathroom and mixed two more drinks. A very light one for myself. Mostly Schweppes. I resisted the temptation to cold-cock his drink. I didn't want him passing out on me. I had to keep him drunk but conscious.

"Feel better?" he asked.

"Yeah. I've been drinking too much in the interest of research."

"I hear you went to see Carol."

"Who told you that?"

"Who had to tell me? How was she?"

"As you so charmingly put it, none of your goddamned business."

"She studied under a master. Too bad you're going to dump her."

"You've got dump on the brain. Who said anything about dumping her?"

"I did, kid. Just now. She's out. So are the rest of the Family. You start clean. You get yourself a whole new crew. You want to pay Carol's rent for a while, that's between you and Carol. She's sung her last bad note on the air."

"You coach your team, I'll coach mine."

Now he had me talking that way.

"Kid, you got a lot of learning ahead of you. I call the signals and I give the signs. All of them. Carol and the rest of them are out. *Fini. Kaput.* Just because I said so."

"We'll talk about it later."

"The hell we will. There's nothing to talk about. Just be satisfied to be the best paid puppet in the history of the world, don't talk back and let me pull the strings and we'll get along fine. Understand?"

"Screw you, Sid."

I picked up the script and handed it to him.

"Let's get something straight. You can cut out that puppet crap right now. Here. I make you a present of a nice rough-draft script. Go ahead, you read it into an open mike on Friday night. Don't get the idea you can push me around and play God. I'm up to my ears in people who are playing God."

"Calm down, Ed."

"Who the hell do you think you are?"

"Take it easy, Skipper."

"Easy, my ass. Just calm down yourself, Sid, or you can take this script and the whole goddamned Amalgamated Broadcasting System firmly between the thumb and forefinger and shove."

"You got spirit, kid."

"I mean it, Sid. Cut it out."

"I'm sorry, kid. I'm not pushing you. Believe me, kid, I'm in your corner. I'm like your brother."

"I thought we were father and son."

"Let's have a drink and forget all about it."

So we drank some more.

I lit a cigarette and handed one to Sid. He lit it. We sat quietly for a couple of minutes.

"I got an idea, Ed," he said. "After this is all over, after you've taken over and Operation Harris is on the rails, maybe we could take off together and go to Paris. Do some remotes with a tape recorder. How about that? Would you like that?"

"Sure. I'd like that fine."

"And this time I wouldn't have to leave Paris by myself."

"You wouldn't have to what?"

"I wouldn't have to leave by myself. You didn't know that, did you? You didn't know I hightailed myself to the Siegfried Line alone, did you?"

If this were a movie this is where the musical score would have been sneaked in under the dialogue, ominously. I was suddenly cold sober and listening.

"What do you mean, Sid, alone?"

"You didn't know that, did you? You're so smart. Such a wise guy. You liked those tapes, didn't you? They were heartbreaking, weren't they? You could smell the sweat and the blood, couldn't you? And wasn't the quality good for stuff done on a wire recorder in the field? Bull . . . my friend. They were as phony as a nine dollar bill. Fuller never left Paris."

I didn't say a word.

"He was loaded and shacked up from the minute we stepped off the plane. I let it go for a couple of days. What the hell, I was having a ball myself, but when the time came for us to leave for the front with the blood, he told me to go take a flying screw at the moon. He wasn't leaving. I did everything but hit him over the head with the bottle of plasma. And I kept stringing the Army along. Along and along. Mr. Fuller is sick. Mr. Fuller will be ready to leave in a couple of days. For a week I kept this up. And then the dirty son of a bitch disappeared on me. He just didn't show up at the hotel for two days."

"A spot," I said.

"What would you do?" he asked.

"The same thing you did."

"Sure. And what did I do, wise guy?"

"You went up to the Siegfried Line yourself."

"And then what?"

"All right, Sid, what did you do?"

"Just like you said, I went up to the Siegfried Line myself. I gave the Army a snow job. Sure. A snow job, but there was one PRO kid who didn't fool worth a damn. He knew what was going on, so I told him the truth. He promised to make some inquiries . . . discreet inquiries, he called them . . . and find Fuller for me."

"Did they know about this in New York?"

"Are you crazy? Of course they didn't know about it in New York."

"So you went up to the Siegfried. Then what?"

"I had the wire recorder with me. I figured I'd get started and this PRO kid I told you about was going to find Fuller and send him on up. I figured I'd do some of the recordings and then, when Fuller showed up, we'd knock the blood bit off and get back. Fuller never showed up."

"So you recorded that piece in the Battalion Aid Station? It was a great piece."

"Yeah. It was great. I remember doing it. It was just outside a town called Wattweiller, on the other side of the Siegfried Line. It was a funny feeling going through those concrete dragon's teeth they put up to stop the tanks. It was like going through the gateway to hell. This Aid Station was set up in an old barn. One side of it had been knocked out by an artillery shell and the battle was going on just over the hill. We could hear the machine guns firing and once in a while a German shell would come whistling over. Scared the bejesus out of me. All I could think of was Fuller shacked up back in Paris. I figured I was going to get my tail shot off while he was goofing off. Anyway, I set up my machine in this Aid Station. It was just like you heard it. I recorded about twenty minutes of it. They were amputating a kid's leg. He was all coked up with morphine or something and he was talking in a kind of monotone. The operating table was a stretcher put on top of a table with a G.I blanket on it. There was a headlight, a headlight off a jeep, suspended over the table and attached to the battery of a jeep parked outside the barn."

"Did they really use the blood you brought with you?"

"Sure. The Medic told me it saved the kid's life."

"How long did you stay around?"

"Not long. I'm no hero, Skipper. I hauled ass out of there and got back to the press headquarters by jeep."

I kicked my shoes off and put my feet up. Sid had his shoes off and his feet on the coffee table. I felt lousy.

Sid stopped to put out a cigarette.

"Why don't you make a phone call and get us a couple of girls up here?"

"Maybe later. Not now. When did you find Fuller again?"

"When? What?"

"You went back to the press headquarters by jeep after you got the recording. Then what?"

"You're a curious little bastard, aren't you?"

"Sure. What happened at the press headquarters?"

"I had great recordings. I thought so. But when I played them back on the machine there, I had nothing. The machine hadn't been recording. I had nothing. Not a goddamned thing. All that great stuff I'd recorded in that barn up in Wattweiller was gone. I didn't have a stinking thing."

"But I heard them, Sid. They were great."

"Relax, kid. Take it easy. Let me tell it my way."

He took another pull at his drink. He lit a cigarette and his hand sent a shower of sparks all over the couch. We slapped at the cushions putting the sparks out.

"Clumsy," he said and mashed the cigarette out on the coffee table. He got up.

"I'm gonna be sick," he said and stumbled across the room into the bathroom. He was. He came back a minute or two later.

"I put some coffee on," he said.

"Fine. Come on, Sid, what happened?"

"How the hell do you stay so sober? You've been matching me drink for drink and you're sober. Goddamned sober. Too goddamned sober. You've been pumping me. What the hell business is it of yours what happened in Paris? You go to hell, Ed Harris. You go to hell. I'm not going to tell you another goddamned thing."

"You don't have to, Sid. I can take it from here. Let me tell you something first. I'm so fed up to my teeth with that dirty son of a bitch Fuller, I want to puke. I've been doing a mental coin-flipping bit. You don't know what it's like to get handed all his filth in a couple of days. You've lived with him for years. You got the lousiness spread out over a lot of time. I didn't. I got it all at once. I'll tell you something, Sid."

"Don't get so serious."

"Why not? This is a serious time of my life for me. What happens in the next couple of days is going to change everything. And I've been flipping a coin in my head. Heads I go through with it, tails I walk out. Walk out on the whole stinking deal."

"Now wait a minute. Wait just a minute. You're not walking out. Herb Fuller is dead. What difference does it make to you whether he was a little gentleman or the bastard he was? He's dead. Good and dead. What are you afraid of, kid?"

There was that word again.

"Afraid? Who's afraid? What the hell am I afraid of? You shouldn't have told me about the trip, Sid. You don't know what those tapes meant to me. For once I heard this guy being a human being. But he wasn't. He was still being Herb Fuller. The whole thing was another phony. Another con game."

"What kind of a business do you think you're in? You're a con man. We all are. We're pushing cigarettes and beer, soap and furniture polish instead of gold bricks or the Brooklyn Bridge, but we're all con men. So we got an electronic gadget that amplifies our voice, but we're still con men. And Fuller was the king of them all."

"And the King is dead."

"The King is dead."

I lit a cigarette. "All right," I said. "All right. You faked the tapes. Where?"

"In Paris. After I got back. After they found Fuller. It wasn't hard. I was worried at first about the Aid Station tapes. I couldn't go back and hire a couple of AFRA actors. The word would have gotten around. Then I had a great idea. The Army ran a whole radio network in Europe during the war. I sat down and batted out a script on the Aid Station. Just like it was and then I went over to the radio station and told them I needed some G.I. actors to record a dramatic show. I forgot to tell you, I wrote a whole script. This was just one scene in it. I told them it was a recruiting drive show that we were putting on and that we were recording shows all over Europe with G.I. casts for a special series. They went for it. I threw the rest of the script out and just kept that one part. I figured they wouldn't remember that one hunk if they did it that way. And besides, they wouldn't hear it when it went on the air back in the States. I was taking a chance, but not much. And then later I recorded Fuller's introduction and his finish spot and put it all together. You coulda fooled anybody with it. When I got finished blending and re-recording even Fuller himself would have thought he'd been there. There ain't no flies on

Sid Moore. There may be flies on some of you guys but there ain't no flies on me."

"You fooled me, Sid. Ten years later you fooled me."

"There may be flies on some of you guys but there ain't no flies on me."

"And this was your hold over Carleton and the network? You figured if you told your story you'd have blown the Fuller legend sky high? You think you can still do it?"

"What the hell," said Sid. "You know this much, you might as well know the rest of it. I still hadn't found Fuller when I recorded that piece at the radio station. Two days after that, this PRO kid I was telling you about came to my hotel about midnight. He'd found Fuller."

"Where?"

"In the hoosegow. In the can. In short, in jail. The French police were holding him."

"What had he done?"

"Like I figured, he'd been shacked up with a dame. The only thing wrong was the kid was fifteen. She'd run away from home, from one of those towns in the provinces. Came to Paris to be a model or an actress or something. Fuller picked her up in one of those cellar bars over on the Left Bank. They had a room out near the University. Thing they didn't know was the place they were living was a kind of storehouse for the black market operators. The police raided the place and pulled everybody in, including Fuller and the kid. As soon as they got to the police station the kid started crying and blew the whole bit. She told them her name, they notified her family and when Papa and Mama showed up they started yelling 'Rape!' Fuller was in a hell of a jam. I pulled him out of it. Old Fireman Sid Moore pulled the game out of the fire."

"How, Sid?"

"With a checkbook. With a checkbook and just about

every dime I had in the world. I hustled him out of there and got on the first plane out of Europe. All the way over the ocean, I kept thinking, 'Now I got them where the hair is short.' 'Now they can't brush me off.' Fuller did everything but lick my hand. I was his old buddy again and he was never going to forget what I did for him. When we got back to New York, I had him record his end of the tapes and then I went to see Carleton."

"And got thrown out on your ear."

"Yeah. On my ear."

"And you took it?"

"I took it. They gave me back the dough I'd spent to get him out of the jam. Period. That's all, brother. Bye-bye, baby. Wave bye-bye, Sid. I was running scared. I chickened."

"And what makes you think you won't be running scared now? If they weren't afraid of you then, what makes you think they'll scare now?"

"It had to be then or now. Then it was right at the beginning of the build-up. I could have killed the build-up. I didn't. Now Fuller is news again. Big news. The papers will print anything about him they can get their hands on. A story like mine would hit most of the front pages. It could blow the legend wide open and maybe even put Amalgamated out of business."

"Maybe. Maybe not."

"Don't you see it, kid? With all this build-up for you, they got Fuller sounding like he was Jesus Christ. You ride in on his obituary notices. If all of a sudden something happens that shows him up to be a Class A bastard, the build-up doesn't work. His name becomes a dirty word. Sponsors pull out of the Ed Harris show because they've built you into the heir to the throne. I could hurt them, Eddie boy. Hurt them bad. They won't dump Sid this time. This time I'm not scared of them. I got some dough stashed away. I can sit out their goddamn black list."

"You could hurt me, too, Sid."

"You're an innocent bystander. You don't count. You're on the gravy train because I put you there. If I have to yank you off, I have to yank you off."

"That great big zero, Ed Harris. Ed Harris, boy puppet. What makes you think I won't turn into just as big a bastard as Herb Fuller?"

"You will, kid. Believe me. Six months from now you'll be just like he was. You won't be able to help yourself. But this time I'll be prepared for it."

"Suppose I walk out right now?"

"Walk. Go ahead. There's the door. Who the hell are you? A snotty kid who never threw a strike in his life being given a chance to pitch the opening game of the World Series. The woods are full of snotty kids. I got a whole station full of them. You just got picked because you were handy. You don't think that half-ass interview program with your wise-guy play reviews made everybody suddenly realize you were the Great Man, do you?"

"You put it so charmingly. You fat little chiseler, you put it so charmingly."

"You'll do fine, kiddo. You got a nice voice. Given the kind of build-up you're going to get, you'll do fine. Don't boot a million dollars a year away, kiddo, just because you don't like the way the air smells once in a while."

"What you're saying is, if I don't do it, somebody else will. If I'm not the Great Man, somebody else will be. Right?"

"Right. Right. Right as rain. Right. Right, right, right. You got the message?"

"I got the message."

"Now, you want to walk?"

Sid got up and opened the door.

"All you do is follow the banister down to the street floor and head east."

"Sit down, Sid," I said. "Sit down."

Sid sat down.

He punched me playfully on the arm.

"You're a good kid. Like a son to me. That's what you are, Ed. Like a son to me."

"Yeah," I said. "Yeah. Like a son."

I picked up my shoes and put my feet into them.

I had a little trouble tying the laces.

"Where you going, kid?"

"Out. . . . Outside. I'm going to follow the banister. Don't worry, Sid. Don't worry. I'll finish your script and I'll read it into the microphone. Don't worry."

"Who's worrying?"

"Me," I said. "Me. I'm worrying. I'm like you, I'm running scared right now. Scared silly. Scared because I haven't got the guts to take the kind of a walk you suggested. Scared because I didn't think money was that important to me. You're right, you know."

"About what?"

"About my being like him in six months. Make it three. I know that. Every lousy thing he did was something that I could do. I know that. Maybe everybody could. Maybe there's some of that in everybody, but most people don't get a chance to find out. Most people don't get to be king where they can do any goddamned thing they want to do. I'm going to and in three months I'll be just like him. And I haven't guts enough to walk out of here and go back to being Ed Harris."

"We'll make a lot of money for each other, Coach."

"What time is it?"

"You got a watch on, look at it."

I looked at my watch. It was a quarter after one.

"I told you, kid, you can spend the night here."

"You know what I want right now, Sid?"

"A drink?"

"A woman."

"I told you, kid. I'll call up and get us a couple of girls."

"On the cuff? On the expense account?"

"Any kind you want. Short, tall, fat, thin, blond, brunette, redhead . . . "

"Any fifteen-year-old French girls, Sid?"

"Relax, Ed." He put his hand on my arm.

I brushed it off and got to my feet.

"Thanks, Sid. Thanks for a wonderful and instructive evening."

I stood up. I felt dizzy.

"Just let me use your phone for a minute."

"On the end table," Sid said.

I picked up the phone and dialed a number.

It rang five or six times. Finally the receiver was lifted off the hook at the other end.

The voice at the other end sounded sleepy.

"This is Ed," I said. "I'll be over in about fifteen minutes. Fifteen minutes, got it?"

I hung up.

Sid was smiling.

"Say hello to your French girl for me," he said.

I got out of Sid's and hailed a cab on the corner. I sat back on the seat. Once I almost leaned forward and told the cab driver to take me home instead. Almost. I started to laugh to myself and the hackie looked back at me. "Just happy," I said. "Just happy."

I gave the cab driver a fifty-cent tip and when I rang the bell the buzzer sounded immediately letting me in. Carol was waiting for me. Waiting for me.

THURSDAY

When I woke up, I had a bad couple of minutes trying to figure out where I was. I opened my eyes tentatively and looked around the room without raising my head off the pillow. Over by the door I saw my clothes in a heap on the floor. The ash tray on the bedside table was choked with cigarette butts. There were two half-filled glasses beside my wrist watch. I slid my hand out from under the covers. The movement disturbed Carol in the bed beside me and she turned over and flung her hand out. It fell across my stomach. I slid myself slowly out from underneath it and put my feet on the floor. My head was spinning and I felt lousy. All I wanted to do was get out of there without waking her up. I couldn't stand looking at her or talking to her now. I picked up the watch on the bedside table and looked at it. It was twenty after seven. I looked around for a cigarette. I walked across the room and went through my pockets. No cigarettes. I opened the door of the bedside table. No luck. I took one of the bigger butts out of the ash tray and lit it. The first drag gagged me and started me coughing. Carol turned over again and brushed her hand through her hair. I got up again and walked through the bedroom into the bathroom. I put some cold water on my face and in my hair. I looked at myself in the mirror over the sink. God. My eyeballs looked as if they were swimming in a sea of tomato juice. I gargled with mouthwash and combed my hair. I opened the medicine cabinet and reached for a shaving brush and a razor. My hand stopped halfway.

A shaving brush and a razor.

His.

I left them there and went back into the bedroom and climbed into my clothes.

I tiptoed out of the apartment and closed the door carefully behind me. Outside on the street, I walked out to the gutter and waited for a cruising cab. It was drizzling and the wet rain blowing in my face felt good. There was no sign of a taxi, so I walked west to the corner and got one almost immediately. I climbed in and gave my address and sat back in the seat with my eyes closed. I rested my head against the cold window glass.

When we pulled up in front of my place, I handed the driver a dollar bill without looking at the meter.

"Enough?" I asked.

"Plenty. Thank you."

"Merry Christmas," I said.

I walked up the stairs, holding onto the banister. Outside my door, I leaned over and picked up the morning paper. I had trouble finding my key but finally opened the door and walked in. I'd left all the windows closed and the room smelled damp and musty. I flung open the window and threw myself on the bed. I must have fallen asleep because the next thing I remember was looking at my watch. It was five to nine. I had to straighten myself out. I was due in Carleton's office for a meeting at ten. I stripped again and climbed into the shower. I shaved, brushed my teeth, washed my mouth out again and got dressed. I went out to the kitchen and made some coffee. I lit a cigarette and felt almost alive.

Almost.

Not quite.

But almost.

I sat down at the table and propped up the paper with the sugar bowl. I drank my coffee and shuffled through the paper. There was a picture of me on the theater page. The caption said: "Ed Harris, who will narrate the Amalgamated Broadcasting System's hour-long Memorial Program to Herb Fuller. The tribute to the late radio personality will be heard over the full Amalgamated Radio Network tomorrow night at 10 P.M. E.S.T."

A story in the right-hand column was headed: "Amalgamated Plans Hour-Long TV Memorial Program for Fuller."

I took another swallow of coffee and read the story.

"Philip Carleton, President of the Amalgamated Broadcasting System, announced today that an hour-long TV Memorial Program, similar to the one scheduled for Friday night at 10 P.M. on the radio network, is in the planning stage. The radio program, which will be narrated by Ed Harris, will include taped excerpts from Fuller broadcasts of the past and Mr. Carleton said that the Television Memorial would undoubtedly include kinescopes of Fuller television broadcasts. No specific date has been set for the TV show as yet and Mr. Carleton said that the narrator had not, as yet, been decided on. According to Radio Row gossip, Ed Harris, who runs a local radio program in New York called 'Metropolitan Memo,' was scheduled to replace Herb Fuller on his radio and TV shows. Mr. Carleton denied that any decision on Fuller replacement had been made. 'Mr. Harris,' he said, 'has been engaged to write, produce and narrate the Radio Memorial Program. No decision has been made on Fuller's successor. No decision has been made on the narrator of the TV Memorial Program.' "

What the hell did that mean?

Was I being quietly eased out?

Was I being kissed off with a one-shot hour radio show?

I'd know in less than an hour. Maybe that explained the sudden summons by Carleton to a meeting. Maybe I was about to be shown the door and told to follow the banister.

I put the cup and saucer in the sink, took two aspirins, took my raincoat out of the closet and left the apartment. Outside, I debated walking or taking a cab. I decided I needed the air, so I headed west. The rain in my face felt good. I went through the usual dialogue with Peter, the doorman, with the starter and John, the elevator operator, and got off at my floor. The receptionist was in her usual place.

"Good morning, Mr. Harris," she said.

"You look fine."

"Thank you."

She smiled at me.

"You've made my day for me," I said.

She went back to stuffing program schedules into envelopes.

A mole the size of a half dollar.

"Has Mr. Moore come in yet?" I asked.

"A half hour ago."

"How did he look?"

"Like he'd had a big night."

"I hear he did."

I walked through the door and headed for my office. Lillian was bent over her typewriter.

"Good morning, Sexy," I said.

It was nice and reassuring to fall back into a routine.

I walked past and all she could manage in return was a leer and a wink.

Ginny was sitting at my desk, opening mail.

"Anything interesting?"

"Did you see the paper this morning?"

"Yeah."

"What does it mean? I thought you had the job sewed up."

"So did I."

"Mr. Carleton's secretary called to remind you of the meeting in his office this morning."

"Did she say who was going to be there?"

"No. She just said to remind you that Mr. Carleton was expecting you in his office at ten."

"Do I have time for a cup of coffee?"

"You have twenty minutes. I'll go down and get it for you."

"Thanks, kid, I need it."

"Hangover?"

"Right. Hangest goddamned over you've ever seen."

"Bromo as usual?"

"As usual. And get Sid Moore for me, will you? I have to find out in a sneaky sort of way if he's going to be at the Carleton meeting."

Ginny went out to her desk and a minute later buzzed me to say that Sid Moore was on the phone. I picked up the receiver, pressed down the button and said, "Good morning, Sid."

"Good morning, champ," he said.

Who had I ever licked?

"How do you feel this morning, Sid?"

"Like the last of the fifteenth with the bases loaded."

"Is that good or bad?"

"Bad. Bases loaded against me. How did you make out last night?"

"Bases loaded with me. Anything I should know this morning?"

"You know too much you shouldn't know right now. What are your plans for the day?"

"Editing. Script. From here on it's just work pulling the script together."

"It looks great, kid. Maybe I didn't tell you that firmly enough last night, kid. The script looks great."

"Yeah. Great. Did you see the paper this morning?"

"I saw it."

"And?"

"And what?"

"What does it mean?"

"Carleton's just playing it close to his chest."

"Or has had a second thought."

"Don't let it worry you."

"Why should I let it worry me? Don't I work for this best of all possible networks in this best of all possible worlds?"

"Thataboy."

"Sid, you sure it's the size of a half a dollar?"

"What?"

"You don't retain well, do you? The mole."

"Oh sure, kid. At least the size of a half dollar. If seeing is believing, I can fix up a demonstration for you. What are you doing for lunch?"

"Eating."

"Where?"

"Probably at my desk. The script is still rough as hell. I don't think I'm going to have much time for eating until tomorrow night at eleven."

"I thought maybe you'd join me and Gordon at the Pig Pen."

"I'll try. What time?"

"One-ish."

"O.K., Sid. Maybe I can make it. I'll try."

"See you, Coach. If you need any relief hurling, let me know."

"Right. So long, Sid."

I hung up. Sid didn't know anything about the meeting with Carleton.

I looked through the mail Ginny had been opening when I walked in.

A bill from Saks for two suits and three button-down shirts.

Tickets for the opening of a new musical Friday night. I put them on the corner of the desk to remind me to pass them along to Ginny. I wouldn't be seeing any new musical this particular Friday.

Press releases from the Museum of Modern Art, M-G-M, Paramount and the Theatre Guild.

Two fan letters.

Ginny walked in with my breakfast in a brown paper bag. She put it on the desk and I handed her a half dollar. I started to grin. From now on I'd never be able to look a half dollar in the eye. She gave me a dime in change, took the top off the cardboard container and put in the sugar.

"The ET came in from Beaseley."

"A sixteen-incher?"

"Yes. It's pretty dusty. I sent it up to Engineering. They're going to clean the grooves out with some carbon tet and then they're going to dub it onto tape for you."

"Did you listen to it?"

"The beginning of it. The quality is fine. A little gritty, but the carbon tet will take that out."

"Good. You're a dear, sweet animal."

"I know. You have ten minutes to finish your breakfast and get up to Carleton's office."

"Right."

I gulped down the coffee and followed it with the Bromo. I belched. Loud and clear.

"You were expecting maybe chimes?" I said.

"By the way," I added, "Here are a couple of tickets to the opening tomorrow night. Can you use them?"

"If I can't, I can sell them."

"That's my girl. Wish me luck."

"Luck," she said.

I took the elevator up to the executive floor. The receptionist was expecting me and ushered me right into Carleton's office. Well, not quite his office. His secretary's office. She was expecting me and ushered me into Carleton's office. Really Carleton's office this time. He was busy talking on the phone in a low monotone, so I looked around.

Class.

Real class.

The walls were hung with tan drapes. There were what I suppose you would call non-objective pictures hung on the wall and lit by small spotlights screwed into the brown-colored ceiling. The furniture was blond and modern. Real modern, not on-the-cuff-fairy-decorator modern like Sid's. Carleton was sitting in a heavy brown overstuffed chair next to a wall cabinet that contained a phone and a dictaphone machine. No desk. I sat in a steel and canvas contraption that looked like half an umbrella turned upside down. Beside it was a huge ash tray on a stand that looked like a ruptured penguin. I lit a cigarette and wondered what was going to happen now.

Carleton finished his phone call and got up and came over to me, extending his hand.

"Don't get up, Ed," he said.

I hadn't made a move.

"It's good to see you. I know how busy you must be. I appreciate your taking time out to see me."

This was the first time I'd heard him speak more than a couple of words and I found myself fascinated by his voice.

It had a kind of purring quality. It was a kind of furry monotone. It also had a kind of force that kept you leaning forward listening to it carefully.

"Are you expecting anyone else?"

I purposely didn't use his name. I wasn't quite sure yet what kind of a basis we were on. Was he Mr. Carleton to me? Or Phil? Or Philip? Or Coach? Or Skipper? Or what?

"No, Ed. No one else. I thought it was about time we got together. We really don't know each other at all, do we?"

"No, I suppose we don't."

"I want to rectify that. That's why I asked you here this morning, Ed. Do you smoke cigars?"

"Not usually, but I can learn."

I took a cigar out of the box he offered to me. It was a black lacquer box with a gray and gold painting of the Amalgamated call letters on the top. I bit the end off the cigar and lit it.

"I suppose you saw the piece in the paper this morning, Ed?"

"I saw it."

"I suppose you wondered about it?"

"Yes, I wondered about it."

"You thought we had decided on you as the Fuller replacement at the last meeting. You thought it was definite. You had the job. Isn't that what you thought?"

"That's what I thought."

"You were right."

"I was?"

"You are. You do have the job. Both jobs. Radio and TV. As of this moment you and I are the only ones who know that. As far as the rest of the world is concerned, nothing has been decided yet. The only assignment definitely made is the memorial show tomorrow night."

"You'll forgive me, Mr. Carleton," I said, "but you've succeeded in confusing me. Can we talk plainly? Can we start at the beginning?"

"Certainly. What I'm about to tell you is in confidence. It's for your information exclusively. If you try to quote me on it or pass it along to anyone else, I'll deny it completely. Do you understand that?"

"Yes. I understand that. But that's about all I do understand."

"Just be patient, Ed. In the next half hour you'll understand a lot of things. For instance, did you know that we have had our eye on you for quite a while? Long before Fuller piled into the side of that hill?"

"No. I didn't think anything that was on a local station had any existence up here in the rarified atmosphere of the network."

"Did you know that we were seriously considering breaking our contract with Fuller before his death removed that necessity?"

"No."

"And did you know that we were considering moving you into his place then?"

"I won't interrupt you with any more no's, Mr. Carleton. You can just assume I didn't know any of the things you're about to tell me."

"That piece in the paper this morning was the opening gun in a campaign that I will try to make plain to you in the next couple of minutes. Starting next Monday afternoon you will read some other stories. One columnist will have a big scoop to the effect that Amalgamated has decided to dump Ed Harris. The story will be that a dark horse from the Pacific Coast is about to be brought east as Fuller's replacement and that you will be let out. We will neither confirm nor deny this story except to reiterate that no arrangements had been made with you beyond Friday night's broadcast."

"All right. I have that."

"Right now the rumors are being circulated around the agencies that you are on your way out. Not only are you not the heir apparent to the Fuller throne, but after tomorrow night you won't even have a local show. You're finished. You can take my word for it, Ed, when we want to circulate a rumor, we can do a bang-up job of it. And we want to circulate this one. By Monday night you won't be able to buy a morning newspaper on credit."

"Thank you, Mr. Carleton. You've made my day."

"There will be only two people in the world who will know that the rumors and the column items are phonies. You and me."

"Stay healthy, Mr. Carleton. I wouldn't want to be the only one who knows it."

"Perhaps you're asking yourself why. Are you?"

"No. I'm asking you, Mr. Carleton, Why?"

"I think I can tell you why in two words. Sid Moore."

"Oh," I said. There was a big "Oh" in my stomach too that slowly dissolved. "Oh."

"Precisely," said Carleton. "Sid Moore. You signed a contract with him, didn't you?"

"Yes. I signed a contract with him."

"We have had some trouble with Mr. Moore in the past in the matter of contracts. In the past, however, we have been able to convince Mr. Moore that it was to his advantage to tear up contracts when they conflicted with what we regard as the general good. It might be a little more difficult to convince him of it this time. In short, Ed, he sees in you a chance to recoup his fortune."

"I know the details of the last contract dispute, Mr. Carleton."

"All the details?"

"All the details."

"I see. You're a very astute young man. In that case, I think the rest should be very plain to you."

"I'm afraid you're assuming a little too much intelligence on my part, Mr. Carleton. Suppose you spell it out for me."

"All right. Sid Moore has a contract with you. He has a certain hold on us. He can threaten us and by so doing force us to include him in on any deal we make with you. In short, he becomes something like a manager to you and in the process earns himself a percentage of your earnings, which incidentally will be considerably more than you even dream they will be now. He has a good case. He recognizes the fact that all our publicity on you has attempted to set forth certain personal relationships between you and Herb Fuller. We know those relationships didn't exist. The public does not, and if Sid Moore succeeds in destroying some of the Fuller legend, he destroys you in the process. He is willing to play that way . . . all or nothing. He is banking on the fact that we have chosen you to be Fuller's successor and banking on the fact that we will not permit him to destroy Fuller and you. Do you follow me this far?"

"This far, yes."

"Fine. Now we turn the screw a little. We decide that you are not network caliber. You are a fine young man and capable of being a big success on a local level but you do not have the network potential we need, so we decide to dispense with your services. We start with column items. Follow that immediately with agency rumors and blind items in the trade papers. We announce that we have made no commitment with you beyond the radio memorial show. How does this sit with Mr. Moore?"

"It sits on his small intestine and presses."

"Presses hard, Ed. He has a contract, but the contract isn't worth anything to him unless we buy you, and we have looked over the merchandise and decided we don't want it. What can Sid do? Shoot his mouth off? Not now, because he has nothing to gain by doing that now. He can't threaten to destroy you in the process because we have already eliminated you with our complete disinterest in your future. Now this is where you come into the picture."

"I thought you'd be getting around to me."

"Sid Moore is sitting with a worthless contract. You are hopping mad. He told you you'd be sitting pretty and you've been double-crossed. You've been left waiting at the church."

"Out trying to stretch a single into a double."

"I see you've acquired some of Mr. Moore's colorful patterns of speech. You are mad, Ed. Very mad. Meanwhile we have planted other items, other rumors about possible successors to Fuller. Sid Moore doesn't know what has hit him. You demand your contract back. You tell him he couldn't manage . . ."

"A girl's softball team?"

"Yes. A girl's softball team. You tell him that you still have faith in yourself and then you offer to buy the contract from him."

"He knows I haven't got a dime in the bank."

"We will pay you five thousand dollars for the memorial show. You offer that to him for your contract. I think he will sell it back to you."

"Just so it wouldn't be a total loss?"

"Mr. Moore has a native shrewdness. As far as he's concerned, you're a washed-up nobody and five thousand dollars is five thousand dollars. The day you buy that contract back you walk into this office and sign another one, a contract to take over the Fuller radio and TV shows. Everything is simple if you approach it with the proper orientation."

"And what makes you think Sid Moore will sit still and

take it? What makes you think he won't start talking his head off then?"

"Mr. Moore has an instinct for self-survival. As long as you were the white-haired boy and he held your contract in his pocket, he was capable of anything, even blowing the whistle on us. But now, remember, he has nothing. He has no contract with you. He has nothing to gain by going through with his threat. He has everything to lose with no gain or possible gain to counterbalance it. He knows for a certainty that he will lose his job and find it impossible to get another one. He's leading from weakness rather than from strength and we will be willing to make some concessions. We are not completely heartless. We can afford to show mercy in victory."

"What kind of mercy?"

"We can allow Mr. Moore to keep his job on the local level, just as we did in the past. We can even promise him a sizable increase in salary. You will find, I think, that Mr. Moore is a realist."

"Now all I have to do is buy back that contract?"

"Oh, not right away, Ed. All you have to do is prepare yourself for the discouraging things you'll be reading about yourself in the newspapers and be satisfied to realize that you and I both know they don't mean a thing. Then, by—say, the end of next week, you have to have a scene with Sid and buy back that contract. Once you've taken the loaded gun out of his pocket, you'll find he isn't such a tough hombre after all. Trust me that he can be handled without too much difficulty."

"And suppose I can't buy back the contract?"

"Of course you'll be able to do it."

"And suppose I can't?"

"In that case, I'm afraid only you will know that the

stories in the papers aren't true. I'm afraid we'd have to be forced into dumping you and finding somebody else to take over the Fuller programs."

"If you'll pardon me for picking up your figure of speech, Mr. Carleton, you're the one with the loaded gun in your pocket and it's pointed straight at my head."

"I suppose it does seem that way to you."

"You're not afraid of my shooting my mouth off, are you? I know everything that Sid Moore knows."

"Ed, you know that nobody pays any attention to what the rejected suitor of the bride has to say at the wedding. And believe me, son, by next week you will be the most rejected suitor in history."

"You're not going to reject me so much that it will be impossible to salvage me, are you?"

"Build-ups are always effective, if we want them to be. We haven't said anything about not wanting you. We have neither denied nor confirmed anything that's been spread around columns and small talk. When we get around to making you the white-haired boy again, we do it with the biggest exploitation budget in Amalgamated history. We slap you on every billboard and car card in the country. We slap your voice on every station break all day and all night. We put your mug on the front of every fan magazine on the stands. We throw cocktail parties for you every hour on the hour. We guest-star you on every radio and TV show in the Amalgamated stable. We sell you the way Procter and Gamble sells soap. That we can do, believe me."

"Mr. Carleton, may I ask a silly question?"

"You may ask any question you want to."

"Why me? What's the special talent I have that you need? You say you were thinking of me even before Fuller was killed. Why?"

"I didn't intend going into such great detail with you, Ed, but since you ask, I'll tell you. As you may or may not know, we had a lot of trouble with Fuller. He had delusions of grandeur. The hold he had on his audience went to his head. He didn't realize how much of that hold was a direct result of the exposure we gave him. How long would his hold last, if we just turned off his microphone and covered up his television cameras?"

"And how long would Amalgamated have stayed in business?"

"There you have put your finger on the crux of the problem. We had created Fuller out of whole cloth and suddenly the tail was wagging the dog. It was an interesting problem. Was Fuller, as he believed so firmly, bigger than the Amalgamated Broadcasting System? Could he bankrupt us by moving over to CBS or NBC? Or could we survive his loss? Could we take anybody and, by creating a character, hiring the best writers and directors, putting him on a great many programs, build him up eventually into as big a drawing card as Fuller? It was an interesting question and one we were about to attempt to answer when an auto accident made it unnecessary."

"And at the time when you were considering that question, you thought of me?"

"You and several others."

"Your thesis, Mr. Carleton, was that you could take almost anybody and with all the machinery of radio and television build him into a star. You could dump writers, directors, money for exploitation and time for exposure into a pot, stir it around and come up with a success. You must have a great contempt for performers, Mr. Carleton."

"No, I don't think that's true. I have a great respect for the mass production mind of the American Public. They have likes and dislikes. We can find out what they are by making surveys. They are suckers for certain subjects, certain material. We can find that out, too."

"And you can create something that you know by pretesting, by surveys, by impartial laboratories will be a big success. You have a great contempt for your audience, don't you, Mr. Carleton?"

"Don't you?"

"No, I don't. Maybe I'm naive, but I have a certain respect for my audience."

"Your audience, may I remind you, is a local audience in New York. And what is your audience, Ed? It's the bartender in Shor's who tells you he liked that story you did the other night. Or the people you run into at cocktail parties. Or the press agents who rupture themselves being nice to you because they want to get their clients' names on the air. You wouldn't know an audience if you fell over it. You're playing to yourself. You want to know what your audience is like, go down to one of the playhouses some afternoon when a quiz show is breaking. Look at the faces of the fat old ladies with the shopping bags as they come out. That's your audience. Don't kid yourself that they're anything else. The intelligentsia has long since left us. They're listening to hi-fi phonographs or WQXR. And good riddance to them, too. They don't buy detergents or soap or cigarettes just because we ask them to. The sooner you discover that, the better off you'll be.

"You have an infinite capacity for contempt, Mr. Carleton."

"I have an infinite capacity for facing up to the truth. I don't try to convince myself that I'm slaying dragons when all I'm doing is running an electronic pitch game. You have an educational process ahead of you, Ed."

"What kind?"

"Come to the office with that contract in your hand and you'll find out."

"All right, so I come to you with the contract and my hat in my hand. What kind of a show will I be doing?"

"I don't know yet. I do know this, it will be whatever the best brains around me tell me is sure-fire at that particular moment. I can tell you this, the first thing you'll have to do is lose Ed Harris."

"I thought Ed Harris was important. I thought you were considering him long before the Fuller accident. I thought he was a commodity you wanted."

"Certainly. That's true, in a small, specialized sense. Except for one thing. When we get through with you, you won't recognize the new Ed Harris. We will create a character that you will play, that we will label Ed Harris. I don't know yet what it will be. I know only that it will be successful because every cent and every craftsman in this organization will see to it that it is successful."

"You'll pardon my puritanical streak, Mr. Carleton, but isn't that a little dishonest?"

"Dishonest? Is it dishonest when Judith Anderson comes out of the stage door and isn't arrested for killing her children? Is it dishonest that she can be Medea on a stage for three hours and revert to being Judith Anderson when the curtain goes down? Is that dishonest?"

"That's different."

My head was splitting.

"Why is it different? Why do we have to turn up with the Holy Grail every hour on the hour? We're getting awfully philosophical, aren't we?"

"Yes, aren't we?"

I put my hand to my head. Carleton noticed it.

"You have a headache, Ed?"

"A terrible headache."

"I'm sorry." He pressed a buzzer on the cabinet and talked into an intercom in the wall. "Miss Carlisle, would you bring two aspirins and a glass of water, please?"

He turned back to me.

"You've been working pretty hard on this broadcast for tomorrow night, haven't you?"

"Pretty hard."

"Been seeing a lot of the Fuller people?"

"Some of them."

"You've found, I assume, that there are certain advantages to being the Great Man?"

"Did you call him that too?"

"The 'Great Man'? Everybody called him that. He liked it."

"Yes, I suppose he would."

"I never liked him much, Ed. Did you know that? On or off the air, I never liked him much. He was crude and loud and dirty. He was a dirty little boy who had suddenly gotten too big to spank. That was my fault."

"You won't make that mistake with me, will you, Mr. Carleton?"

"I won't have to, Ed. I think we understand each other."

The door opened and the secretary walked in with a glass of water. She carried two aspirins on a water carafe tray like they were crown jewels. I picked them up, put them on my tongue and washed them down with the water. I put the glass back on the tray and she exited.

"My secretary said you wanted to see the script."

"I realize you haven't finished it. I'd just like to see some roughs on it. Do you have it with you?"

"I forgot it. It's down in my office. I'll send it up by page when I get back."

"That will be fine. When do you think you'll be finished with it?"

"Sometime tonight or early tomorrow. I plan to stay until it's finished."

"Good. I wish you'd let me see the finished air copy when you have it. Don't get that look on your face, Ed. I'm not going to butcher it on you. I'd just like to look it over. Who knows, I might even be able to offer a usable suggestion or two."

"I'll send the roughs up to you right away. And I'll send you the finished copy when I have it."

"You feel better now?"

"The headache, you mean?"

"No. Just generally better. Now that you know which wheels are going which way and why."

"Yes. I feel better. I feel a little like I've just heard General Quarters ring on the ship. At least I'm not rolling in my bunk imagining that Kamikazes are heading straight for the deck. At least now I know I'm in for a battle, but I know where it's coming from, how and why."

"You were in the navy, weren't you?"

"Yeah. Four years."

"It must have been quite an experience. Those of us who were left back here in essential positions can never, I'm sure, really understand that particular segment of history. I can tell you it wasn't easy, being shut off from that experience."

"I knew a lot of guys, Mr. Carleton, would have settled for being shut off from that experience. Well—is there anything else I should know?"

"I think you know quite a lot now, don't you?"

I didn't answer and he continued.

"Yes. Quite a lot. Don't let the column items get you down next week. Don't let the sudden case of leprosy bother you too much."

"I won't."

"Good boy."

We shook hands and I left the office. I thanked the nice lady for the two aspirins and took my headache out of her impeccable office into the hallway. I pressed the down button and waited.

What the hell was I getting myself caught up in?

I couldn't figure the casting. I didn't know whether I was Judas Iscariot or Lochinvar. And how about Carleton? Was he leveling with me or was the dump going to be permanent? Who was double-crossing whom? Who was doing what, with what and to whom?

I felt lousy.

When I got down to my office, Ginny got up off the couch.

"Did you ask him about my raise?" she asked me.

"Funny thing. It slipped my mind."

"I can't trust you out of my sight, can I?"

"No jokes, Ginny. No fast patter. I feel lousy."

"Sorry."

"Now, don't get hurt."

"Who's hurt?"

"You are. Every time you give me that 'Sorry' bit, I know that your delicate soul has sprouted a brand new pair of bleeding ulcers. I just feel lousy and I'm not up to ad libbing funny."

"Why don't you conk off on the couch and grab some sleep? I have the tape rooms working on the new stuff that came in. They'll pipe them to Ediphone and you'll have transcripts this afternoon. I re-typed the script. I found the carbon in your top drawer and I made a nice clean copy for you. I corrected your lousy spelling too."

"Thanks, honey. You're really a very sweet girl."

"Get that. A very sweet girl. Who hit you on the head?"

"Mr. Philip Carleton hit me on the head. Mr. Philip Carleton, who looks like a lightweight but hits like Rocky Marciano."

"What happened?"

"Nothing. Will you send that nice clean copy of the script up to him by page boy?"

"Sure."

"I think I'll stretch out on the couch for a couple of hours. Wake me up around two, will you?"

"Sure. Oh, your French girl called."

"And?"

"She's hopping. Mad, I mean. She says you better call her by three o'clock or you're dead."

"Call her for me and tell her I'm not in the office. Tell her I'm in a meeting with Carleton and can't get to a phone. Tell her I love her *beaucoup* and any other clean French words you know."

"What other kind of French words do they teach at Julia Richman High School?"

"And keep Sid Moore away from here while I'm sleeping."

"Right."

"Now you're doing it."

"Doing what?"

"Turkey trot. God, I'm tired."

"You just stretch out and Momma will cover you up."

"Thanks, Momma."

I stretched out on the couch and Ginny put my topcoat over me. I wadded my raincoat up into a ball for a pillow and kicked my shoes off.

"Comfy?" Ginny asked.

I nodded my head.

"Good night, sweet prince," she said.

I closed my eyes and fell sound asleep.

I woke up with a start. I had that familiar falling sensation and it took me a minute or two to shake it off. I looked at my watch. It was a quarter after three. I got up and buzzed for Ginny. She came in.

"I thought you were going to wake me at two?"

"I came in at two, but you were sleeping so soundly that I thought I'd let you sleep a little longer."

"Anything happen?"

"Nothing much. Sid Moore called and wanted to know why you hadn't joined him for lunch. I told him you were busy on the script and weren't going out for lunch."

"Anything else?"

"Nick Cellantano called. I told him you were out. He wants you to call him when you come in."

"Where is he, in his office or uptown?"

"In his office."

"Get him for me."

Ginny dialed his number. I combed my hair, buttoned my shirt collar and closed my tie. I put my coat on and felt a little more human. The headache had gone. I just felt weary. Not tired. Weary.

Ginny held the phone out to me.

"Nick," she said.

I took the receiver.

"Hello, Nick. Ed Harris."

"Ed. Are you busy? Can I see you for a couple of minutes?"

"Have you had lunch yet, Nick?"

"A couple of hours ago."

"I haven't. I thought I'd go out and eat. Could you join me for a cup of coffee?"

"Where?"

"There's no use trying Marcel's or any of the other regular places. They'll be closed down by now. How about Schrafft's?"

"Fine. I'll meet you there in ten minutes."

I hung up.

"You feel better?" Ginny asked.

"Much better. Can you stay around tonight? I have to get the script written. I'll need your help."

"I can stay."

"I'm sorry to spring it on you like this at the last minute."

"It's all right. I didn't have anything to do, anyway. You've had a rough couple of days."

"You'll never know how rough. Too much booze, too little sleep."

"You've been learning a lot, though, haven't you?"

"I sure have. I've been learning a lot. What would happen to you if I just walked out?"

"You're serious, aren't you?"

"Yes. I'm serious."

"You've had a rough time?"

"I'm on a Ferris wheel. Lots of lights, lots of loud music, but I'm just going round and round. One minute I want it so bad I can taste it. The next minute I don't want to touch it with a ten-foot pole. Almost immediately after that they start to make a motion to take it away from me and I want it bad all over again. Then I get a couple of hours sleep and I start to tote things up in my head and I want out again. Is a puzzlement."

"You talking just about tomorrow night or the rest of it?"

"The rest of it. Tomorrow night I'll do. I guess. Right now, I'll do. Program subject to change without notice. Honest to God, Ginny, I never knew I had an ethic to my name. Or a moral. Or a scruple."

"You're loaded with them. You got scruples you haven't even used. Are you real serious now?"

"Real serious."

"Don't worry about me. I'll be fine. Somebody can always use a secretary. The way I'm built they'll take me because they figure they can make time. By the time they find out they can't, I'm too much involved in their business to get rid of."

"Is that the way you worked it on me?"

"You don't know the first thing about the way I'm built."

"There seems to be a certain amount of regret in your tone."

"That way lies madness. Cut it out. If you're talking serious, talk seriously. If you want me to make with the wisecracks, O.K. Just don't throw them in now."

"You're a nice kid, Ginny."

"Brother! First a very sweet girl, now a very nice kid. What have you been drinking?"

"It wouldn't be too much of a curve for you if I walked out on the whole deal?"

"Are you going to?"

"I don't know. Probably not. Let's just say I'm entertaining the idea. I'll be over at Schrafft's, with Nick, if you want me."

"I stuck my nose into your business a little while you were sleeping."

"How deep into my business?"

"All the way. I called Nicole."

"And?"

"I told her you'd pick her up for dinner at the hotel at seven-thirty."

"Why did you tell her that?"

"It seemed like a good idea at the time."

"Thanks, Ginny. It was a very good idea."

"I thought so."

"Don't be so smug."

"I can call her back and cancel, if you want me to."

"O.K., Ginny. O.K. Your point. I'll be at Schrafft's with Nick. When I get back I want to work on the script. We'll knock off at seven and then I'll meet you back here at nine and we'll stay around until we finish."

I left the office, stopped in the washroom to pour some cold water on my face and comb my hair again and went down in the elevator. I got the glad hand from all hands. I wondered how many of them would still be throwing bouquets at my feet after the campaign kicked off in the columns Monday.

Nick was sitting in a booth when I got to Schrafft's.

He had a cup of coffee in front of him. I ordered a bowl of soup, a ham on rye and a cup of coffee.

"Did you get sprung from the funeral parlor?" I asked him.

"We had a meeting this afternoon. I had to come back for it."

"How is the wake going? Still packing them in?"

"Still packing them in."

Nick was sitting looking down into his cup as he stirred the spoon around.

"What's the matter, Nick? Anything wrong?"

"I don't know," he said. "Maybe I should be minding my own business."

"About what?"

"I think you oughta know, Ed. It's none of my business and maybe I'm sticking my neck out talking to you about it, but I think you ought to know."

"Know what, Nick?"

"You're getting the finger. They're sharpening the knives."

"What do you mean?"

"The meeting this afternoon. We're planting stories that Amalgamated is getting rid of you. You saw the *Tribune* piece this morning? That was a sort of range finder, I guess. Starting Monday, the word gets out that you're finished at

Amalgamated. Not only are you not Fuller's successor, you don't even have your local show."

"Thanks for telling me, Nick."

"You don't act surprised."

"Why should I?"

"You knew about this?"

"In a way. How are they going to do it?"

"It's routine, Ed. I've done it before. All the guys in Press Info have their own special feeds. We use them as a feeler. For instance, maybe the Program Board is thinking of doing something and they're not too sure what the public reaction will be, they sic one of us and we let it leak to a column. That way the brass can get some ideas of public reaction and can either officially confirm it or deny it."

"And this is like that?"

"No, I don't think it is, Ed. I think this is firm. I think you've had it. What happened? Did you get caught in bed with Mrs. Carleton?"

"No. Not Mrs. Carleton. The way I feel she's maybe the only girl in New York I haven't been in bed with this week."

"A big week?"

"The biggest."

"What are you going to do about it?"

"About being dumped? What can I do about it?"

"You've got a contract or something, don't you?"

"Sure. I've got a contract with Sid Moore. That will do me a lot of good. It'll get me all the station breaks I can eat."

I felt like a heel playing it dumb with Nick. I was strangely touched by the fact that he'd come to me with the information. It was a decent thing to do and he had no ax to grind. I resisted the temptation to tell him that I knew all about it and that there was a twist to it, a hidden zinger on the end working for me. I even started wondering if there was. If maybe Carleton wasn't smarter than I gave him credit for and wasn't really dumping me. That couldn't be true. He didn't have to play games that way. My soup came and I started to eat.

"You take it pretty calm," Nick said.

"What did you expect me to do, tear the buttons off my shirt and beat my breast?"

"Something like that. For Christ's sake, Ed, don't tell anyone I tipped you. I just thought you should know."

"Maybe I should walk out now, Nick. Maybe I should just head west and leave them a nice big hour hole to fill on the network tomorrow night?"

"I wouldn't do that, Ed."

"Why not?"

"First off, because you're not that kind of a guy. This show tomorrow night is a job to do and you'll do it. Second, I've seen them call signals off on these things before. Maybe they're just going through the motions to talk you down a little on the price side. Maybe they figure somebody would leak it to you and they'd have you in a much better frame of mind to talk the kind of figure they want you to talk."

"Do you really believe that, Nick?"

"Do you?"

"No."

"Me neither."

"You sure you don't want some soup? Very good."

"No, thanks. You know something, Ed? Maybe you're better off. I was around Fuller a long time. Maybe you're better off out of the whole setup."

"You don't believe that either, do you, Nick?"

"Yes. I believe it. Leveling. I believe it. You're a nice guy, Ed. Oh, sure, on the surface you're a wise guy with a lot of answers. But under that thin veneer, you're a pretty decent guy."

"Thanks. Who told you?"

"All right, forget the whole thing."

"Wait a minute, Nick. Don't get sore."

"Then don't be such a goddamned wise guy when somebody's doing you a favor and putting his neck on the line to do it."

"I'm sorry, Nick. Go ahead."

"It's nothing, really. It's just that I've been around the Fuller setup for a while. And you're a nice guy and I'm just as happy you're gonna continue being a nice guy instead of a well-heeled bastard. That's all I had on my mind."

"That's plenty. And I'm grateful to you, Nick. Really I am. Grateful as hell. I'll tell you why, someday."

"O.K., Ed. That was all I had on my mind. You finish your sandwich. I've got to get back uptown. Big doings tonight. Eulogies all night long. Georgie Jessel at eight-thirty. That I can't miss."

Nick got up, left a dime for his coffee and left the booth. He smiled and waved his hand.

I applied myself to the ham sandwich and the coffee.

On the way back to the office, I stopped off at the newsstand and picked up the afternoon papers. I stood on the corner and worked my way through the columns. Nothing in Leonard Lyons. Earl Wilson was reporting on strange marriage customs of the American Indians. Barry Gray was rediscovering Rome. Nothing in Dorothy Kilgallen. Sobol and Louella Parsons ditto. I felt better.

Back at the office, I took my coat off, opened my collar, rolled up my sleeves, locked the door and went to work. By a quarter after six, I'd finished the first draft of the script. I rough-timed it and it was about twelve minutes over. That was fine. That gave me time to move around in for the final polishing and cutting. It was a great script—if you had a strong stomach.

I shuffled through the transcripts of the tapes and put

them in the order they came in the script. I buzzed for Ginny.

"I'm going home and shower and change my clothes and then I'm going to dinner with Nicole. Why don't you knock off for dinner and then work with the engineer in the tape room?"

"I don't think I'll go out to eat. I think I'll just have something sent in."

"O.K. Here are the transcripts. Mike has most of the tapes isolated and on the show reel. Take the carbon of the script and put the tapes in order on a reel. When I get back from dinner, I'll go to work on cleaning up the script and we should have the whole thing wrapped up by midnight."

"Give my love to Nicole."

I promised that I would.

My place smelled damp and musty. I opened all the windows. All two of them. I stripped, shaved and showered. I sat around bare-ass, listening to the radio and smoking. I did a little thinking, too.

In the middle of it, my phone rang.

"Hello."

"Is this Ed Harris?"

"Yes."

"This is Rickie Tyler."

"Hello. We've been missing each other."

"I called your office and got your secretary. She said I'd be able to reach you here."

"Well . . . here I am."

"I'd like to talk to you, Mr. Harris. I know you're up to your ears with the broadcast for tomorrow night, but I think it's reasonably important that we sit down together for a little while. I think we can be of mutual assistance."

"I'm a great believer in mutual assistance."

"So am I. When can I see you? Tonight?"

"No, I can't make it tonight. I'm on my way out to dinner and then I'm going back to the office to finish up the script. How about tomorrow?"

"What time?"

"You say."

"In the afternoon."

"Fine."

"Where? I'd rather not come up to your office. The fewer poeple at Amalgamated that know we've gotten together, the better. How about coming up to the hotel? I'm at the Astor."

"The Astor. How about two o'clock?"

"We can have lunch in the room."

"All right, Miss Tyler, two o'clock tomorrow. I'll see you then. Good-by."

"Good-by."

I hung up.

Now what the hell had I done that for? By tomorrow at two the script would be finished, rolled up, if you will, into one ball of wax. Why was I bothering with Rickie Tyler? Rickie Tickie Tyler, the shadowy figure in Fuller's history. A great subject for a Sunday feature in the *American Weekly*.

"Was This Girl Really the Power Behind the Throne?"

"Who Was the Great Woman Behind the Great Man?"

"I Made Herb Fuller!"

Didn't she just?

Anyway I was going to see her. I was going to see her, talk to her, drink with her, eat with her and, judging by my past track record, probably wind up sleeping with her. All in the interest of science, research and the pursuit of the Great Man. That was tomorrow. Right now there was another woman I had to see, talk to, eat with, drink with and, God willing, sleep with. I put on my nylon shorts (sexy as hell), my blue serge suit, white madras shirt and my most conservative blue tie. I looked fine. I even felt pretty good. It was ten after seven. I had plenty of time, so I walked. I strolled slowly up Fifth Avenue, looking in the shop windows. I'd talked myself into a sort of Scarlett O'Hara or "I'll Think About That Tomorrow" frame of mind.

The dinner was a huge success. I was relaxed and the French have a wonderful quality of picking up your mood and going along with it. By the time the Cherries Jubilee arrived (Nicole's only direct challenge to her tendency to get plump), we were back together again.

We had brandy with our coffee and held hands under the table. I got back to the office at a quarter to ten feeling great. Ginny noticed it immediately, when I walked into the tape room.

"Nobody ever looks like that after having dinner with me," she said.

"They will," I told her. "Someday Ginny, somebody is going to take a good look at you—"

"And get me a raise," she finished.

"Very romantic girl," said Mike Jackson, working at the tape machine.

"How are you doing?" I asked.

"Just about finished," he said. "I think you're way over. You have exactly forty-one minutes and ten seconds of tape."

"That much?"

"That's without counting any music you're going to dub in for opening and closing billboard. You have another forty minutes of narration. Ginny and I figure you're about twenty-two minutes over."

"I'm going to start on the final script right now. I'll cut the narration down. I'd like to keep as much tape as I can. Does any of it sound cuttable to you?"

"The Christmas Eve broadcast you're using is a little

soggy. I'd cut a full two minutes out of it. It runs four fifteen now."

"It's awfully good right there though. I'll tell you what . . . maybe we can pull it down behind narration after two and a half minutes. That way we'll have the flavor of it and save ourselves some air time. I'll write the narration in that spot over for tape behind. Anything else?"

"I think you ought to cut the Carol hunk right out of the show."

"It's only the lead-in to her song. And I have tapes with the rest of the Family with lead-ins to songs. I'd like to save it."

"She sounds loaded," Ginny said.

"She probably was," said Mike. "I think you ought to cut it. To hell with time. I'm not talking about time now. I'm talking about content. Ginny's right. She does sound loaded."

"All right. Cut it. How much time do we pick up there?" I asked.

"One forty-three," said Mike.

"That means we've pulled out about two minutes and ten seconds. Anything else that sticks out?"

"Those are the major ones," said Mike.

"You go ahead pulling that stuff out and I'll go to work on the script. When I finish, we can run all the tapes and listen to them with the script."

I went back to my office and started on the script. I started right from the top. I slashed, rewrote, rearranged and by a quarter to twelve I was finished. For better or worse the script was finished. It was a kind of a milestone.

It was a good job too. Slick, but not too apparently so. It had a kind of authentic emotion to it. Professionally authentic, maybe, but if you didn't know Fuller, you came away from it feeling that he really was a wonderful guy. I had to fight the tendency to pile it on and I somehow managed to do it.

After another hour in the tape room, I was all wrapped up. The script was down to time and we'd eliminated the questionable tapes and cut down the good ones. It was tight. A good job.

I dropped Ginny off at her apartment by cab, kissed her quietly on the forehead and went home. I was in bed by one. I felt lonesome at first. I read for about fifteen minutes, smoked two cigarettes and turned the light out. I lay awake in the dark for awhile. Twenty hours from now it would be all over with. Twenty hours from now I'd have done the broadcast and started a lot of wheels turning. Twenty hours from now I'd come into my inheritance.

In the back of my head a little thought was pounding away like a pulse beat.

"Don't do it. . . . Don't do it."

I was getting five thousand bucks for the broadcast. Carleton had said so. Right now, twenty hours from air, I had no chains, no commitments. I was free to walk out. I could head west . . . for the Coast. Nicole would be going back there in a couple of weeks. I could get some kind of job out there. In radio, TV . . . maybe at one of the studios. Five thousand bucks wasn't much, but it was a stake. And if I married Nicole, she could carry us for a while, until I landed something.

"What the hell am I talking about? What's the matter with me? Talking about settling for five grand. I'm out of my goddamned mind. Five grand. Christ! The League I'm stepping into, five thousand is tie money. Who am *I* to get so goddamned finicky all of a sudden?"

"Don't do it."

"Don't do it."

"Don't cold-bloodedly turn into a son of a bitch."

"Don't think the money is that easy. Don't think you can get home free."

"Don't cold-bloodedly make yourself into a Herb Fuller."

"Don't be the Great Man."

"Don't do it."

"Don't do it."

"Tell them to shove it."

"Five grand is a stake."

I finally fell asleep.

I didn't dream at all.

FRIDAY

THE PHONE woke me up. I could hear it ringing. It cut into my sleep, but it was a long time before I could pull myself back to consciousness and answer it.

I finally did.

"Hello."

"Ed?" It was Ginny.

"I've been calling you for the past hour."

"What time is it?" I asked.

"A quarter to eleven. Brother, when you sleep, you sleep."

"Anything the matter?"

"Not now. We were worried about you."

"Who's we?"

"Me. Can't I worry about you?"

"Sure. I'll be in in about an hour. I'll stop for breakfast on the way."

"I retyped the script and sent copies to Carleton and Sid. Was that all right? You mentioned that you wanted them to see it when it was finished."

"That's fine."

"Is there anything I can do for you before you come in?"

"No, nothing. I'll see you in an hour."

"Ed? You still there?"

"Yeah."

"You're all over the papers. Nick got out a big release on the show tonight and it hit everywhere. The *Tribune* and the *News* have your picture and Nick Kenny devotes his whole column to your bio."

"In poetry?"

"Prose. Hang on a minute, will you? The other phone is ringing."

I cradled the phone between my chin and my shoulder and reached for the pack of cigarettes on the bedside table. I lit one and took a deep drag. I suddenly realized something.

No hangover.

No headache.

No cough.

I felt great.

Maybe there was something to this celibacy routine after all.

"Ed? Still there?"

"Still here. Who was it?"

"Sid Moore. He wants you to cut some thirty-second spots that they can use on station breaks starting at one o'clock and continuing on through to air time of the show."

"Who's going to write the copy?"

"You are. That's what he said."

"Great. I guess I'd better dictate it to you now. You ready?"

"Just a minute. O.K. Shoot."

"This is Ed Harris. Like the rest of you, I felt a great sense of personal loss when I heard about the death of Herb Fuller. And like the rest of you, I didn't want him to pass, unnoticed, unremembered. I hope you'll be listening tonight at ten on this network when I'll be back with the Herb Fuller Memorial Show. I hope you'll be with me then and remember, as I'll be remembering, a Great Man . . . and a great loss."

I stubbed out the cigarette.

"Did you get it, Ginny?"

"I got it. How can you do things like that on an empty stomach?"

"That's the old American know-how that won the war. Let me read it over at normal speed and clock it with my stop watch. Hang on."

I found my stop watch in my pants pocket and came back to the phone.

"I don't remember the goddamned thing," I said. "Will you read it the way I would. I'll clock you at this end."

Ginny read it. It clocked at thirty-three seconds.

"Fine," I said. "I can do it in thirty seconds. You'd better set up a studio and a tape room for noon so I can do it."

"Right."

"I'll see you in about an hour."

I hung up, took a shower, got dressed and pulled out the door that hid the kitchenette. I made myself a big breakfast. The works. Tomato juice, bacon and eggs, toast and coffee. I pulled up the shade. It was a beautiful day. Bright and sunny. I felt a sort of excitement. Maybe it's just because I'm a ham at heart. I was looking forward to the actual job of broadcasting the show tonight. I always get a boot out of sitting in front of a mike with a script in my hand and talking. And I knew I had a good script. The tapes were fine too. Put everything else aside. Forget that it's about Fuller. Just looking at it as a show, as a performance, it was good. I was looking forward to doing it. To the actual doing of it, that is. I purposely wasn't thinking beyond that. I purposely wasn't thinking of what the papers used to call the "Big Picture."

I stacked the dishes in the sink and went into the bathroom and brushed my teeth. In the middle of it, the phone rang again. It was Ginny again.

"Ed? Studio Nine at noon. For the promos."

"Studio Nine. Where is that?"

"On the sixth floor. I'll meet you there with the script."

"Don't bother, Ginny. I'm leaving now. I'll come into the office first."

"All right."

I hung up the phone and left the apartment.

I walked to the Amalgamated Building. Peter was opening the door of a taxi when I walked up. I waved and walked into the building. Peter came up behind me and poked me in the kidneys. I resisted the impulse to turn around and poke him.

"You can be replaced, peasant," he said.

I kept walking. He kept following. Right up to the door of the elevator.

"The Book of the Month to you," he said and poked me in the kidneys again as I walked into the elevator car.

John was singing. We were alone in the car.

"You notice the difference in my voice?" he asked.

"Yes. Big difference," I said.

"New teacher. She has me singing more like through the mouth. She says I was singing through my nose before. She is just great. Told me I had to keep in mind like that the song was rolling over my tonsils on its way out. You noticed the difference right away, didn't you?"

"Right away," I said.

"She has me singing all those arias and things . . . like that thing from *The Chocolate Soldier*. She told me more good voices have been ruined by not singing the right songs. She is just great."

Artie, the starter, clicked and John closed the door regretfully and we started up the shaft.

"The acoustics in here aren't very good," he said. "You don't get the full appreciation like of the tones. I don't know why I never thought of this before. But if you just keep a mental picture like of your tonsils while you're singing, you'd be surprised what it does. Like you noticing the difference right away. You know how I do it?"

"No," I said. "How do you do it?"

"I make it a game like. Like the song starts from down in your stomach and on the way up from the stomach it's like on a ski tow. You know? Then when it gets up to the throat it kind of takes off like in skiing. Right over the tonsils it goes . . . zip and out. It's amazing what a good teacher can do for you. She said herself, a little thing like remembering the tonsils can make ten or fifteen thousand dollars' difference a year."

I was sorry when we arrived at the ninth floor.

There was a new receptionist at the desk.

"What happened to the other girl?" I asked.

"She left," I was told by a tall, willowy brunette. Sid Moore must have been changing his type. This one was different. She was not blond, she was not smiling. I sneaked a quick look. Thank God, he hadn't lost his head completely. She had the standard cute fanny that all WBSR receptionists sport.

"I'm Ed Harris," I said.

"Yes?"

"I work here."

She nodded. She accepted it but wasn't impressed by it.

I walked through the door into the office. Lillian wasn't at her desk. Ginny was.

She handed me an envelope. It was sealed and the embossed lettering in the corner said simply "Philip Carleton."

"You don't know how close I came to opening it," she said. "It made me nervous sitting there on the corner of my desk."

"When did it come?"

"About ten minutes ago. By page."

I ripped it open. Inside was a handwritten note. It said:

"Script is fine. Excellent job. Because of the normal delay in company checks, I'm taking the liberty of enclosing my personal check for the amount we discussed." It was signed with the initials "P.C." I filed that away for future reference. Not Mr. Carleton. Not Philip. Not Phil. Not Skipper or Coach. P.C.

Attached to the note was a check for five thousand dollars. I flashed it at Ginny.

"A tip?" she asked.

"Dinner money for working late last night."

I folded it carefully and put it into my wallet.

My mad money.

I wondered what I would do with it.

"It's five to twelve," Ginny reminded me. "You'd better get down to Studio Nine. Here are the scripts."

I took the papers and went down to the studio.

It took about five minutes to record the station-break announcements. I did them three times. I hit all three of them at thirty seconds on the nose.

When I got back to my office, Sid Moore was sitting at my desk talking on the phone. He waved his hand at me and I sat on the couch. When he finished talking, he lit a cigar and leaned back in the chair.

"Calling my bookmaker over in Jersey. Have a hot filly running at Bay Meadows. Want me to put something down on it for you, Skipper?"

"No thanks, Sid. What happened to the girl with the fifty-cent can?"

"We had a jurisdictional dispute. We disagreed not about end result but about method. How do you like her replacement?"

"A little on the frigid side."

"That adds a certain spice."

"Did you want to see me about something, Sid?"

"I read your script."

"And?"

"Great."

"But . . ."

"No buts. Great. Big League all the way."

"And you came over here to shake my hand and wish me Godspeed."

"Something like that. I don't have to tell you how important this thing tonight is. To both of us. This is the World Series, kid. The seventh game. The clutch. The pay-off."

"In a word, Sid. This is . . ."

"I don't have to tell you, boy. I'm thinking of throwing a big party at my place tonight. How about it? You feel like celebrating?"

"You really think we're in, Sid?" I made my voice grave and questioning. I was probing around. If rumors were flying, some of them were bound to come zooming in Sid's window.

"You think we've really pulled it off?" I asked. "You don't think Carleton is going to change his mind and get himself another boy?"

"Another boy? Ed, you're his boy. He thinks you're the greatest."

"That's not the way you were talking the other night."

"Ed, I was loaded. I talk too much when I'm loaded."

"I have news for you, Sid. Drunk or sober, you talk too much."

"What does that mean?"

"You were just talking off the top of your head the other night. Just noodling around. Is that it?"

"Sure, that's it. Just running up and down the sidelines, warming up. I was loaded. Anybody knows me knows enough not to believe a word I say when I'm loaded."

"Meet the exception. I believe everything you say when

you're loaded. On the other hand, I pay absolutely no attention to anything you say cold sober. I'm a real perverted guy, that way."

"You're in a good humor, kid. I can always tell. When you're real nasty, you're in a good humor. Well . . . I have to get back to the old ball game. Just wanted you to know I'd be in the stands, rooting tonight."

"Fine. I'll be on the mound with my old bag of tricks. My sharp ball will be breaking fast. The slim portsider will be in his usual sharp mettle."

"You're feeling great. I'm glad, Coach. How about tonight? *Chez moi.*"

"I don't think so, Sid. I have a date."

"The French one? Bring her along."

"We're going to the top of the Empire State Building together."

"Well . . . if you change your mind, drop over. I'll call you after the show, anyway."

"O.K., Sid. And God bless you for your many kindnesses, for your warm heart, your understanding and your good offices."

Sid laughed. His phlegmy laugh.

"You're funny when you're snotty. I love it. We're going to have a million laughs. Have fun."

Without thinking I gave the countersign.

"Likewise."

Sid left.

Ginny came in.

"Can I talk?" she asked.

"I think so," I said. "I've heard you do it once or twice."

"You were talking big last night."

"About what?"

"About quitting. About walking out."

"I was talking."

"That's all?"

"Yes, Ginny. That's all. Don't you pay any attention to what your little playmates say."

"Can we be serious?"

"Sure. What's on your mind?"

"You. I told you I worry about you. I don't know why I should bother when you don't even try to get me a raise. But I do."

"And?"

"And you don't like the setup, do you?"

"Not much."

"And every once in a while you get the feeling that you want out."

"Every once in a while I get the feeling that I want out."

"Why?"

"Why? I don't know. Maybe I can make you understand it. Maybe I can't. I'm not sure I understand it myself. I'm Ed Harris, right?"

"Right."

"In the larger scheme of things I don't amount to a hell of a lot, right?"

"Qualified right."

"Thanks. O.K. But I like being Ed Harris. I have enough to pay my rent, buy my drinks, take my French girl out to dinner. I enjoy."

"You enjoy."

"All of a sudden, I'm not Ed Harris. I'm a big deal. I'm an influence on my time. People start paying attention to what I say. Maybe I even affect their lives. Maybe not . . . but maybe yes. Skip that. Stick to Ed Harris. Who isn't really Ed Harris any more. He's a sort of cog in a big, successful steamroller. He affects the bank balance, the happiness, the life of everybody connected with him. He isn't so important any more. He's a prime mover. He's a corporation. He's a big deal. He's the Great Man."

"That's bad?"

"Not yet. It could be. It could be if in the process Ed Harris gets lost. How long do you think it would take me to be a thorough bastard?"

"You being serious?"

"Dead serious."

"You're not like that. You know you're not."

"No? I'm so close to it right now I can touch it. I feel like Gulliver. These little bastards got their ropes around me right now. I'm on a conveyor belt headed for the buzz saw. And there won't be any goddamned hero around to pull me off in the fifth reel, pay off the mortgage and shoot the villain. You don't believe it? How long do you think it will be before I start making passes at you in the afternoon just because there isn't anything better to do and Carol is a forty-cent cab ride away? And how long will it be before you start wearing a pair of round heels and start getting calluses on your can from that leather couch?"

"Come off it, Ed."

"You know, I think I've finally figured part of it out. Not in Fuller's case. I'm convinced he was a bastard to begin with. He just had a little more scope for his talents when he became the Great Man. Now, I'm talking about me. I've got it figured out. You know what it is? When you get to be the Great Man, nobody has any real respect for you as a person. Nobody you work with, I mean. You're just a meal ticket to them if they're under your thumb. Or you're just a financial sheet to them if they're big brass. But they don't give a hoot in hell for you as a person. It would never occur to them to question any decision you make or are forced to make, to stop and say, does this violate this guy's integrity? Am I making any sense?"

"How does walking out solve it?"

"I walk out as Ed Harris. I'm no longer a cog. I'm me. I'm allowed a little integrity . . . a little moral standard . . . a scruple or two. If I act like a thorough bastard, I have to take the consequences for it. There are consequences for the Ed Harrises. For the Great Man there are no consequences. Too many people get too much out of him for there to be any consequences, and besides, who gives a goddamn about him personally?"

"You're really afraid of doing it, aren't you?"

"You might say it's the complications that worry me. I'm not afraid of the disease. I'm afraid I'll die of complications. You didn't think I was such a forthright bastard, did you? You didn't think I had that much moral fiber, did you?"

"But why does it have to be the way you just said it would be? Why can't you be the Great Man and still be Ed Harris?"

"Because you can't be both. Ed Harris wouldn't do the things the Great Man has to do to be the Great Man. The Great Man would laugh his head off at the scruples of that ridiculous schnook, Ed Harris."

"So you're going to walk out? You're really honest-to-God going to walk out?"

"I didn't say that. I don't know what I'm going to do. Maybe I just need a psychiatrist. Maybe I just have a complex about being successful. You know, in a lot of ways I feel sorry for Fuller."

"That's a new one."

"No, I mean it. Right from the start he never had a chance to be a human being. I have. When I came out of the navy, when the war was over, I had a strange attitude about everything. I'd spent a couple of years of my life with no real certainty that I was ever going to be given the chance to grow old. For a couple of years my life was up for grabs three times a week. Any goddamned minute, a plane flying out of the sun could louse me up. Any goddamned minute a torpedo could cancel out my chances of a normal life . . . a life with kids and a wife. You make adjustments to it after a while. You concede that maybe you're going to be killed. You accept it.

"And then all of a sudden the war is over and you have to make another adjustment. You have to start thinking in terms of staying alive. Barring an accident or some germs, you're going to live your life out. You get careful. You look both ways crossing the streets. You don't want to louse up the life that's been given back to you. I guess a million guys came out of the war feeling that way. Feeling like every day they were living was velvet because they somehow managed to survive all the planes, all the torpedoes, all the bombs. Maybe you weren't old enough to be aware of it, but 1945 and 1946 were strange years to live through. Every one of us who'd been away to a war was living a careful life, moving around slowly, getting used to being alive. Christ, we were careful! Most of us got over it. Most of us are back to normal. But not completely. Me, I got a new appreciation of what it means to be alive, what it means to be able to make a date for next Tuesday and know for sure that I'd be around to keep it. You're wondering what that has to do with what we've been talking about, aren't you?"

"Yes."

"I'm not sure that I want to screw my life up by being the Great Man. I'm not sure that it's a fair trade. I'm not sure that the money and the power are that important. When it happened Monday, when the wheels started turning, I considered myself the luckiest guy alive. The world was being dumped in my lap. I've had a liberal education since then. I'm scared, Ginny. Scared to death. Now they're nominating me for God."

"And you don't want to be God?"

"Does anybody? Every decent instinct I have says walk out, there are lots of ways of getting rent and eating money, but can anybody really walk out on a pass key to Fort Knox?"

"You want to know what I think?"

"What do you think? Tell me, Ginny. Give me the Word."

"I think you're dramatizing hell out of yourself. I think you're enjoying searching your soul. I think you have no intention of walking out. I think you're trying to justify your not walking out to yourself. And I think you'll succeed beautifully. The fact that you know all these things, that you're afraid of them, is the best insurance that you won't turn into a Herb Fuller."

"So I'll marry the legend and live happily ever after."

"I can't help you on this, Ed. Nobody can. This is a decision you have to make for yourself."

"O.K., Ginny."

"And don't worry about my heels or my calluses."

Ginny walked out of the office. What the hell was she getting so peeved about?

I looked at my watch. It was a quarter to one. In a little over an hour I'd be seeing Rickie Tyler. I needed a briefing session. I knew who could give it to me.

I dialed Nick Cellantano's office. His secretary answered.

"This is Ed Harris. Is he there?"

"He's grabbing a sandwich in the Rose Room, Mr. Harris. After that he's going back uptown to the studio."

"Thanks, honey, I'll see if I can find him."

I found Nick at the bar with a ham sandwich and a glass of beer in front of him. The stool next to him was empty so I slid onto it.

"Hi," I said. "Obviously you're not eating on the expense account today."

"Sure, I am. Just take a look at it next time you're in the

office, you'll find I have a twelve dollar meal at Twenty-One with a contact. Want a sandwich?"

"A bottle of beer will be fine."

Kimo, the bartender, heard me and the beer was put in front of me immediately. I get great service in the Rose Room. I keep all the waiters supplied with passes to the Roxy, the Capitol and the Paramount. It works wonders.

"How's the script?" Nick asked.

"Finished. Good," I said.

"Anything else new?"

"You mean what you were telling me the other day?"

"Yeah."

"Not a thing."

"It figures. Monday is D Day."

I sipped the beer.

"I want to know something, Nick."

"Anything I can tell you, Ed. What?"

"I'm going to see Rickie Tyler at two."

"I thought you said the script was finished."

"It is."

"I don't get the Tyler bit."

"Just say I'm curious. I've had calls from her all week. We finally got together by phone and set up a date. I'm going to keep it because . . . I don't know. Just because."

"Because you're curious?"

"All right. Because I'm curious. I want a fill-in on her. From you. It doesn't make any difference now to anybody, so I figured you'd level with me about her. Get the furrows out of your forehead, Nick. I'm just seeing her for kicks, for what killed the cat."

Nick put his sandwich down.

"Why don't you just forget it? Why get yourself mixed up with Rickie?"

"Listen, goddamn it! Give me some credit for a little understanding, a little normal human curiosity. I've spent a whole week digging into the manure pile. Whether I wanted to or not, I got screwed up in Fuller's life. O.K., I got fascinated. O.K., I'm hooked. O.K., for my own personal information I want to put all the pieces together. She's a big piece."

"She sure is."

Nick smiled.

"The biggest piece he ever had," he said, "and the most important."

"Why?"

Nick looked around the bar. There were two empty stools on each side of us. The tables were filled, but the bar trade was thinning out. He lowered his voice anyway.

"All right," he said. "I don't know what harm it can do. You want to know about Rickie Tyler, I'll tell you about Rickie Tyler. I was there before she was. As soon as Sid brought him down to New York from Worcester, I was assigned to him by the Publicity Department. After he was on the air about three weeks, Rickie showed up."

"What do you mean, showed up?"

"Just that. Personnel sent her down to see Fuller as a possible secretary-assistant. Fuller, of course, took one look and flipped. She was gorgeous. A little corn-fed, but gorgeous. Fresh and young and unspoiled. Just ripe for plucking. Fuller fired his secretary and hired her. He set her up in a place in the Fifties just east of Lexington. She was a good kid. I liked her a hell of a lot. In the back of her head, I think, she thought he'd divorce Fran and marry her someday, but meanwhile she wasn't wasting any time. She moved in on him. After a while, if you wanted to do any business with Fuller, you had to go through Rickie. She made the decisions. She was concubine, personal manager, agent, secretary and wet nurse all rolled into one. It was fun to watch. She almost made him respectable."

"Was she making anything out of it?"

"Her salary and whatever he let her chisel on the side. She used to set up personal appearances for him around the New York area. She always got a rake-off on that. She programed all the records on his show and so she handled the song pluggers. Figure she made a couple of hundred a week in payolas on that. But she was more ambitious than that. Long before anybody realized it, she had Fuller pegged as a potential national celebrity. She sunk his dough back into good writers. She was always hiring package outfits to come up with a network program idea. She was always on my tail to get him some national publicity."

"Where does Sid Moore fit into this picture?"

"Now you've hit it. Sid spotted her right away. But he sat back on his can and let her have her head. What the hell did he care? She was breaking her back promoting Fuller, making some small change. Sid didn't worry too much. He discovered Fuller. He had a contract. He figured, in a way, she was working for him, and how tough is it to dump a secretary when you figure she's outlived her usefulness?"

"How about Fuller all this time?" I asked. "How did he feel about Rickie?"

"The bed part didn't last very long. After a couple of months the bloom was beginning to fade on Rickie. After a while he found himself a replacement in the bed department, but in the office, Rickie had become the most important part of his life. He trusted her. Maybe he was flattered by the way she felt about him. Nobody else had ever thought about him in quite the terms she did. She fed his ego, took care of all his business problems and by the time she'd been with him eight months he couldn't have gone on without her. She knew that. She'd been counting on that. That was something smart old Sid Moore hadn't figured on."

"So there was a showdown?"

"Sure. You didn't know that Rickie is the one that came up with the successful format, did you?"

"No."

"A couple of the writers she'd been supporting came up with it and she was smart enough to recognize it as the road map to where she wanted to take Fuller. She took it to Moore and demanded an in. She owned the package. She'd created it on Fuller's money but put it in her own name. Sid spotted it immediately too and tried to buy her off or scare her out of it. She didn't scare. And she had an ace going for her in the hole. Fuller himself. He wouldn't make a move without Rickie being in the picture. So Sid cut her in. Nobody ever knew that. Nobody but Sid, Fuller, Rickie and me. That was while Sid still had something to cut somebody in on. Rickie, like I told you, was a smart girl. She didn't trust Sid and she spotted him as a likely candidate for liquidation any time anybody wanted to get tough. Very quietly, she signed a contract with Fuller that gave her a piece of anything he ever did. That was the equalizer she had to protect her against Sid Moore."

"Smart girl."

"The smartest. You know, I told you she was pretty. Even after she'd been around Fuller a while she was still quite a dame in the looks department. I think she was in love with the son of a bitch. All the time. Any other dame, when he kicked her out of his bed and started tom-catting around, would have walked out. Her pride wouldn't have been able to take it. Not Rickie. It was like she closed the book on the sex side of it. She never made a peep about his whoring around. Only when it looked like it might get him into trouble professionally. I used to wonder how she felt around the Fuller Family. Around Carol and the rest of the dames on the show he was knocking off regularly. If it was me, I think I'd have scratched their eyes out, kicked them in the pratt and raised hell. Not Rickie."

"Maybe she was getting her kicks some other way?"

"You mean some other guy?"

"Maybe."

"No. I said she was a smart girl. But maybe she wasn't so smart after all in one thing. I think in the back of her conniving little head she thought some day Fuller would come back to her; some day he'd finally get his fill of all the other women and come back to her. Another funny thing. Fuller was a tom cat, but he had a kind of respect for Rickie. You and me in that situation would figure, once in a while, what the hell, it's there, it's easy, I've had it before, I'll knock it off now and then as a kind of fill-in. Once he stopped with her, he never started again. She wasn't getting anything in that department, from him or anyone else."

"What happened after Sid Moore got dumped?"

"Sid Moore got dumped. Period. End of sentence.

"They didn't try dumping her?"

"Maybe they tried. Maybe they didn't. They didn't succeed. They'd have lost Fuller if they did. Any deal he made in those days included Rickie or he walked out. Besides, Carleton recognized her value. He didn't buy Fuller at the beginning with his eyes closed. He knew he was buying a louse. He knew he was buying the kind of egomaniac bastard who would walk all over him if given the chance. He figured Rickie was worth her price as the sane influence, as the gal who could handle him and keep him under control."

"And she did?"

"As much as anybody can keep a guy put in that slot under control. She kept him from blowing up the world, if that's what you mean. She gave him enough of his head to let him play the Great Man. It was about here that she took over another title and another job. She became Fuller's Gestapo. If something was going on in the Family that he didn't know about, you could bet your bottom dollar Rickie knew it and when it became important enough or big enough to threaten Fuller's position or his peace of mind or his reputation she stepped in. Carol got mixed up with one of the announcers on the show and Fuller didn't know about it. Rickie did. Me, I'd have let them go on, what the hell, Carol had been sleeping with Herb . . . you'd think Rickie would be damned glad to have Carol revolve her pelvis in somebody else's bed. She told Fuller and he took care of it. There wasn't anything went on she didn't know about. He did the slapping down, the terrorizing of the kids on the show, but she was behind him feeding him ammunition to fire at them. Maybe that's what you meant when you asked if she was getting her kicks somewhere else. Maybe that was one way she had of getting them. . . . I always figured she and Fuller would have kept a whole school of head doctors in material for ten years."

We ordered two more bottles of beer. It was one-thirty. Nick and I were the only two customers left at the bar. We sat quietly for a couple of minutes, sipping the beer.

Nick took another slug at his beer and continued.

"When he got really big nationally, she damn near ruptured herself being the power behind the throne. She dealt with all the agencies, handled the commercials, the endorsements, picked the summer replacement shows and argued contract with Carleton and the big brass when option time rolled around. I make her sound awful, don't I?"

"You don't make her sound like Whistler's Mother."

"She wasn't. She was hard, cold, shrewd, calculating. The kind of female I usually can't stand being around for ten minutes, and yet somehow she was also a nice gal. Maybe she just figured I could be useful to Fuller, and therefore to her, but she was always nice to me. We got along fine. Once in a while she'd stick her nose a little too far into my business, but most of the time she left me alone. To tell you the truth, once in a while I even thought of making a serious pass at her. I used to think of all that energy at work in bed. It was an awe-inspiring thought. You're going to see her in a half hour. You'll see what I mean."

"How does she look now?"

"Did you ever see an overage Rockette? Did you ever see a female tennis star who's somehow gotten to be forty-two? She's kept her figure. She dresses well and she looks fine. She looks fine until you take a second look. Until you take a close look. Then suddenly you see a kind of hardness you see in people who have devoted their lives to one idea or one movement or one conviction."

"What happened between them?" I asked.

"I don't know where it started. Maybe the Great Man got a little sick of having an almost Great Woman behind him. Maybe it was something personal. Who knows? All I do know is that he suddenly wanted to get rid of her. He called me in and told me from here on out he wanted no publicity on Rickie. Before that I'd been using her for a lot of things. She was always good for a column item or a layout in the women's magazines. He told me to lay off. She was through and he didn't want to see her mentioned in any clippings from then on. I layed off. But she wasn't through, not yet. He found out it wasn't easy getting rid of her. She didn't want out and he suddenly found out that she knew too much about him and was too mixed up in his business life to be kicked out."

"But he finally got rid of her?"

"Sure. He got rid of her. In typical Fuller fashion. The Great Man was nothing if not consistent. It was at a meeting in his office when he laid the plans. 'O.K., she won't leave nice and quiet,' he said. 'I guarantee you in six months she'll be begging to be let out.' He was wrong only about one thing. It took him fourteen months. From then on she had it. He really socked it to her. He had a great talent for obscenity and filth and he gave it full reign. He turned her into a pimp. She had to get him girls. She finally knew more call girls than the D.A. Skip the details . . . just believe me, he made it rough on her. But she gritted her teeth and took it. Again, if it was somebody else, you might figure pride would enter into it. You might figure somebody that knew that plain she wasn't wanted would have picked up her marbles and walked out. Not Rickie Tickie Tyler. She stuck. She stuck until Cleveland. He was out doing a show at some damned centennial celebration or something and she went along. By this time his campaign to get rid of her was in high gear. She experienced every degrading, filthy thing he could think up and he had a genius in things like that. But finally in Cleveland he did it. He put on an orgy in a hotel room with himself as the central figure and made her stick around, watch and pick up the pieces afterwards. That did it. She gave up. They made a deal."

"What kind of a deal?"

"I can't quote you figures. I can tell you what the talk was."

"What was the talk?"

"A million cash and a percentage of Fuller for the rest of his life."

"Which brings me around to a question. Why does Rickie Tyler want to see me?"

"I thought you wanted to see her."

"I do. But she started it. She wrote me a note asking me to get in touch with her at the Astor."

"Maybe she just wants to make sure you don't do anything

to tarnish the bronze idol she's devoted her life to. Maybe she wants a little posthumous credit and identification. Maybe she wants you to record her for the memorial show. Who knows what she wants? You'll find out pretty soon."

Nick fingered his beer glass . . . revolved it around in his hand.

"Maybe I'm cockeyed," he said. "Maybe my sense of values are all screwed up. I told you, I liked Rickie. I still do. I haven't seen her in a couple of years, but I'm fond of her in a peculiar way and I figure that of all the dirty, slimy things that bastard did, his treatment of Rickie was the slimiest."

"Why? She made plenty out of him."

"Sure. That's true. But she earned it. Every goddamned cent of it. Whatever he wanted from her, she gave him. He wanted her to sleep with him, she slept with him. He didn't want to sleep with her any more, that was all right too, if that was the way he wanted it. She made him. Without her, he wouldn't have been able to keep his mask on for a week. The whole listening world would have known what a sadistic, drunken, vicious bastard he was. He couldn't have hid it. She created him and made him live up to it, most of the time. Without her, he'd have been a five-line obit in *Variety* instead of a front page story in every paper in the country. After she led him by the hand into the big money, he figured he could take it from there himself, so he booted her out."

"With a million dollars and an annuity."

"That wasn't because he wanted it that way. That was because, in addition to everything else, Rickie was a smart girl with a great instinct for self-preservation. That's all I can tell you about her, Ed, except one thing. When she left, Fuller started rewriting history. Rickie Tyler never existed as far as he was concerned. Nobody ever mentioned her name when he was around. It was a guarantee of his getting into one of those rages. You never saw a Fuller rage, did you?"

"No."

"It was awe-inspiring. He broke things. He threw things. He screamed and bellowed. Obscenities belched out of him. It was something. After a while, Rickie just disappeared. Physically she left right after the settlement. Nobody knew where she went. I figured she went back home. She just took off. But six months after the break-up it was as if she had never been. You knew you weren't allowed to talk about her and after a while you didn't even think about her."

"But he got along all right without her, didn't he?"

"He made mistakes at first. For instance, he used to get snotty with the kids in the Family on the air. Rickie wouldn't have allowed the mask to slip that much. Under her regime he could tie them to a pillar in the basement and beat hell out of them with a cat-o'-nine tails, but on the air it was one big happy family and Fuller was the kind, understanding Papa. He forgot that for a while. He used to hold the kids up to ridicule on the air. You could see the iron fist slipping out of the velvet glove. He made mistakes and damn near destroyed himself. He was petulant and nasty. He was snotty and superior. He was way out of character. He missed Rickie, who had a kind of instinct for what he could and could not say or do on the air. For a while his rating took a nose dive. A couple of national sponsors pulled out. The columnists had their hatchets out for him and were taking potshots at his hide every day."

"He finally straightened himself out though, didn't he?"

"He was smart, too. He finally figured out that he was in trouble. He went back to the sure-fire things."

I sneaked a look at my watch. It was ten minutes to two.

"I have to get out of here, Nick."

"Me too. I have to get back uptown. Did you know we were closing up the studio during your broadcast tonight?"

"Why?"

"Who knows? Orders. At first there was some talk of having an invited audience, government officials, civic leaders, movie stars, people like that on hand and we'd pipe in the broadcast over the loudspeaker. A kind of ghoulish personal appearance. Cooler heads prevailed on that, thank God, but the order came down to close down the mortuary during the hour of your broadcast."

"You gonna hear the show?"

"Are you kidding? I wouldn't miss it for anything. I have a portable backstage in that office. Me and Jack Hoxie and Colleen Moore will be listening."

"Nick, about that thing you were mentioning the other day . . . about a job for you."

"Yeah."

"I'll swing it."

"Aren't you whistling in the dark, kid? What makes you think you'll have a job come Monday?"

"And what makes you think I won't?"

"You know something I don't?"

"That's possible."

"You got something going for you?"

"I got something going for me. It's too involved, too melodramatic to go into now, but don't hold onto the stained glass windows and the organ for my funeral. I may just have a wonder drug all my own to spring on you."

"I hope so."

"Then again I may not."

"Then again you may not."

"Have fun," I said, as I slipped off the bar stool.

"Likewise," said Nick.

I slid a buck across the bar to Kimo and left.

I went out through the lobby and Peter got me a cab immediately. I slipped him a quarter.

"Twenty-nine Wistful Vista," he said to the cab driver.

This must have been a new cab driver, not one of the usual crew that services the feedline outside the Amalgamated Building.

"Twenty-nine what?" he asked as we started rolling north.

"Wistful Vista," I said.

"Where's that?" he asked. "I'm not allowed to go out of the five boroughs."

"I'll direct you," I said.

And I did. Right to the Hotel Astor.

"This is it?" he asked.

"This is it," I said and overtipped him outrageously.

It was two on the nose when I knocked at Rickie Tyler's door.

I knocked and in between the knocking and the opening of the door I tried to imagine what she looked like now. Strangely enough, standing there in the long carpeted corridor of the Astor I felt awkward, ill at ease and a little excited.

The door opened.

"You're Ed Harris." It was a statement. "It's nice of you to come. Come in, won't you?"

I followed her into the room. I noticed that there was a table, set for lunch, at the window.

She was wearing a white blouse and a blue skirt. Her hair was pulled back and tied with a ribbon. She looked much younger and much prettier than I thought she would. Her figure was fine.

"I know how busy you must be," she said, "so I didn't have them send lunch up. I thought I would call when you got here. Can I give you a drink?"

"I'd like a drink very much," I said. I sat down in an armchair beside the double bed that dominated the room.

She called room service, gave her name and room number and told them to send up lunch, that we were ready to eat.

"I look the liberty of ordering in advance," she said. "I hope you'll settle for steak."

"Any time," I said.

"How about that drink? Will Scotch and water be all right?"

"Scotch and water will be fine," I said.

She disappeared into the bathroom and I heard the clink of ice cubes.

She came out carrying two drinks and sat on the edge of the bed next to me.

"You must be very tired," she said. "It must have been a hellish week for you."

"Pretty hellish," I said.

"How is the script?"

"Finished. I make no claims for it beyond that. I'll fill an hour. That's the only promise I'll make."

"It will be very good," she said. "I took the trouble of finding out something about you. The script will be very good."

"Why should you take the trouble to find out anything about me?" I asked. We were fencing. I felt myself slipping back into my old defensive technique of answering questions with other questions.

"I was interested in you," she said. "When I read in the paper that you'd been picked to do the memorial show, I was interested and I started finding out about you."

"And what did you find out?"

"Enough to know that you'll do a good job on the show tonight."

"Have you been up to Studio 41?"

"No, I haven't."

"You live in New York now?"

"No. I came up to see you."

I let that hang. She'd tell me sooner or later why. I had the feeling we were both making small talk until lunch arrived. After lunch, I figured she'd get down to business.

We talked about the weather, about mutual friends and finally there was a knock on the door and the waiter came in pushing the food cart in front of him. He pulled back the covers like a magician doing a specially difficult trick. It was sort of an anticlimax to disclose nothing more magical than steak, French friend potatoes, peas and bread and butter.

We sat down and ate and made some more small talk. We had a second drink with our lunch and when we finished Rickie opened a door and I followed her through it into a sitting room. We sat down with the remains of our drinks and I had the feeling that finally, as Sid Moore might have put it, infield practice was over and the game was about to begin.

"Were you disappointed?" she asked.

"About what?"

"Me. You've been studying me all through lunch."

"No," I said, "not disappointed a bit."

"You know a lot about me, don't you?"

"Some. Not a lot. I know who you are."

"And who I was. Who briefed you?"

"Briefed me?"

"Briefed you. I'm willing to admit I found out all I could about you. I can't believe that you didn't do the same about me. Who filled you in on the details?"

"Is that important?"

"Very important. Your whole attitude toward me in our discussion now will depend on what you heard about me and from whom."

"Nick. Nick Cellantano."

"A good choice. Nick's a good boy. Was he fair?"

"I don't know. You'd know that better than I would. He seemed to me to be fair."

"Nick was a good choice."

"I like Nick," I said.

"So did I."

I took a pack of cigarettes out of my pocket, offered her one and lit it for her. I lit one for myself. I walked across the room and took a large ash tray off a table and put it on the floor between our chairs.

"I'm ready, if you are," I said.

"All right," she said. "To put it right on the line, I want to handle you."

"I thought you'd retired."

"What you mean is you thought I'd taken my boodle and gone off to retire to my rose garden somewhere, to grow prize tulips or collect antiques."

"Something like that."

"What was the figure Nick gave you? A million dollars and an annuity?"

"Something like that."

"Just between us, that's close. Maybe I'm just an old fire-horse that hears the bell ringing."

"And maybe you're not. Let's get something straight now, Rickie. I'm no Herb Fuller. Whatever that means to you, good or bad, I'm no Herb Fuller."

"Nobody expects you to be. He was one of a kind. A collector's item. Nobody can ever be a Herb Fuller. And I mean that good and bad."

"I think you should know too that I'm paid to do this one show tonight. That's the only commitment I have. Anything else you may have heard or read is premature. I'm not the heir apparent. I'm not necessarily going to inherit his radio and TV shows. Now I'm laying it on the line."

"No, you're not."

"I'm not?"

"No. I've been around a long time, Ed. If I want to know what's going on, I can find out. I know, for instance, about your contract with Sid Moore. I know, for instance, about the newspaper blitz that starts Monday. I know, for instance, Carleton's fine, Italian hand. I know quite a lot, so don't start off by oversimplifying. Don't try throwing this particular bird dog off the scent. This particular bird dog has quite a nose."

"The rest isn't bad either."

"And you can forget that routine too. I want to talk straight. Did Nick tell you that you could trust me?"

"He hinted at it."

"Well, you can. Fuller always knew that. He always knew that I'd chisel, lie and cheat for him, but he also knew that he could trust me. Unless you take that on faith right now, at the beginning, you might as well thank me for lunch and take off."

"All right. Your point. I accept that. Where does that leave us?"

"At the very beginning. You know, it's funny, but life has a kind of continuity. And you and I sitting here now are proof of it. Without me, you're nothing. Without you, I'm nothing. Together we're quite an unbeatable team."

"That's something Nick neglected to tell me."

"What is?"

"Your disconcerting habit of saying nasty things that make sense."

"You mean about you being nothing without me?"

"Yes. Suppose I don't accept that on faith?"

"You don't have to. Will you accept it on logic?"

"Probably."

"You, Mr. Ed Harris, are a babe in the woods. In the

jungle, if you like it better that way. Animals like Philip Carleton and Company eat you for breakfast. Even over-age lions like Sid Moore take big chunks out of your hide. Can I outline the plot for you?"

"It's your hotel suite."

"You've got a contract with Sid Moore. That was a mistake you fell into because you didn't know any better. If a dog gets fleas he gets rid of them. He doesn't stand around begging fleas to hop on. But you did. You didn't know. You thought Sid still had some weight to throw around. You mistook nuisance value for power and now you have to retrace your steps and get rid of him, don't you?"

"You're outlining the plot. Not me."

"All right. So you have to dump Sid Moore. On Carleton's orders? Or didn't they think it was even important enough to have him put the pressure on you? I'll give you the benefit of the doubt. Carleton's told you to get rid of Sid Moore. He's given you a couple of suggestions about how to do it, but he won't have anything to do with you until you come to him cleansed of your fleas. And when you do, what happens? You sign a contract with Carleton and Amalgamated. Before you do you'll have been reading all the nasty innuendos about yourself in the papers. Oh, sure, you know it's all part of the plot. But that won't keep you from wondering if it is or not. And when you finally succeed in delousing yourself and Carleton puts a contract in front of you, you'll sign it. Then you're really hooked."

"Why? It's to Carleton's advantage for me to become a star."

"Why? What makes you so important? You're nothing. Just like Herb Fuller was nothing until he was put into a mold, until a little world was created for him to rotate around. Signing the contract isn't the end of the rainbow. Contracts, particularly the kind you'll sign, can be broken.

Carleton isn't risking anything. If you fall flat on your face, you're out and another Ed Harris is thrown into the breach. And there's another behind him. There's a whole line of Ed Harrises, stretching right across the country, in every local station on the network. Did you think all you had to do was sign your name to a contract and wake up the next morning as the Great Man?"

"I guess I did."

"It wasn't even that easy with the authentic, original Great Man. I know. I helped create him."

"And wound up in a rose garden, raising prize tulips and collecting antiques?"

"Do you mind if I talk straight and risk hurting your feelings . . . risk insulting you?"

"I haven't so far."

Rickie smiled.

"You got a bellyful of Fuller this week, didn't you? You really dived into the cesspool, didn't you?"

"Right off the high board."

"And you didn't like it. You were thinking of walking out on it because you thought you might turn out like that, weren't you?"

"Take off your turban, honey, and put away the crystal ball."

"You just took for granted that at 10:01 tonight you were going to fall heir to the whole shooting match. It isn't that easy. Unless I'm very wrong, you don't have the natural equipment yet. You can't tell a filthy joke and have all the old ladies in the country thinking you're a darling boy. You can't spout religious clichés and make them sound sincere. You can't use the word God out loud without being a little self-conscious about it. You can't be a son of a bitch to everybody you work with, terrorizing them through four hours of rehearsal, and make the big switch on the air and sound like their good-natured lovable old father. You can't sleep with a girl all week end and convince forty million people on Monday morning that you've never had a carnal thought about her in your life. You can't do any of those Great Man things yet. And maybe you never will be able to. Maybe you don't have to. Maybe that isn't the world you play sun to. Maybe you haven't got a chance in a thousand of being anything more than just what you are, a local radio performer without any particular claim to national attention. Say what you will about Fuller, people noticed him. People had opinions about him. People were aware of his existence."

"Do you mind if I tell you that I don't give a good goddamn about Fuller?"

"You don't have to. Just don't forget that he had that special quality that makes a great entertainer. It doesn't matter a damn whether he ate his grandmother for breakfast or burned down the orphanage. What does matter is that he was able to get on the air and convince a lot of people that the phony character we'd built for him was real. And in the process sell somebody's toothpaste, somebody else's cigarette and back the opposition on the other networks right against the wall. Can you do that yet?"

"No."

"That's where I come in."

"You can wave your magic wand and turn me into a national celebrity, is that it?"

"That's it. Except that there is no magic wand involved. Just a lot of work. A lot of caring that you make it. To Carleton you're just one in a series of possible replacements. The truth of the whole thing is, Ed, that nobody really gives a damn about you, at this point. I would. I'd believe in you, work for you and together we'd pull it off."

"Why? The money?"

"No. I have more money than I'll ever be able to spend. Not for the money."

"The power?"

"Not even that. Not the way you mean it. I did it once, with Fuller. I had to ad lib the whole thing. I had to learn how to do it, while I was doing it. Now I know how. Maybe it's something as simple as personal satisfaction. Maybe, in a cockeyed sort of way, I'm just trying to destroy Herb Fuller by proving that he wasn't such a Great Man after all."

"Maybe you have a God complex all your own, Rickie. Maybe you just want to prove you can make the Great Man out of even the most unpromising material. Me."

She didn't deny that.

"Don't think I won't take money for it," she said. "Lots of it. You'll get full value for your money."

"Suppose I buy this? What's the plot from here on?"

"The same old plot. Sid Moore gets the boot. I'll take care of that. You won't even have to soil your hands picking the fleas off. I can handle that end of it. Then we take on Mr. Carleton. I take care of that too. The first thing we do is kill the Monday stories. We don't get you off on the left foot and we take away Carleton's 'out.' He's on record now picking you as the heir apparent. He doesn't welsh on that. I'll take care of that too. Then we find you a format. We spend a lot of money on writers. We throw Ed Harris out the window and create a fictional character that you become. That may take a while. It may not. It will take a lot of money."

"Which I don't have."

"If I know what I'm doing, it will be Carleton's money, Amalgamated's money. If necessary, it will be my money. With the build-up you're getting tonight on Amalgamated and a foolproof format we can walk into any network in the country and write our own ticket."

"What's to prevent me from following that script without you?"

"You couldn't do it. You couldn't handle Moore or Carleton. You couldn't find the right format and you wouldn't know what to do with it if you did."

"You make me sound like a sure bet for the Hall of Fame."

"Wait'll you hear how I make you sound after we sign that contract. Get that straight too. The minute we're working together, you're the greatest. I don't know whether Nick told you about that or not. I'm telling you, if we're together, we're together. I'm with you all the way down the line. There isn't anything I wouldn't do for you."

"I'd like another drink," I said.

"I don't know you well enough to know whether you should have one or not. Whether we work together or not, you better be sober on the air tonight. And every other night. You can have all the contempt you want to for any ideals you want to spit at. Just don't get any contempt when you're working, for the people you're working to. In plain language, stay sober on the air. That's for free. Now, can you still take another drink?"

"I can still take another drink."

She walked into the other room. I heard the ice tinkling in the bathroom sink again and a minute later she came back with two more drinks. She handed me mine and put hers on the floor next to the ash tray.

"That's all I had on my mind. Now you know the setup. You know where I fit in. You have to decide."

"I'll think it over," I said. "God, how I'll think it over."

"I think, between us, we can make it."

"If we want to."

"Sure. If we want to. Can I pull out the crystal ball again?"

"Wheel it out. Put on your turban too. Do you need tea leaves or can you read ice cubes?"

"I told you I checked up on you. A lot. You're a pretty decent guy and that's why you're all screwed up now. You found out a little too much about our mutual, dearly departed friend. You may have even nibbled a little at the cookies on the shelf and you're a little afraid you're going to turn out the way he did. Don't be. You're a pretty decent guy. I said that, didn't I? He wasn't. He never was. He was a bastard and he had a lot of scope to be one. He didn't change. He just expanded his normal base. That's what you'll do. You'll be all right."

"Will I, Rickie?"

"I can help you there too. You had the feeling that if you walked out you'd be doing a big dramatic thing. You'd be exploding H-bombs. Ed, you aren't even a two-inch salute. Nobody would lose a thing by your walking out except yourself. Carleton would get himself another boy and in the process, he'd give you such a newspaper black eye that you wouldn't even be able to get a job in a 200-watt foreign language station."

"Suppose I talked?"

"About what? You got a Sid Moore complex. You going to spill that French blood bank story? Everybody in the industry knows the story. Oh, sure, you'd cause a little ripple, but the ripple wouldn't reach up to the executive floor at Amalgamated. They made the last dime they're ever going to make out of Herb Fuller. What do they care if he's burned in effigy at every American Legion meeting from now until Christmas? That's Sid Mooreism. He thinks he's a blackmailer. He's just a charity case. Carleton could slap him down like a mosquito on the back of his hand any time he wanted to. Carleton probably played up the Sid Moore exposé big for you. Sure. If you get rid of Sid, that's fine, it saves him the trouble. That was just a windmill for you to tilt at so you came back to the throne room with the proper frame of mind."

"Nick told me something else about you, Rickie."

"What?"

"He told me you were in love with Fuller. True or false?"

"True and false. At the beginning I was in love with him. You know Carol?"

"Carol Carson? I know her."

"You know about her?"

"Carol and Fuller? I know."

"Just use the same story. Replace her name for mine. For a while anyway. Same plot. The only difference was she had a voice and I had a brain. I got a boodle and she got the DT's."

"Nick told me too that you blew the whistle on her and the announcer."

"Sure. I blew the whistle whenever I thought I had to. I told you, the only thing that was important to me was Fuller and his career. She was threatening that. She could have been the chink in the armor of the Fuller Family. She could have started a revolt. It was important then that the Family stay together. It was important that the audience retain the father picture of Fuller and the kids. It was important that she get back in line."

"You're a regular Burr Tillstrom, aren't you?"

"Maybe it looks that way to you. You believe in the existence of Kukla, Ollie and the rest of them, don't you?"

"Sure."

"Have I hurt your ego?"

"A little. The facts of life always hurt the ego a little. The stork theory is a much prettier story than the birds and the bees."

"I assume your script is a great big puff about the Great Man?"

"You assume right."

"Amalgamated's done a good job of publicizing it. You'll have a huge audience tonight. What's the script like? What technique are you using?"

"Bastardized documentary. Narration and tape cut-ins. Short sentences. A little irony here and there. Good script. As a piece of craftsmanship."

"You going to think over what we've been talking about? There's nothing I can do unless you give me the go ahead."

"And suppose I don't give you the go ahead?"

"I'll go back to my tulips, my roses and my antiques. I'd like to come out of retirement. I think we could pull it off."

"Let me think it over, Rickie. Let me think the whole thing over. If you don't hear from me by midnight, go back to your roses."

"Fair enough. Let's leave it at that."

I stood up, finished the dregs of my drink and put it on the table. Rickie walked to the door with me. I turned at the door and put my hand out. We shook hands formally, like a couple of diplomats. I even bowed a little from the waist.

"It was nice meeting you," I said.

"It was nice meeting you," Rickie answered.

I waved my hand and walked down the corridor to the elevator.

I ignored the cabs parked at the curb outside the hotel and walked north up Broadway. I walked past the haberdashery shops, the record stores with jazz blaring out of them, the shooting galleries and the orange juice stands and the candy stores with the cloying sickening sweet smell of caramel and popcorn. I stopped and had a glass of synthetic orange juice. I leaned against the counter looking south toward Times Square.

I could hear a loudspeaker blaring from the store next door where a phony auction was going on. I paid for the orange juice and walked another block. I walked past a store selling junk jewelry for forty-nine cents, past a store selling elaborate practical jokes and another selling hats with your name stitched across the brim.

Broadway was in its usual form, dirty, smelly and cheap. I picked up a newspaper at the stand on a corner and hailed a cab.

"The Amalgamated Building," I said and sat back and opened the *World-Telegram.* I turned to the radio page and found myself looking at my own picture. There was a big plug for the show and Harriet Van Horne had finally gotten around to doing a respectfully snippy biography of Fuller. I looked up from the paper. We were crossing Fifth Avenue, heading east. I leaned forward and tapped the cab driver on the shoulder.

"I've changed my mind," I said. "Take me to Eighty-first and First."

"We may have a little trouble getting up there," the driver told me. "That's where they have Herb Fuller's body and the crowds are very big."

"Let's try, anyway. Get me as close as you can."

He got me to Seventy-eighth and First and I walked the rest of the way. The crowds were just as big as they had been the last time I was there. I finally fought my way into the stage door and walked backstage to the office Nick Cellantano was using. It was empty. There was a half-empty bottle of liquor on the table and I reached for it and turned it around so I could read the label. The same lousy booze.

I walked out through the side aisle and into the auditorium. It was exactly the same. The organ music, the dimmed lights, the crowds shuffling quietly by the coffin. I stood there for a full minute, just looking. I moved up the aisle and climbed a flight of stairs that led to the balcony of the theater. I sat in the front row looking down. From here I could see the coffin. The spotlight picked out the face so sharply that it looked like bas-relief.

I sat there for a long time.

Looking.

And thinking.

A long time.

EPILOGUE

I'M SITTING now in my office on the ninth floor of the Amalgamated Building. It's getting dark. I know that if I turn around and look out the window at my back, I can see the sun setting behind the RCA Building. I can just barely hear the music blaring out of the loudspeaker in the reception room around the corner of the office.

It won't be long now. In two hours, I'll pull the string on the light over my head, pick up the script in my top drawer, lock the door carefully and go around the corner to Studio 23. Or maybe I'll just pull the string on the light over my desk, lock the door carefully, throw the key away and catch the first plane headed west.

Maybe.

Then again, maybe not.

That's why I'm sitting here, running up a trial balance.

It's hard to believe Fuller died only last Monday.

It's hard to believe the whole thing started only five days ago. And what am I trying to prove, sitting here flipping mental nickels, trying to decide what to do?

All I have to do is pick up that script in the drawer, walk around to Studio 23, spend the hour from ten to eleven reading it into an open mike and I've started the wheels turning.

It's simple.

That's all I have to do.

The question is, will I do it?

Will I?